THE CURSED WRITER

THE BAKER STREET MYSTERIES

HOLLY HEPBURN

B

Boldwood

First published in Great Britain in 2024 by Boldwood Books Ltd.

Copyright © Holly Hepburn, 2024

Cover Illustration: Shutterstock and iStock

A CIP catalogue record for this book is available from the British Library.

Paperback ISBN 978-1-83533-753-0

Large Print ISBN 978-1-83533-754-7

Hardback ISBN 978-1-83533-752-3

Ebook ISBN 978-1-83533-755-4

Kindle ISBN 978-1-83533-756-1

Audio CD ISBN 978-1-83533-747-9

MP3 CD ISBN 978-1-83533-748-6

Digital audio download ISBN 978-1-83533-749-3

Boldwood Books Ltd
23 Bowerdean Street
London SW6 3TN
www.boldwoodbooks.com

To Sir Arthur Conan Doyle, for creating Sherlock Holmes in the first place.

'There is nothing more deceptive than an obvious fact.'

— SIR ARTHUR CONAN DOYLE, *THE BOSCOMBE VALLEY MYSTERY*

1

It began, as so many adventures did, with the arrival of a telegram for Sherlock Holmes.

That the message was for Holmes was not unusual – Harry White opened and read hundreds of similarly addressed letters each week and she had, by and large, grown used to the idea that so many otherwise sensible and intelligent people believed the celebrated master detective was a real person. They came from all walks of life, as far as she could tell, earnestly writing to seek assistance with all manner of mysteries and suspected crimes. And since the newly built head offices of the Abbey Road Building Society spanned the detective's famous Baker Street address, that was where the letters were delivered. They had accumulated in the post room of the bank for months, growing in volume every day, until it became clear something needed to be done about them.

By dint of an unpleasant but well-timed collision between Harry's knee and her lascivious manager's groin, she found herself unceremoniously demoted from the plush upper floors of the bank to the basement, and what she supposed was the most menial role an enraged Simeon Pemberton had been able to find. For the best part of two months, Harry had worked her way through the backlog of letters, responding to each in the same brief but sympathetic manner: *Mr Holmes has retired to Sussex to keep bees and is regretfully unable to help.* At least her reply to *almost* each letter had been the same, and a glance at that morning's newspaper headlines reminded her she did not regret a single moment that had followed from her one deviation, even if her true role in the events that followed would never be publicly known.

But the arrival of a telegram for Holmes stood out from the other correspondence, by virtue of its novelty as well as its urgency, and it caused Harry to sit up straight at her desk to open it.

SHERLOCK HOLMES. PHILIP ST JOHN AT DEATH'S DOOR. TIME OF THE ESSENCE. REPLY IMME-DIATELY.

It came from a John Archer, Esq, of Thrumwell Manor in Cambridgeshire, and although Harry read it four times she still felt herself none the wiser. The telegram was reserved for news and information of vital importance and, at face value, a mortal illness certainly qualified. Moreover, Philip St John was a man of considerable literary repute – both her father and grandfather had waxed lyrical about his novels and her mother had complained on more than one occasion that he had snubbed all her invitations to the illustrious dinner parties she threw at their family home, Abinger Hall.

The revelation of his apparent indisposition was both unexpected and alarming. But Harry could not fathom why this Mr Archer had felt the need to advise Sherlock Holmes of the unhappy situation, and to spend a not insignificant amount in doing so. Even if she overlooked the fact that Holmes did not exist, surely Dr Watson was the more qualified resident of 221B Baker Street in matters of health. Perhaps Archer suspected foul play and wanted Holmes to investigate, but if that were the case, why not say so?

Shaking her head in bewilderment, Harry read the terse message again. It made little sense, which she supposed at least put it in the same category as much of the other correspondence she dealt with on a daily basis. What she ought to do was place it at the bottom of the date-ordered pile and respond in the usual way when it reached the top, without being swayed by the urgency of the message. But even as she forced herself back to the task of opening yet more envelopes, she knew she could not ignore the telegram that long. It smouldered like a sullen coal beneath a blanket of tinder. Sooner or later, it would catch light and she would need to attend to it.

Despite the burning presence, it took Harry until three o'clock that afternoon to finally give in. The latest batch of correspondence was typical of that received by Holmes, veering between the scandalous, the libellous and the merely dull, but it did succeed in distracting her. A woman in Margate was unsure whether the man she was set to marry was who he claimed to be. A gentleman in Dulwich alleged his neighbour had poisoned his honeysuckle. Another asked for help in retrieving his late father's missing Last Will and Testament, promising a handsome reward if Holmes was able to restore his rightful inheritance.

Harry allowed herself a moment to imagine how the detective might approach the case; undoubtedly, he would deduce within seconds that there was more to the matter than vanished paperwork. At first glance, it appeared Mr Stubbs might be the victim of an unscrupulous relative who had stolen his father's fortune, but the jagged zigzag of his signature would tell Holmes the man was hiding a dark personality and could not be relied upon for the truth. And then Harry felt a faint sting of guilt, because Mr Stubbs was not a character in a Sherlock Holmes story but a real person in some distress – she had no right to second-guess the circumstances that had brought him to write to Holmes.

Reining her imagination in, she filed it at the bottom of the pile and settled herself into typing up standard responses. But her fingers, usually speedy and nimble, felt slow and fat. All too often, the keys jammed, creating letters that were smudged and littered with mistakes, forcing her to start again. The constant clack-clack-clack sounded like pistol shots and, to make matters worse, she had the start of a headache that she suspected was due to a lack of sleep and an overabundance of excitement. And every time she closed her eyes, John Archer's words swam before her eyes: *time is of the essence... reply immediately...*

At length, she sat back and was instantly overtaken by a yawn so vast and unladylike that she was grateful she had no colleagues to witness it. Giving up on her infernally possessed typewriter, Harry reached for her notepad. Surely it wouldn't hurt to ask Mr Archer for more information, if only to set her own mind at rest. After several attempts, she managed to draft a reply that was probing yet succinct. Conscious of the need for brevity, she decided against mentioning Holmes' retirement and focused instead on the question of why Mr Archer had sought his help at all.

Sincere condolences. Request more details to assist. S.H.

Once the message was crafted to Harry's satisfaction, she checked the return address on the telegram from John Archer and added it to her notebook, below the message she had composed.

As another yawn overtook her, she decided enough was enough – she had not taken her lunch break after all. Gathering up her belongings, she locked the door of her tiny office and made for the fresh air of Baker Street.

Newspaper sellers called out the headlines of the evening edition. '*American Drug Lord Arrested at Southampton!* Read all about it!'

'*Suspect Released in Lord Robertson Robbery* – read all about it!'

Harry couldn't help glancing at the newspapers as she passed. Her own role in exposing the criminal gang behind Lord Robertson's burglary was a closely guarded secret, and the whole sequence of events that had led to her chasing the true culprit around the alleys of south London felt like a bad dream, although she still had the bruises to remind her it had been real. All that mattered was that justice had been done, and the innocent maid accused of the crime had been set free.

At the post office, Harry transferred her message to a telegram form and slid it beneath the grille to the clerk. 'Standard or greeting?' he asked, without looking up.

Greetings telegrams were reproduced on decorative paper by the receiving post office, and were commonly used for birthday messages, congratulations and other good wishes. Harry could only imagine what Holmes, or even John Archer, might make of such frivolity. 'Standard, please.'

The clerk nodded. 'Two shillings and sixpence, if you please.'

Harry paid the fee without complaint, glad she had chosen not to use the telephone in her office to reply to Mr Archer. The cost would have been added to the bank's bill, and while she felt reasonably confident it would have gone unnoticed among all the other correspondence sent on official Abbey Road Building Society business, it was much better not to leave any trace of her actions. Harry's immediate manager, Mr Babbage who ran the post room, had once warned her she had a powerful enemy within the bank and she had no wish to draw attention to herself, and if she was caught in such a flagrant breach of bank procedure, it would mean instant dismissal.

The faint flutter of anxiety that thought caused stayed with her all the way home to her small but elegant apartment in Hamilton Square. For the second time in her official capacity as secretary to Sherlock Holmes, she had deviated from her duties as required by the bank. For the second time, her curiosity had been roused, leading her to indulge a most un-Holmes-like whisper of intuition that nagged at her in much the same way as Esme Longstaff's letter about her missing sister had some months earlier, prompting her to launch her first investigation into the case of the missing maid. And for the second time, in spite of her anxiety, Harry felt certain she had done the right thing.

* * *

Harry was intrigued but not surprised by the speed of John Archer's response. It came by telegram the next afternoon, much to the interest of Bobby the post boy, who presented it to her with an expression of unbridled curiosity. 'Another urgent message for Sherlock Holmes,' he said, wide-eyed beneath his red velvet cap. 'It must be something serious.'

'Thank you, Bobby,' Harry said mildly, taking care to ensure her expression revealed nothing of her own interest in the contents.

He waited, an expectant look on his face, until it became clear she wasn't going to open it. 'Have an 'eart, Miss White,' he begged. 'The lads in the post room gave me hell yesterday when I said I didn't know what the big mystery was.'

Harry placed the telegram on the desk in front of her. 'We

receive hundreds of letters to Sherlock Holmes every week. Do they ask you about those?'

Bobby scratched his chin. 'No. But a telegram – two telegrams, even. That's different.' He paused. 'My money's on murder.'

'You've been reading too many detective stories,' Harry said, mildly amused by his ghoulish certainty. 'Assuming this telegram is from the same person as yesterday then I can assure you it is nothing so sensational. And it is quite common for those who seek the help of Mr Holmes to write more than once.'

Bobby shrugged, apparently unconvinced. 'Letters are cheaper than telegrams. Whoever sent it really wants your attention.'

'Not my attention,' she corrected gently. 'The attention of Sherlock Holmes, who is unable to help, for obvious reasons.'

'But what if it really is murder?' the boy persisted. 'Shouldn't you tell the peelers?'

Harry thought about the hundreds of letters she had read, alleging everything from embezzlement to grave robbing, and it was true that several had claimed to have uncovered the darkest crime. But in those cases, they had only turned to Holmes after the police had refused to entertain them and Harry felt certain their accusations must have already been investigated. Besides, she did not want to encourage the idea in Bobby's head that she might do anything other than answer the letters in the way Mr Babbage had instructed her. She liked the post boy, but she had no idea whether she could trust him, or anyone else at the bank.

'The people who write to Mr Holmes are not – well, let us say they are confused about what is real and what isn't.' She held up a hand as Bobby opened his mouth to object. 'But it isn't my job to pass judgement on them, nor to consider the truth of what they say. I open their letters, I read them and I send a standard reply.' She crossed her fingers under the desk. 'Without exception. Not even telegrams.'

He frowned. 'You must get some real nutters writing to him.'

'Some of them are a little strange,' Harry conceded. 'But I suppose it's simply a testament to the excellence of the stories. They draw the reader in, make them want to believe someone as brilliant as Sherlock Holmes could be real.'

'Maybe,' Bobby said. 'Do you reckon other detectives get letters, then? Miss Marbles and that?'

Harry smiled. 'Possibly. But not all of them have such a famously recognisable address.'

'Lucky for you that he does,' Bobby observed, then blinked nervously as Harry stared at him. 'After... well, after what happened and all. With your last position, I mean.'

Harry knew her expression must be glacial but she couldn't seem to unfreeze it. She hadn't realised the reason for her move to the post room was common knowledge. 'What exactly do you mean?'

He shifted from one foot to the other. 'I don't mean nothing, Miss White. Except that it's a good thing there's all these letters to answer and this little room, so you can keep out of his way. I don't doubt that he didn't dare give you the sack, not after what happened the last time.'

He trailed off, staring at the floor as Harry's thoughts jumbled together and cleared. 'The last time,' she repeated slowly. 'You're telling me there was someone Mr Pemberton harassed before me?'

But even as she said it, she knew it must be true. A man like Simeon Pemberton had a lecherous eye and a great opinion of his own worth; he would undoubtedly have used his position of power to bestow his attentions on other young women at the bank.

Bobby cleared his throat and glanced over his shoulder into the corridor as though checking he could not be overheard. 'A secretary in the typing pool. She didn't – what I mean to say is, she left of her own accord. But the other women all knew what had happened.'

He eyed Harry expectantly. She drew in a breath and forced herself to be patient. 'Which was what?'

'That she didn't say no like you did,' Bobby said in a low voice. 'People started to talk. She couldn't keep working at the bank then. Not with him being married.'

She shook her head. 'How long ago was this?'

Bobby pursed his lips. 'Must have been six or seven months ago now. I'm surprised you didn't hear about it.'

But Harry was not surprised. As Mr Pemberton's personal assistant, she had kept herself to herself on the bank's upper floors, preferring not to indulge in gossip. She'd known some of the women in the secretarial pool by name, recognised more to nod to in the corridors, but she wouldn't have known if one had left, even under such a cloud. And then Harry herself had fallen victim to Mr Pemberton, although her own experience hadn't been anything like as terrible. Even so, it appeared she had been the subject of gossip too. 'But what happened to her?' Harry asked.

'No one knows,' Bobby said, shaking his head. 'One of the secretaries who'd been friends with her called at her lodgings and discovered she'd left. Maybe she went back to her parents.'

Which would probably have meant admitting she had lost her job, Harry thought. 'Poor girl,' she murmured. 'And Pemberton forced her out?'

Bobby gave a short laugh. 'Not directly – he made it seem like it was her choice to leave. But that's why he couldn't risk sacking you, see? If you'd started blabbing – well, the gossip would have been even worse. The higher-ups might have heard about it and questions might have been asked.'

Harry nodded to herself. Hadn't Pemberton said as much when he'd despatched her to the basement? *I would remind you that everything occurring within these walls remains highly confidential...* And she had kept quiet, determined not to let him force her out even though the repetitiveness of typing the same letter almost drove her mad. Until she'd opened the letter from Mildred Longstaff's sister and everything had changed.

'I reckon he thought you wouldn't last a week down in the post room,' Bobby went on. 'But Mr Babbage was too sharp for him – he found you this place instead. That's what I mean by lucky, see?'

Harry stared at him, then gave herself a mental shake. It wasn't his fault – compared to the other secretary, she had got off lightly. And she still had a job, albeit considerably less well paid, as she'd discovered when she received her first wage slip after her altercation with Mr Pemberton, but that didn't matter so much. Bobby couldn't know Harry worked because she wanted to, not because she needed to; the granddaughter of a baron was not expected to earn a living. But the alternative was submitting to her mother's well-meaning efforts to find her a suitable husband and the very thought of that made Harry shudder. Married women were expected to give up their jobs to devote themselves to their husband, and the kind of match Harry was expected to make also came with the distinct requirement of providing an heir. It wasn't that she was against marriage, if she met the right person, but she was not ready to give up her freedom yet. Working at the bank allowed her to live in London and enjoy some independence, away from the watchful eye of her mother. It had also enabled her to reunite Mildred with her family and reveal the criminal gang who had set her up. Perhaps Bobby was wiser than he knew, Harry thought ruefully. She had enjoyed an awful lot of luck in her life so far.

'Yes, I do see,' she said quietly. 'I am very grateful to Mr Babbage, and to you too, for helping me to settle in so well.'

He nodded, although she thought his chest puffed up a little under the smart burgundy jacket. 'You sure you can't give me a hint about what's in that telegram?'

Harry smiled at his persistence. 'Quite sure. See you later, Bobby.'

'Maybe,' he said, and turned towards the door with a melodramatic sigh. 'If the lads in the post room don't kill me first.'

2

Harry sat at her desk for quite some time, staring at the rectangular telegram without truly seeing it. Her thoughts were jumbled – mostly focused on Bobby's revelation about the poor woman who had paid the price for Simeon Pemberton's lustfulness. Would he risk attempting to seduce another of the bank's employees? It seemed likely, although the fact that Harry was still a member of staff might help to deter him. Should she have spoken up instead of meekly accepting her demotion? If she had, it was likely both she and the other secretary would be unemployed. But perhaps so would Mr Pemberton. Was that a sacrifice Harry ought to have made?

Still troubled, she turned her attention to the telegram, hoping it might distract her. The message was shorter than the previous one and contained only four words.

GARSTON CLUB. TOMORROW. 5 P.M.

Harry sat back in her chair. She had hoped Archer might give more information about why he sought the help of any detective, let alone Holmes, but he had only deepened the mystery. Rather than satisfy her curiosity, the imperious summons to the Garston Club in Piccadilly only fanned the flames of her interest; if such a telegram had arrived at 221B Baker Street in a Conan Doyle story, Holmes would undoubtedly have been similarly intrigued, which she supposed might have been Archer's intention. The trouble was that Harry could not go to the meeting – not as Harry White, nor using the pseudonym of R. K. Moss, the name she had invented for the secretary of Sherlock Holmes. She could not go because she was a woman, and under the Garston Club's archaic but inflexible rules, women were expressly forbidden to enter.

It boasted an impressive list of members, Harry knew; her two elder brothers had both undergone the strict vetting process to join the ranks of well-known actors, authors, artists and aristocrats who met there. The fact that this John Archer was also a member only increased Harry's puzzlement. If the grand-sounding address of Thrumwell Manor had not signalled he was a man of some importance, his membership of the Garston Club made it clear, and once again, Harry found herself wondering what he hoped to gain by contacting Holmes.

But it appeared the pieces of the puzzle would only be revealed in full by meeting him and that was what frustrated Harry the most. Could she send a telegram requesting an alternative venue? Archer might very well do it, for the great Sherlock Holmes, but it would mean the arrival of yet another telegram at the bank, which would raise still more questions in the post room, and Harry would rather not undergo another interrogation from Bobby. Tapping her fingers thoughtfully on the desk, she considered the problem. What would Holmes do, if he were in her shoes? The answer was obvious and offered no help at all: he would simply meet Archer at the Garston Club, because he could go anywhere and do anything, by virtue of being a man. Moreover, he had Sir Arthur Conan Doyle to remove such inconveniences with a clever sentence or two. Harry had no such advantages. She would have to decline the meeting and hope Archer did not decide to present himself at 221B Baker Street, demanding to see the detective in person. He might even produce the telegram she had sent on behalf of Holmes, which while laughable might also set alarm bells ringing among those who knew the bank did indeed employ a secretary to Sherlock Holmes. There was, in short, a risk that the trail might lead back to Harry and she would find it extremely difficult to explain the coincidence away. And it was a scenario she felt all the more likely to occur if she did not cancel the meeting and no one turned up to meet Archer at the Garston Club. Harry rubbed her temples, wincing as her fingers brushed the bruises that were a souvenir of her desperate chase through London a few days earlier. She was beginning to regret following the impulse to reply to Archer at all.

Harry did her best to focus on her work but, as the afternoon wore on, the problem gnawed at her. The unpredictability of what might unfold if she followed either course of action troubled her; both carried risk and she couldn't settle on the best path. But eventually, she decided with regret that the meeting must be cancelled, and in such a way that it was clear that no further correspondence would be undertaken. It was, she thought, something of a shame not to learn more about Mr Archer's problem, but there was no help for that. She could not meet him, yet couldn't chance going. The only way to nullify the danger was draw a line under the matter entirely.

She remained convinced of this as she made her way once more to the post office and copied the message she had composed onto the telegram form.

Regret unable to help. Matter now closed. S.H.

Her determination did not waver as she joined the queue, which was longer than it had been the day before and slow moving. Harry allowed her mind to drift, studying the other customers to pass the time. The woman directly before her was clearly impatient, tapping a well-heeled shoe and huffing. From the back, Harry guessed she might be in her forties; her coiled hair was shot with grey. A fellow secretary, she decided, impatient to complete her errand and be away home. The man ahead of her was tall and smartly dressed in a pinstripe suit, with a dark grey trilby hat that covered most of his head. He carried himself stiffly, with two brown paper packages under one arm, leaning heavily on a mahogany walking stick. Perhaps a war veteran, Harry thought, watching him move slowly forwards in the queue.

Holmes would know from his gait exactly which part of his leg had been injured, and from that deduce which of the armed forces he had served in. There would be some other barely perceptible clue that told him where the man had served. But for Harry, who had no superhuman intellect to rely on, there were no such remarkable revelations. She might not even be correct in assuming he had been injured in the Great War – his disability could have been caused by a car crash, a workplace accident, a debilitating illness – but she thought there was something military in his straight back and proud bearing.

And then he turned his head to the left, only a little, and she caught the unnatural curve of a smooth, hard cheek. It was painted to mimic the colour of the man's skin tone but somehow that only made it more obvious to Harry. The breath caught in her throat as she hurriedly looked away, feeling suddenly intrusive. So many men had returned from the war horrifically disfigured and not all were able to face the world again, even with metal masks to hide the damage or skin grafts to try and repair it. That this man could was a testament to courage. She watched him turn to face the front, noting how many of those around him averted their gaze. Such men were undoubted heroes, but, even fourteen years on, they were also an uncomfortable reminder of the terrible cost the war had exacted. A price some would continue to pay for the rest of their lives.

The queue moved again, although not fast enough for the woman in front of Harry, who muttered under her breath. The man with the walking stick shuffled forward but seemed to get his cane tangled with his foot. He stumbled, throwing his arms wide in an attempt to regain his balance, and the packages he carried tumbled to the ground. The secretary tutted loudly, making no move to help. 'Really.'

Harry's cheeks began to burn with indignation. She stepped past the woman and flashed a smile at the man, who was trying with some difficulty to recover his parcels. 'Here. Let me.'

Once she had scooped them up, she held them out, allowing him to gather them awkwardly under his free arm. She looked fully at him then, saw that the metal mask extended across more than half his face, covering both eyes and the whole of one cheek. It disappeared beneath his hat and Harry supposed the trilby must be helping to keep it in place. His eyes were dark behind the holes but they fixed on Harry and she thought he was trying to return her smile, although his mouth barely twitched. 'Thank you,' he said, the words a little indistinct.

'That's quite all right,' Harry replied. 'Will you be able to manage? I can help, if you'd like.'

Fresh tutting broke out behind them. 'Don't think you're jumping the queue, miss,' the secretary said, and Harry looked back to see a hard-faced woman whose expression was even more sour than her tone. 'I know your game.'

Harry lifted her chin. 'My game, as you put it, is helping this gentleman. Nothing more.'

The other woman scowled. 'Just as long as you remember your place. It's behind me.' She jerked her head at the man. 'He can join you there if he needs help.'

Drawing a deep, calming breath, Harry summoned up a cool smile. 'That won't be necessary.' She turned her attention back to the man, who had been following the exchange in silence. 'I'm happy to carry your parcels to the counter. It's no trouble.'

She sensed rather than saw his indecision and thought she understood. It was probably pride, mingled with a reluctance to draw attention to himself, doing battle with the inconvenience of grappling with the two packages and his walking stick. But it appeared practicality won, because he nodded. 'Thank you. That would help.'

'See?' The secretary raised her voice as Harry took the parcels back. 'What did I tell you? She's trying to jump the queue.'

The unfairness of the accusation nettled Harry. Without stopping to think, she held up her telegram form and tore it in half, then again and again. She crumpled the pieces in the palm of her hand. 'There,' she said to the scowling woman. 'Now I have no business at the counter so I can't possibly be pushing in.'

For a moment, she thought her adversary might argue but she merely pressed her lips together and glared. Deciding the battle had been won, Harry turned to face forwards and waited in silence beside the man. When the queue moved, she kept pace with him, noting that his movements were much easier without the packages to hamper him. As they reached the counter, she slid the brown paper parcels across to the clerk and glanced at her companion. 'You'll be fine now.'

'Yes,' he said. 'Thank you.'

'My pleasure,' Harry said, and resisted the temptation to look at the woman behind them. 'Cheerio, then.'

Still holding the fragments of the telegram form, she made for the back of the queue, which now snaked almost out of the door. She bit her lip. If she joined the queue now, there was no guarantee she would reach the front before the counter closed and she didn't want the man with the walking stick to notice and realise he had inconvenienced her. More than that, Harry was loath to give the sour-faced woman the satisfaction of knowing she had cost her the place. Yet her message to John Archer must be delivered. Disaster would follow if it were not. And then a flash of inspiration struck her – she could telephone Thrumwell Manor once she arrived home, and leave word for Archer that Holmes was unable to help. It was not perhaps quite as official as a telegram, but it would get the message across.

Thrusting the torn-up paper into the pocket of her coat, Harry hurried out of the post office. But as she made her way along Baker Street, it occurred to her that using her own telephone was not perhaps wise. Mr Archer might very well try to call Holmes back, and the local switchboard operator would be able to locate the number Harry had called from. It was better to use one of the red and white public telephone booths that were dotted around London's streets, she decided. The nearest she remembered seeing was on Marylebone Road, a short walk from Baker Street. Harry made her way there.

'Directory Enquiries, how may I help?' The voice was so crisp and efficient that it caused Harry to hesitate, if only briefly.

'Mr John Archer, Thrumwell Manor, please,' she replied, with as much confidence as she could muster. The Directory Enquiries service had only been introduced earlier that year and Harry hadn't needed to use it until now. Would they really be able to find the correct John Archer and put her through without knowing the number?

'Is that Thrumwell Manor, Cambridgeshire?' the operator enquired, after a short silence.

Harry was impressed. 'That's right.'

'Putting you through. Hold, please.'

Before Harry could thank her, there was a series of clicks on the line, which she took to be the effect of the call being transferred. Moments later, it began to ring and shortly after that, an entirely different, much softer female voice sounded in Harry's ear. 'Morden four.'

Hurriedly, Harry pumped some more coins into the slot. She had no real idea how much the call would cost and did not want to risk being disconnected before she had made her purpose clear. 'Hello, is this Thrumwell Manor?'

'That's right.'

Harry allowed herself a small smile of relief. She'd assumed such a grand-sounding house would have a telephone but from the single-digit number, it didn't sound as though there were many others in the area that did. 'Excellent,' she said. 'I'm trying to contact a Mr John Archer. Is this the right number?'

The line crackled. 'It is, but Mr Archer is not here at present.'

So much the better, Harry thought. She didn't actually want to speak to the man. 'That's perfectly fine – I only want to leave a message. Will you see to it that he gets it? It's rather urgent.'

'That might be a problem, then,' the woman said. 'He's in London, see. Not due back here until Thursday evening.'

'Oh.' Harry hadn't considered that Archer might have already travelled to the city for his meeting with Holmes. 'Is there a way I can contact him? Is he staying at a hotel, perhaps?'

There was a noise that sounded very much like a snort. 'You could but I doubt he'd see it. You'd do much better to try his club – that's where I find him when I need him.'

Harry felt a familiar sinking feeling. 'His club. Would that be the Garston?'

'That's the one.' It seemed to dawn on the speaker that she

had given no small amount of information without asking for Harry's name. 'Who's calling, please?'

Rapidly, Harry ran through her options. She couldn't give her own name, and mentioning Sherlock Holmes might raise all kinds of questions she didn't want to answer. But the name she used to sign her letters on behalf of Holmes ought to be safe enough. Surely no one would think to link it back to Harry or the bank. 'R. K. Moss,' she said.

'R. K. Moss,' the woman repeated, as though writing it down. 'Well, like I said, you'll most likely find him at the Garston and if he's not there, he'll be along at some point. Is there anything else I can help you with?'

Harry was about to say no when another thought occurred to her. She placed a steadying hand on one of the booth's window-panes and took a chance. 'How is Mr St John, may I ask? I was so sorry to hear of his illness.'

Was it her imagination or did she catch a sharp intake of breath on the other end of the line? The answer, when it came, was considerably less cheerful in tone. 'Much the same. We can only hope and pray for a miracle.'

'Of course,' Harry murmured and tried to recall the exact wording of the first telegram to Holmes. 'Mr Archer said the malady was serious but I had hoped for some improvement. Has his doctor nothing to say?'

A brisk clucking noise travelled down the line. 'It is serious, make no mistake. But there's nothing any doctor can do, not with the curse hanging over him.'

Harry blinked, assuming she must have misheard. 'The curse?'

'Aye,' the woman said with stout certainty. 'I fear it'll be the death of him, as it has been for many others in these parts.' She sniffed. 'Not that Mr Archer believes, of course. But he will.'

Her tone left Harry in no doubt of what she thought of John

Archer's refusal to accept his uncle's fate. 'I see,' she said, frowning as she tried to make sense of the macabre prophecy. 'But what exactly is the nature of the—'

A faint background ringing seemed to bring the other woman up short. 'That'll be the nurse,' she said abruptly. 'Like I said, try the Garston Club. Goodbye, now.'

She rang off, leaving Harry staring at the receiver as her unused coins clattered into the metal tray. Whatever she'd expected to hear when she'd asked about Philip St John's illness, it wasn't some strange mumbo-jumbo about a curse. It was, she thought, exactly the kind of thing that happened in a Sherlock Holmes story, however, and she began to have an inkling about why John Archer had sought the detective out, although from what the woman on the telephone had said, it didn't sound as though he believed his uncle was under any kind of supernatural thrall.

Pensively, she gathered up the coins and pushed back the glass-panelled door to rejoin the bustle of Marylebone Road and considered what she had learned. It would be safe enough to call the Garston Club from her own telephone at home – they must receive scores of telephone calls each day and hers would not stand out. But an idea was forming in her mind, one so obvious that she didn't know why it hadn't occurred to her immediately. She was not able to go to the Garston Club herself to meet Archer but it didn't follow that no one could. Both her brothers were members, although she couldn't possibly ask them. They had no idea Harry had been demoted, for a start, and she feared Seb in particular would never stop laughing if they learned of her new job and its association with Holmes. And it was unlikely that either would agree to meet Archer, at least not without consider-able explanation.

But Harry did know someone else who was a member of the

Garston Club – someone who already knew all about her position as the secretary of Sherlock Holmes. Someone who had
helped her investigate Mildred's disappearance and pursued the
criminals responsible through the shadowy streets of Elephant
and Castle, much against his better judgement. Someone who
could be relied upon to keep quiet, even if he could also be quite
priggish and intensely annoying. That someone was Oliver
Fortescue, city lawyer and best friend of Harry's eldest brother,
Lawrence. She hadn't spoken to him since Tuesday lunchtime,
when she'd all but hung up on him as Bobby arrived with the
first telegram, but surely he wouldn't object to attending the
meeting with John Archer in her stead. Surely he would understand her curiosity and be equally intrigued, especially if she
added the details of her call to Thrumwell Manor. Once he'd
finished lecturing her about the stupidity of replying in the first
place, that was. But the short-term pain of that was worth
enduring to learn more about the mystery John Archer
represented.

With renewed vigour in her steps, Harry turned towards
Mayfair. She would telephone Oliver the very moment she got
home.

* * *

'Absolutely not.' Oliver's tone was firm. Harry could picture him
frowning, his dark eyebrows beetling together in forbidding
disapproval. 'For heaven's sake, Harry, I'm surprised you'd even
ask.'

Swallowing a sigh, Harry sat up straight on the settee and
adopted her most reasonable tone. 'I'm not asking you to do
anything unethical. All you have to do is meet this John Archer
tomorrow evening and pass on my message.'

'Your message,' Oliver said flatly. 'Or that of an imaginary person?'

'Technically, it would be from Holmes,' she conceded. 'But it's me you'd be helping. I just need to make sure Archer doesn't get angry and turn up at the bank, demanding to speak to him.'

There was a long silence. 'You shouldn't have got involved in the first place. Haven't you learned anything from the business with Mildred?'

She had, Harry wanted to say. She'd learned that she wasn't a bad detective, if not quite in Holmes' league. She'd learned how to impersonate a Cockney to obtain information, to dress like a man and chase a suspect through the back streets of the city. She had discovered a hitherto unsuspected talent for digging up clues, for following their trail and using what she found to right wrongs. And most of all, Harry had learned she could make a difference, to do something that mattered instead of just finding ways to dodge her mother's matchmaking efforts. 'I know I shouldn't have answered,' she told Oliver, taking a sip from the bone china cup that held her tea. 'But I did and there's no help for it.'

He huffed in irritation and now she could imagine him pushing his black hair back from his forehead. 'What sort of person consults a detective instead of a doctor, anyway?'

'I don't know,' Harry said honestly, because she had wondered the same thing. 'I thought perhaps you might know him, actually, since you're both members of the same club.'

'The name isn't familiar,' Oliver said, sounding thoughtful. 'But the Garston has a few hundred members. I haven't met them all.'

Harry weighed her options up. When she'd first thought about asking Oliver to help, she had only wanted him to pass on the message that Holmes was unable to assist. But as she'd made her way home, she'd begun to wonder whether he might find out a little more about Philip St John's strange malady. Now she wasn't sure sharing the details of her odd telephone conversation with the woman at Thrumwell Manor was a good idea. Oliver, she knew, was a believer in science and the law, and cold, hard logic. He would not be swayed by tales of a mysterious curse, and Harry decided she would do better to keep that part of the story to herself. Instead, she waited in silence. She'd asked for his help. The only thing that remained to be seen was whether he would agree to give it to her. And if he said no, she could fall back on the plan to leave a telephone message of her own at the club. At length, Oliver let out an irritable sigh. 'When did Archer tell you to meet him?'

'Five o'clock tomorrow,' Harry replied. 'Although he's expecting Sherlock Holmes, of course.'

Oliver gave a humourless laugh. 'Then he's going to be very disappointed.'

Harry felt a warm rush of elation. 'So you'll do it, then? You'll meet Archer and tell him Holmes can't help?'

'I'm not sure you've given me much choice,' Oliver grumbled but she didn't think he was as annoyed as he was pretending to be. 'But that's all I'm doing – I'll make sure he understands the message and then I'm leaving. And you agree not to send any more telegrams, yes? It's too risky, you're going to land yourself in hot water. If Pemberton ever finds out—'

He stopped and, for a moment, Harry was reminded of the other revelation she'd uncovered that day, the news that she was not the only one to fall foul of Pemberton's grubby hands. But as with the story of the curse, she wasn't sure there was anything to be gained by sharing the discovery with Oliver. 'I know,' she said. 'No more telegrams.'

'Standard replies only,' he went on. 'No more risks.'

He sounded so severe that Harry couldn't help smiling. 'Standard replies only. And thanks awfully, Oliver. I really appreciate you doing this.'

He grunted. 'As you should.'

Harry hesitated for a moment, then decided to throw caution to the wind. 'And if you do happen to find out why Archer wrote to Holmes in the first place—'

'No, I will not tell you,' he cut in. 'I'm not even going to ask.'

She gave in. 'Of course not.'

'And you owe me a drink.'

'Actually, I think you owe me one,' she said brightly. 'A pint of mild from our trip to Elephant and Castle, although I'd much rather make it a cocktail. Why don't we meet after you've seen Archer. At the Savoy, say six o'clock?'

There was a brief silence, which caused Harry to wonder if she had misjudged him. Was he so exasperated with her that meeting for a drink was out of the question? 'An excellent plan,' Oliver said at length, and she was relieved to hear he did not sound exasperated at all. 'See you tomorrow. Do try to stay out of trouble until then.'

'See you tomorrow,' she said, and put the phone down to gaze into the flames that danced in the fireplace opposite the settee. She ought to feel as though a weight had been lifted from her shoulders but instead, she was filled with a strange tingling sensation that she suspected might very well be excitement. Whether that was due to the strange conversation she'd had with the woman at Thrumwell Manor, or the thought of seeing Oliver, Harry did not want to speculate. Perhaps, she thought, it was a little of both.

3

As Simeon Pemberton's assistant, Harry had always endeavoured to be at her desk early. She enjoyed the quiet of the office, the opportunity to review the day ahead without interruption, and the sense that she was completely in control of her domain. After her demotion to the post room, interruptions were few and far between and Mr Babbage left her to manage her own work, which meant her office was always quiet and she always felt in control of her admittedly much smaller domain, but she had maintained her practice of arriving early. Apart from anything else, it meant she had rarely had to worry about running into Mr Pemberton in the bank's hushed, marbled lobby while waiting for the elevator.

But delays on the Underground system the following morning conspired against Harry and meant she found herself hurrying through the front doors later than usual. She was not late, but she was later than she liked to be. And then her morning was made a thousand times worse. She glanced across the lobby and realised with a sinking heart that the day she had been dreading had arrived. Waiting by the elevator, with a neatly furled umbrella in one hand, a briefcase in the other and a black bowler hat on his head, was Simeon Pemberton. From the back, he looked very much like any one of the managers who worked on the bank's upper floors but Harry had taken that hat and coat to hang up every morning for months. She knew it was him.

She almost walked out, but she could already sense a curious gaze being directed her way from the doormen standing outside. Slowly, she forced herself to cross the lobby, her heels tapping with each reluctant step. Was it too much to ask that the lift might arrive before she did, whisking Pemberton out of her sight without him ever knowing she was there? Or perhaps she could take the grand, red-carpeted marble staircase that swept away to the left of the elevator. The problem with that was that Pemberton was sure to see her and she would really rather avoid him altogether. Even so, it was the lesser of two evils. Making up her mind, she dipped her head and made for the stairs. Just as a cheerful ding proclaimed the lift car had reached the ground floor.

There was an understated swoosh as the doors opened. Harry kept walking, hoping Mr Pemberton would enter the lift without noticing her. But it seemed her luck had run out. 'Miss White,' a familiar, peevish voice called as she passed. 'Won't you take the lift?'

It was more of a command than a question but even so, Harry was tempted to ignore it. Could he object to her taking the stairs? The thought of being in an enclosed space with him made her stomach churn and she could always claim she was on a health kick. But the thought withered almost as soon as it had arrived. Simeon Pemberton was an important figure at the Abbey Road Building Society. He could make her life difficult if he chose, as he had already demonstrated once, and she did not want to be summoned to Mr Babbage's office again to explain herself. As much as she hated to admit it, Pemberton held all the power.

She did not smile as she turned back to face him. 'Of course. I didn't realise it was there.'

Pemberton's bottle-brush moustache quivered as he licked his lips. His eyes glittered with unconcealed amusement at the lie. 'It's lucky I called out, then.'

On legs that did not feel like her own, Harry stalked to the elevator doors and stepped inside. Pemberton followed. Stabbing the button for the second floor, she resisted the temptation to close her eyes, relieved to observe he had at least kept a respectable distance between them. Perhaps he remembered the pain her knee had inflicted the last time he had got too close, Harry thought as the doors slid shut. She kept her gaze fixed straight ahead, painfully aware of his too-strong cologne, the underlying hint of the pomade he used on his ridiculous moustache. The journey would not be long but she would hate every second. Just as she was certain he would enjoy the discomfort he must know she was feeling. 'How is your new position? I trust you are better suited to the simpler requirements of the post room?'

Harry wanted to grind her teeth but she would not give him the satisfaction of seeing just how rattled she was. 'Quite suited, thank you.'

From the corner of her eye, she saw the gleam of his teeth as he smiled. 'I've been keeping an eye on your performance, of course, as I was the one who put you forward for the role. It seems Mr Babbage has no complaints.' He paused and she knew he was watching her. 'So far.'

Harry watched the gold arrow crawl past 1 and move towards 2, willing it to move faster. 'Mr Babbage is an excellent manager.'

She shouldn't have said it but being so near to him was grating on her nerves. Pemberton clicked his tongue. 'Babbage is a fool but he serves a useful purpose within the bank. All the same, don't think you can use your charms on him when you make a mistake. I haven't forgotten the way you encouraged my affections, Miss White. A woman might get a reputation for that kind of thing if she is not careful.'

Indignation bubbled up in Harry's chest. 'Encouraged your affections?' she echoed in disbelief. 'That's hardly how things were. You forced yourself on me and sent me to the post room when I refused your advances.'

His face reddened. 'How dare you accuse me of such a thing!'

Heart thudding, Harry forced herself to look into his pudgy eyes. 'But it isn't the first time it's happened, is it? There was another secretary, before me, although you did a better job of getting rid of her. She lost her job entirely, didn't she?'

Pemberton's mouth opened and closed like a carp gasping for air. 'I don't know what you mean. The very idea – you have no proof I was in any way involved.'

'So far,' she whipped back, using his own words against him. 'Furthermore, please don't suggest that I am the kind of woman who dallies with married men. If the truth ever comes out, I think you'll discover you have much more to lose than I do.'

The arrow reached the second floor and Harry felt a flutter of relief as the bell chimed and the doors slid open. 'Have a pleasant day, Mr Pemberton,' she said as she sailed past and into the safety of the corridor. 'I do hope we understand one another better now.'

Her nerves did not stop jangling until she had reached the safety of her office and closed the door behind her. She stood leaning against it, waiting for her breathing to return to normal before she removed her hat and coat and took a seat at her desk. Either she had fired a warning shot across her enemy's bows, or she had scuttled her own ship. Only time would tell.

* * *

It seemed to Harry that the American Bar at the Savoy Hotel was never busy. That was to say, she had never seen the elegantly curved room crowded, although its tables were seldom empty and the seats at the bar always occupied. She had often seen would-be drinkers turned away at the gleaming walnut doors, even when there appeared to be room to accommodate them, and she knew there must be some unwritten rule about who could, and could not, enjoy its understated elegance. Regardless of how full it was, the buzz of conversation was never loud, no matter how many cocktails the clientele had consumed, and the tinkle of the grand piano in the background meant confidences were not easily overheard. It was part of the reason Harry had chosen it to meet Oliver. That, and the excellent cocktails, although she'd learned early that less was definitely more when it came to the bar's signature dry Martini.

Oliver was uncharacteristically late. Harry sat back in the velvet chair, allowing the alcohol to smooth away the final trace of her encounter with Simeon Pemberton at the start of the day. She'd spent most of the morning worrying he would hammer on her door, with Mr Babbage on his heels, but as lunchtime came and went, she began to put the matter into perspective. She had not been wrong when she'd said Pemberton had more to lose than she did; she doubted his wife would appreciate his lasciviousness, for a start. But the more Harry thought about it, the more she realised a run-in like that had been bound to happen eventually. At least he understood she was not entirely defenceless now.

To occupy herself while she waited, Harry observed her fellow drinkers. There were several she recognised without being personally acquainted – the world-famous opera singer Giuseppe Carina, who must have the night off, judging by the way he and his group were downing champagne; an American actress who was the darling of the silver screen was deep in conversation with the bartender; and a well-known author whose latest novel was taking the London literary scene by storm. Harry kept herself entertained by studying each of them in turn, observing their clothing and mannerisms. She might very well be at the start of an Agatha Christie novel. It was exactly the kind of glamorous setting where motive, means and opportunity might come together to spell murder. But despite the entertainment supplied by her fellow drinkers, by the time Oliver arrived at just after seven o'clock, breathless and apologetic, Harry had eaten two bowls of peanuts and was starting to feel drawn towards a second drink.

'I'm so sorry to keep you waiting,' Oliver said, draping his coat over the back of the empty chair and drawing admiring glances from both the actress and the opera singer. 'I couldn't get away.'

Harry raised her eyebrows. 'From the Garston Club in general? Or from Mr Archer?'

'From Archer,' he said, and shook his head in wry amusement. 'It turns out the man's an actor by trade and he certainly knows how to spin a tale.'

Harry absorbed the news with fresh puzzlement. As an actor, Archer must understand the line between reality and fiction better than most. Somehow it made even less sense that he had contacted Sherlock Holmes for help. 'I see,' she said, as Oliver ran a weary hand through his hair and reached for the menu. 'I take it he wasn't too unhappy not to be met by Holmes himself.'

An impeccably dressed waiter appeared at their table. 'I'll have a Scotch on the rocks,' Oliver said, and glanced enquiringly at Harry.

'A gin and tonic, thank you,' she said, and held up a hand. 'Please ask Mr Craddock to go easy on the gin, however. That last Martini nearly blew my head off.'

The waiter gave a nod and glided away as silently as he had

arrived. Oliver loosened his tie a little and sighed. 'It's a funny thing but Archer didn't seem surprised that Holmes hadn't come personally. When I introduced myself and said I was there on his behalf, he simply nodded and said he realised the detective must be rather elderly by now.'

Harry frowned. 'So he does think Holmes is real.'

'It would appear so,' Oliver agreed. 'Why else would he have sent a telegram to Baker Street?'

Why indeed, Harry wondered, for what felt the hundredth time. She eyed Oliver curiously. 'Dare I ask whether you touched on his reasons for sending that telegram? Since you clearly did much more than advise him Holmes could not take his case.'

Much to her amusement, Oliver looked somewhat embarrassed. 'I may not have been quite as emphatic as I could have been on that front.'

Harry stared at him. The Oliver she'd known and admired since she was a teenager rarely had difficulty putting his point across. 'Really?'

Oliver waved her incredulity aside. 'As I said, he's an excellent storyteller and I may have got caught up in the tale he wove. You'll understand when you hear it, although I can't promise to bring it to life quite so well.'

He had her full attention now. What exactly had Archer told him? 'Go on.'

'It's been something of a long day, Harry. Can't I at least have my drink first?' he asked.

Harry forced down a small surge of impatience. Oliver had just done her an enormous favour, after all, and it sounded very much as though the story he was about to share might be worth the wait. 'Of course.'

Thankfully, the service in the bar was every bit as fast as its reputation. The drinks arrived moments later and Oliver took a long, appreciative sip from his glass. 'That's better.'

Harry's own gin and tonic was much less incendiary than the Martini, for which she was grateful. The bartender, a certain Harry Craddock, had compiled a book containing some 750 cocktails and was always looking to add to his repertoire. He was well known for his heavy hand with spirits, meaning some of his drinks were strong enough to fell a giant, and Harry wasn't among those customers seeking the oblivion alcohol could offer. She wanted a clear head for what she was about to hear. After another swig, Oliver set his glass on the table. 'To business, then. Firstly, you were quite right to suspect Archer would not have tolerated being ignored. The circumstances of his uncle's illness trouble him greatly and I believe he is desperate for help.'

'So are most of the people who write to Holmes,' Harry observed, thinking about the many letters that had begged Holmes to intercede. 'But what is wrong with Philip St John? Is he really at death's door, as the telegram suggested?'

'I can only share what Archer told me,' Oliver said. He glanced around, as though making sure they were not being overheard. 'There are some physical symptoms – fatigue, lack of appetite, convulsions – but the majority of the problem appears to be in his mind. He is, according to Archer, terrified beyond all reason.' He rested a sombre gaze on Harry. 'Scared almost to death.'

The words sent an unexpected shiver down Harry's spine. It was no surprise St John's doctor had been unable to cure him – mental illness was fiendishly difficult to treat, even for those who specialised in psychological afflictions. 'Scared of what?'

'That is what Archer has not been able to establish,' Oliver said. 'The symptoms began around two weeks ago, with a series of nightmares so violent that the poor man's screams woke the entire household. At first, Archer put them down to his uncle's vivid imagination – you'll recall he is an author – and asked the house-keeper to prepare a mild herbal sedative. But the next night proved much worse. Not only did the sedative fail to help, St John was also so distressed that he ran from the house in his night-clothes, stumbling into the fenland that surrounds the manor.'

'How awful,' Harry said, her eyes widening as she pictured the scene. 'Was anyone able to follow?'

'His wolfhound led the chase, it seems,' Oliver said. 'Archer said he was out of the door before anyone could stop him, snarling as though he sensed the devil himself in the darkness. They found St John by following the animal's barking and dragged him from the reeds, back to the house. The next morn-ing, St John awoke with a raging fever, no doubt the result of being drenched in fen water, and the doctor was summoned.'

That St John had caught a chill did not surprise Harry. The last days of November had been bitterly cold, with black ice and snow flurries on London's streets. How much colder must it have been in Cambridgeshire? And Philip St John was not a young man; a fever could lead to something much more deadly if not treated quickly. But Oliver had said the worst of his symptoms were psychological. It was likely they, and not the fever, were the reason for Archer's desperate telegram.

'Having listened to Archer's descriptions of the nightmares St John was suffering from, the doctor prescribed a sleeping draught,' Oliver continued. 'This at least allowed the patient and the remainder of the household to get some rest. But it seemed only to force the terrors into the daytime. St John became nervous and jumpy while awake, prone to fits of hallucination and hyster-ical screaming. He refused to leave the library, although Archer says many of his worst episodes have occurred there. But even when calm and lucid, St John cannot – or will not – tell anyone what he is afraid of, only that his doom is upon him.'

Harry reached for her drink, recalling the dreadful certainty of the woman she had spoken to. *It'll be the death of him, as it has been for many others.* 'And there has been no improvement?'

Oliver shrugged. 'The fever has left him weakened, with a rattling cough that shows no sign of improvement, but that is the least of Archer's concerns. He says his uncle does not eat and fights sleep, in spite of efforts to administer the sleeping draught. He sits hunched in a chair beside the fire, smoking his pipe and muttering endlessly to himself, jumping at shadows. Archer fears he has quite lost his mind, although thankfully he shows no tendency towards violence.'

It sounded like a terrible situation, Harry thought, made worse by both Philip St John's fame as an author and his notoriously reclusive nature. If news got out of a suspected mental illness, it might very well result in a newspaper frenzy. But as shocking as St John's decline was, she could not see what Archer could expect of Holmes, or any detective for that matter. It seemed as though the best course of action would be to consult an expert in psychological disorders.

'I agree,' Oliver replied, when she said as much. 'But Archer believes there must be a reason for his uncle's behaviour. The change in personality has been too sudden and the terror so absolute that something must have triggered it. That's what he wants Holmes to uncover.'

Harry sat back, deflated. 'It could be anything. Does Philip St John have a history of mental illness?'

'None at all,' Oliver said. 'Not even after his return from the war, which is another reason Archer is so convinced there is more to the matter than meets the eye. He wants Holmes to visit Thrumwell Manor and speak to his uncle.' He held up a hand to forestall Harry's interruption. 'Obviously, I explained I was in no position to agree to anything. He urged me to faithfully report everything to Holmes and promised to accept whatever decision he made.'

She sipped her drink, turning everything Oliver had said over in her mind. She could not deny it was an interesting case, one that Holmes would undoubtedly have jumped at, had it flown from the imagination of Sir Arthur Conan Doyle. But, as she had learned from her investigations into the disappearance of Mildred Longstaff, and her efforts to bring the true criminals to justice, real-life detective work was not as simple as it appeared on paper. And as tragic as Philip St John's condition appeared to be, Harry couldn't help observing there was very little of substance to investigate. It was something of a surprise Oliver hadn't pointed out the same thing. She arched an eyebrow over the top of her glass. 'Aren't you going to remind me that none of this is my concern?'

'I could,' he said mildly. 'Would you pay any attention if I did?'

It was a valid point. 'No, but that hasn't stopped you in the past.'

He inclined his head. 'Perhaps I'm learning. But in actual fact I think it might be a worthwhile puzzle for you. There's no crime, no danger that you might cross the wrong person and get hurt. The worst thing that might happen is that you get your feet soggy in the fens.'

There was, Harry observed with some exasperation, a maddening hint of condescension in his tone. It came from a well-meaning desire to protect her but completely failed to acknowledge she had already thwarted one criminal gang. He may as well have patted her on the head as he spoke. 'I am quite capable of looking after myself, Oliver.'

'I know. I've seen you in action.' He sighed. 'Look, you know I think you're taking a risk by investigating any of the letters Holmes receives, but I've also developed a healthy respect for your instincts and, having met with Archer myself, I can't help agreeing that there's something strange about the suddenness of his uncle's decline. Something you might be able to uncover.'

Slightly mollified, Harry frowned and shifted on her chair. 'Perhaps. Tell me, did Mr Archer mention anything about a curse?'

The incredulous look on Oliver's face almost made her wish she'd kept quiet. 'A curse? Why on earth would you ask that?'

'Because when I rang Thrumwell Manor yesterday, to advise Mr Archer the meeting could not go ahead, the woman who answered the phone suggested Philip St John had fallen victim to a curse that would lead to his death.' She paused. 'As it had to many others.'

Oliver puffed out a long breath. 'A coincidence. Fear and ignorance often breed superstition and I daresay it could appear as though someone suffering from a mental affliction might be cursed in some way, although it's a rather medieval view.'

'But the suggestion was that others had been afflicted too.' Harry swirled her drink around her glass. 'Surely that can't be a coincidence.'

He rubbed his chin. 'Archer didn't mention it and actors are generally a superstitious bunch. But I doubt it means anything. It's probably some local myth that's easy to repeat when there's no other explanation for frightening events.'

She had to concede it was a good point. 'I suppose so.'

They sat in thoughtful silence for a moment, the piano tinkling in the background. 'I took the liberty of doing some digging on Archer, incidentally,' Oliver said, as the gentility was broken by an outburst of raucous laughter from the opera singer's table. 'He's had some success as an actor – decent enough roles in several acclaimed theatre productions, although nothing you or I might have heard about. He seems well regarded at the Garston – something of a *bon vivant* – but that's no surprise, since you can't become a member if anyone objects to you joining. Philip St John is his uncle on the maternal side, and the consensus is that Archer is a fond and devoted nephew.'

Which explained his desperate efforts to determine the cause of his uncle's illness, Harry thought, if not his choice of detective. 'But what was your impression of him?' she asked Oliver.

Her friend pursed his lips. 'I'd say he's in his mid-thirties. Tall, with the kind of build that suggests he enjoys a good meal. Affable, despite the unhappy subject of our meeting. He speaks very well and, as I said, knows how to spin a yarn. I imagine he'd be excellent on stage.'

She absorbed the information. 'Is there a Mrs Archer?'

'A confirmed bachelor, by all accounts,' Oliver replied. 'Perhaps he hasn't met the right woman.'

It was on the tip of Harry's tongue to point out that perhaps he didn't want to meet the right woman, but she decided to let the observation go. Instead, she sat back, replaying everything else she had heard. She was still not certain that Watson wouldn't be the better choice to investigate, rather than Holmes, but perhaps there was something to be found that could help Philip St John recover his health. She was just about to say as much to Oliver when a shadow fell across their table. Expecting the waiter, Harry glanced up to ask for their bill and realised it was not the waiter at all. Standing before them, a cool smile playing across his handsome features, was Percy Finchem, son of Lord and Lady Finchem, and a potential future suitor for Harry, if her mother had her way. His gaze travelled from Harry to Oliver and back again. 'What a cosy *tête-à-tête* this is. I do hope I'm not interrupting.'

The sudden tightness around Oliver's eyes left Harry in no doubt that he was less than pleased to see Percy, and she was not the least bit surprised. Oliver had once warned her to take care around the Finchem brothers, said that they were not everything they seemed to be, although Harry herself had never known either of them to be anything less than charming. 'You're not interrupting at all,' she said smoothly. 'In fact, we were just about to leave.'

'Oh, surely not,' Percy said, with flattering dismay. He glanced at Oliver. 'Come, Fortescue, allow me to buy you a drink. Scotch on the rocks, is it?'

Oliver shook his head. 'Thanks but as Harry says, we're leaving. You can take our table if you like.'

'No need, I'm with a group of friends.' Percy turned his blue-eyed gaze on Harry and she saw him frown slightly as he took in the bruising around her eye. He was far too well-mannered to mention it but she knew he had noticed it all the same. She hoped the observation would not make its way back to her mother. 'In fact, it was only the sight of Miss White that tore me away from them. Are you sure I can't tempt you into another?'

His eyes danced as he surveyed her and, for a moment, she was transported back to a conversation they had shared on the starlit terrace of Abinger Hall. She'd suspected him of flirting then – there'd been a moment when she thought he might even have kissed her – and she was almost tempted to accept his offer of a drink now. He really was very good-looking, as well as attentive and amusing and even a little exciting. But Oliver was radiating disapproval; there was a good chance he might walk out if she said yes. And then she took in Percy's formal attire – the suave dinner jacket, crisp white shirt and black tie. 'It seems you're on the way somewhere else. We wouldn't want to hold you up.'

Percy lowered his voice. 'A rather stuffy dinner, since you ask,' he said, then brightened. 'But of course you must join us! I'd be forever in your debt – you'll be saving me from death by a thousand dull opinions.' He glanced at Oliver, whose scowl had deepened, and smiled. 'But I can see Fortescue is reluctant to let go of you. Perhaps another time.'

'Perhaps,' Harry replied diplomatically, as Oliver signalled to the waiter, who was at their table within seconds.

'Charge this to my account, Rolo, there's a good chap,' Percy said with easy authority, before Oliver could say a word.

The waiter hesitated and glanced at Oliver, who stiffened. 'That won't be necessary.'

Percy's smile widened into a grin. 'Oh, buck up, Fortescue, and let me buy you and Miss White a drink.'

For a second, Harry thought Oliver would refuse. But then he seemed to realise Percy would enjoy his refusal much more than his acceptance, and the tension in his expression eased. He downed the last of his whisky and put the glass on the table. 'Of course. Thank you.'

'It's the least I can do after disturbing your little get-together,' Percy replied as the waiter hurried away. 'And do give my very best regards to your parents, Harry. I hope to be invited back to dear old Abinger Hall very soon.'

'I'll be sure to pass on your good wishes,' Harry said, and placed her own glass on the table. 'Thanks for the drink, Percy. I hope you have fun this evening.'

'Not as much fun as I might with you for company.' Percy sighed. 'But I daresay I'll survive.'

Harry smiled with wry amusement. She'd thought when they'd first met that James Finchem was the more obviously charming of the Finchem brothers but she had soon learned that Percy's sly humour was a secret weapon that disarmed all her defences. It was probably a good thing she had turned his offer down. She stood up and hung her handbag over her arm. 'I daresay you will. Goodnight.'

Oliver rose too. He nodded at Percy. 'Goodbye, Finchem.'

'Fortescue,' Percy said, but kept his eyes on Harry. She felt him watching them all the way to the polished walnut doors and it was something of a relief when they swung shut behind them. 'That was an unexpected pleasure,' Oliver said, in a tone of voice that suggested it had been anything but.

'You shouldn't let him provoke you,' Harry replied as they made their way down the marble stairs and into the chandelier-lit magnificence of the Savoy hotel lobby. 'It only encourages him.'

Oliver grunted. 'Men like Percy Finchem don't need encouragement.' Seeming to realise how surly he sounded, he puffed out a breath. 'But enough about him. Have you made a decision about Archer?'

'I'm going to sleep on it,' Harry said promptly. 'Mr Archer was returning home this evening – I have no doubt he can wait until tomorrow to hear from Holmes again.'

'That sounds like an excellent plan,' Oliver answered with an approving nod. He glanced towards the brass revolving doors that led to the horseshoe-shaped courtyard, where the green-liveried doormen waited to guide them towards the bustle of the Strand. 'Will you take a cab?'

Harry considered the question. She loved making her own way around London but it was a good thirty-minute walk to her apartment in Hamilton Square, and while the Underground lessened the journey time, she would still have to change trains at Oxford Circus and she was tired. Moreover, the gin had gone a little to her head, a situation that she suspected would only be made worse by the cold night air. A taxi would have her home in less than ten minutes, if the traffic were kind, and curled up on her settee with a pot of Earl Grey gently brewing within quarter of an hour. The thought was too appealing to turn down. 'Yes,' she said, giving in graciously for once. 'I rather think I will.'

4

Despite her early night, Harry did not sleep well. Her dreams were disjointed journeys along dark alleys and dingy backstreets, punctuated with white-faced figures who loomed out of the shadows and vanished within seconds. She was searching for something but could not grasp what it was, let alone find it, and there was no one to help her. On several occasions she was certain she had been awoken by the mournful howling of a hound, even though none of her neighbours owned a dog. When she finally got up, yawning and unrefreshed, it was to dull grey skies and the persistent patter of rain on the windowpanes.

The wireless did nothing to raise her spirits; she listened for a few minutes but the presenter's voice grated on her nerves and she was forced to turn it off. It was going to be a long day, she decided, as she set a saucepan of water on the stove to make a soft-boiled egg for breakfast. A day in which she had some decisions to make.

The rain turned London's streets into a sea of black umbrellas. The newspaper sellers hunched into their coats, calling the headlines with markedly less enthusiasm than usual, although Harry was still able to discern that the American arrested in Southampton for suspected drug trafficking had been released without charge. The Lord Robertson burglary seemed to have slipped from the front pages, which Harry supposed was to be expected. The news cycle moved fast, after all, and fresh headlines sold more papers. Few were stopping to buy today – her fellow pedestrians hurried to their destinations with grim determination, collars up and heads down against the icy deluge. It was not a day for making eye contact or smiling, Harry thought as she made her way along Baker Street.

Danny the doorman nodded deferentially as he ushered her into the sanctuary of the bank. 'Good morning, Miss White.'

'Good morning, Danny,' she said, shaking the raindrops from her umbrella before stepping through the open door. 'I hope you don't get too wet today.'

He smiled. 'It's good for the garden. Maybe I'll grow a bit too.'

Harry laughed, because the doorman was broad-shouldered and at least six foot four. 'Maybe you will.'

Her good humour faded as she crossed the hushed lobby and pressed the gilded button to summon the elevator. She had always been on good terms with Danny, and his colleague, Patrick, and that had not changed. But she suspected one of them, perhaps both, were spying on her for Simeon Pemberton, and reporting her movements in and out of the bank. As Pemberton had implied, he was looking for a reason to force Mr Babbage to sack her, in a way that could not possibly cast a blemish on his own conduct, but perhaps he would consider his next move more carefully now that he knew she was aware of his secret. Nevertheless, Harry intended to find a way to flush out which of the doormen was the spy. That too might be information she could turn to her advantage.

She knew from the moment she unlocked the door to her

office and stepped inside that someone had been there before her. Pausing in the doorway, she took in the scene, wondering what it was that had caught her attention. Nothing appeared to be out of place: the typewriter sat on the small wooden desk, its empty carriage perfectly centred, just as she'd left it the night before. A cluster of envelopes rested beside the peace lily, waiting for Bobby to collect them. Her chair was pushed neatly beneath the desk; the telephone stood to attention on the tallest filing cabinet in one corner; the hatstand loomed behind the door.

All was as it should be, yet Harry could not shake the impression someone else had been in the room. It could not be the cleaners – her tiny broom cupboard of an office was not important enough to merit their attention and Harry kept dusters and polish, plus a dustpan and brush, in a drawer to use herself twice a week. Frowning, she sniffed the air. Was that cologne she could smell? Faint but woody, with a hint of something like musk – not, she thought, a perfume a woman would choose to wear. And beneath that, the unmistakable odour of tobacco.

A swift glance at the keyhole showed no obvious signs of tampering – if there had been an intruder, they had used a key. Closing the door, Harry approached her desk. The envelopes had been neatly aligned when she'd left for the day, leaning against one another like fallen dominos. Now they were ever so slightly askew, as though someone had rifled through them and not taken the same exacting care Harry had when replacing them. Her gaze came to rest upon the floor at the side of the desk. Fragments of soil lay dark against the plush red carpet. It was not unheard of for Harry to accidentally knock the peace lily to the ground, but she had not done so for several days, and she was sure she had tidied any loose soil that had been spilled.

The hairs on the back of her neck prickled as she turned to

survey the filing cabinets, which contained all the correspondence relating to Sherlock Holmes, both the letters he received and carbon copies of the replies Harry sent back. The taller of the two cabinets was not kept locked – she used that for the letters and standard responses she produced on behalf of Holmes. The smaller cabinet was fitted with a lock, to which Harry held the only key. The top drawer was home to her tin of Fortnum and Mason biscuits, which she usually took with a cup of tea from the drinks trolley that passed mid-morning along the corridor. The bottom drawer was where she kept her cleaning materials, along with several old, discarded newspapers. Slotted among the printed pages was a slender cardboard folder, containing the unauthorised letter she had sent to Esme Longstaff and the second telegram from John Archer, detailing the meeting at the Garston Club.

Pulling open the top drawer of the taller cabinet, Harry cast her gaze over the contents. The hanging folders and their papers were arranged in date order, the original letter plus the corresponding reply, each signed by R. K. Moss, the name Harry had invented for the secretary to Sherlock Holmes. She ran a hand across the metal supports, selecting one at random to pull apart and reveal the letters inside. As with the envelopes on the desk, they had not been replaced with precision. It appeared someone was interested in what Harry had been doing in her official capacity at the bank. But how much had they discovered?

Crouching down, she examined the lock on the filing cabinet, ignoring the droplets of rain that ran from her coat to dampen her stockings. There were no telltale scratch marks to indicate it had been picked. She tugged at the uppermost drawer, relieved when it did not open. If someone had been able to pick the lock without leaving a trace, it was unlikely they would have taken the trouble to lock it again. But she would only know for sure by looking inside.

Taking the key from a zipped pocket of her handbag, Harry eased it into the lock. The top drawer appeared to be undisturbed – her biscuit tin was in the corner where she had left it, an unopened bar of Fry's Chocolate Cream beside it. So far, so good, Harry thought as she closed the drawer and opened the one below. This, too, looked exactly as she'd left it. The dusters were folded, a tin of beeswax polish resting on top. The dustpan and brush lay alongside. Carefully, Harry lifted them out and laid them on the carpet. She surveyed the newspapers with a narrowed gaze. Had they been moved? She thought not. Even so, she held her breath when she shifted their weight to reveal the folder hidden in their midst. Her heart thumped as she flipped back the cover. The letter and the telegram were both still there, perfectly centred the way Harry had left them. She let out her breath in a fast, uneven whoosh. Whoever had entered the office, for whatever reason, it did not appear they had discovered her secret.

Getting to her feet, Harry closed the drawer and set about removing her hat and coat. She had never considered who at the bank might have keys that could open all the doors – the security guards, perhaps? There was a cabinet filled with keys in Mr Babbage's office, down in the post room, but Harry did not think he kept a key to her office, for all that it was technically part of his domain. And it seemed almost impossible that the intruder had been someone from outside the bank – what logical motive could anyone have to break into Harry's all-but-forgotten office and take nothing? It made no sense at all, she thought, as she took a distracted seat at her desk. But it made no sense for anyone who worked at the bank to break in either. Unless—

Harry tapped a fingernail on the wooden surface of the desk. Bobby had told her the men in the post room were burning with curiosity after the second telegram to Holmes had arrived. He had hinted there might even be gambling about its contents. What if one of the post room men had decided to settle the wager and find out what the message had said? Could they have snuck into her office to read the telegram for themselves? She could think of no other reason someone might have broken in, and gone to some pains to keep their intrusion secret. But it was a mystery she did not know how to solve.

Certainly, she could not march into the basement and start throwing accusations around – that would lead to a very unpleasant scene and Harry would not come out of it well. She might question Bobby but she instinctively felt this was not his work. He was too blunt and open for such underhand behaviour. But he might know who the culprit was. It was something she would have to think about. And, in the meantime, she would go out at lunchtime to buy a copy of that morning's newspaper and hide the letter to Esme and Mr Archer's telegram inside it when she went home that evening.

An immovable prickle of unease settled between Harry's shoulder blades for the remainder of the morning. Coupled with her indecision about John Archer, she was restless and out of sorts, and frequently caught herself staring into space. By the time the clock hands had crawled around to midday, she was desperate to escape. Donning her hat and coat once more, she made her way to the nearby gates of Regent's Park, in the hope that its lush greenery might improve her mood. It might also help her decide what to do about John Archer and his ailing uncle.

Thankfully, the rain had stopped but Harry's usual bench was wet and uninviting. Preferring not to mar her afternoon with a damp skirt, she decided instead to take the bridge that crossed the boating lake and stroll along the path that led to the newly established open-air theatre. It had begun life as a makeshift venue in June and rumour had it there were plans for a full production of *Twelfth Night* the following summer. Harry made a mental note to ask Seb, her usual partner for all things theatrical, if he'd like to attend. Perhaps John Archer would be among the cast, if he was as talented an actor as Oliver had suggested.

The thought took her back to the story he had shared the night before. The idea that Philip St John might be cursed in some way seemed ridiculous in the cold light of day – she was sure there must be a more logical explanation for his sudden illness. Would it hurt to travel to his home and see if she could find it? The discovery that someone had searched her office had left her unsettled and she suddenly felt the need to get away from London.

Her instinct was to catch a train to Abinger Hall, to immerse herself in the familiarity and comfort of her family home, where there was always a dog to help soothe her worries away, but perhaps a trip to Thrumwell Manor might provide a different kind of distraction. Hadn't Oliver mentioned there was a dog there too? All she would need to do was notify Archer of her intention to visit, on behalf of Holmes, and decide on the best method of communication. A telegram would be easiest, and perhaps might carry the most authority, but a telephone call would allow her to inform Mr Archer that he should expect the arrival of R. K. Moss, not Sherlock Holmes. Since she would be travelling some distance, and would be alone, Harry was anxious to avoid any misunderstandings. It seemed prudent to ensure Archer understood she was a woman.

Her mind made up, Harry left the greenery of the park and revisited the telephone booth on Marylebone Road. Grateful she'd had the wit to make a note of the number to reach Thrumwell Manor, she dialled it and waited for someone to answer. 'Morden 4.'

It seemed to Harry to be the same voice she had heard on her last call, and perhaps the call before that. 'John Archer, please.'

'Who should I say is calling?'

'This is Miss R. K. Moss,' she said in a crisp tone, 'calling with regard to Mr Archer's meeting at the Garston Club yesterday.'

'One moment.'

The silence on the other end of the telephone seemed to stretch for an age, although Harry guessed it was no more than a minute. 'Archer here. Who is this?'

Again, Harry steeled herself. This was it, the moment of no return. Once she explained who she was and why she was calling, the wheels of the investigation would begin to turn. 'Good afternoon, Mr Archer, my name is R. K. Moss. I'm an associate of Oliver Fortescue, with whom you met yesterday. I understand you want to engage the services of Sherlock Holmes.'

If Archer was surprised, his voice did not reflect it. 'That's right. Does this mean Mr Holmes will take the case? Are you calling to make arrangements for him to visit?'

'In a manner of speaking,' Harry said carefully. 'Mr Holmes has retired as a consulting detective. I work as his assistant, managing his London correspondence. Your uncle's story intrigues him but, as I am sure you will understand, he is unable to travel to Cambridgeshire to investigate himself. He has, however, authorised me to do so on his behalf.'

There was a pause as Mr Archer digested the information. 'I see,' he rumbled at length. 'Then who is the gentleman I met with at the Garston Club yesterday?'

'An associate,' Harry repeated. 'A trusted associate who assists me with Mr Holmes' cases from time to time. On this occasion, it was not possible for me to meet you, so I asked Mr Fortescue to do so instead.'

'And he has made you aware of our situation?' Archer queried. 'You and Holmes?'

'He has,' Harry said. 'I am prepared to call upon you and your uncle when convenient, to see what, if anything, Mr Holmes can do to help.'

She waited, resisting the temptation to hold her breath. Either he would accept the story she had proffered or demand Holmes take the case himself. If he chose the latter, she would have no choice but to wish his uncle well and end the conversation.

'How soon could you come?' Archer said abruptly. 'Is this evening too soon?'

Harry thought fast. She was certain there would be a train that would get her to Cambridgeshire that evening, but she did not want to arrive at the house of a stranger, with no means of getting away if she needed to. 'I'm afraid so. There are certain preparations I shall need to make. Tomorrow is more convenient.'

'Tomorrow, then,' Archer said. 'If you are able to take the 1.34 p.m. train from Liverpool Street to Ely, our driver will collect you from the station. My uncle is a recluse, as you must be aware, so the house is rather isolated. You will not find a taxi willing to carry you.'

'Thank you,' Harry said. 'That's very kind.'

'Not at all – it's the least I can do,' he said, and paused. 'I don't know whether Mr Fortescue mentioned that the manor is surrounded on all sides by ancient fenland. It can be a little windswept. Might I suggest you bring a warm coat and sturdy boots along with your overnight bag?'

Recalling Oliver's comment about getting her feet wet, Harry permitted herself a mirthless smile. 'Advice I shall certainly take. I look forward to meeting you tomorrow, Mr Archer.'

'As do I. Until then, Miss Moss.'

Harry walked back to Baker Street with a determined spring in her step and a tingle of what might just have been excitement in her stomach. Investigating the mystery of Philip St John's illness might not have the same thrill as chasing a dangerous criminal through the streets of London but it was still enough to lift her spirits. Whether it became a case worthy of the famous detective in whose name she was acting remained to be seen.

* * *

After everything Harry had heard about Thrumwell Manor, both from Oliver and during her telephone conversation with John Archer, she was not surprised to experience a faint stirring of unease when the chauffeur stopped in front of a pair of imposing iron gates late on Saturday afternoon. 'Won't be a moment, miss,' the driver said, opening his door and allowing a chilly gust of wind inside the car. 'I need to undo the chain.'

Perhaps the security was necessary in the absence of a gate-house, Harry thought as she watched the driver approach the gates, or perhaps it was evidence of Philip St John's reclusive nature. The property was hidden from the road by a high red-brick wall but the entrance was not entirely unguarded; two stone dragons snarled at each other from turrets on either side of the gates. She turned her head to take in the surrounding area. Archer had not exaggerated when he'd said his uncle's house was isolated. The car had passed through a tiny village a mile or so back; Harry had noted a pub – The Morden Arms – and a village shop nestled among a small cluster of houses, but the land since had been barren and flat in all directions. Spindly hedgerows lined the far side of the narrow road that bordered Thrumwell Manor, overlooking bare tilled fields that bled into distant hedges and more fields beyond. Trees were few and far between but when they did appear, they were leafless skeletons grasping at the leaden sky.

Cambridgeshire was prime farmland, Harry knew, famous for its fertile soil reclaimed from the wetlands. She'd expected it to be dotted with farmhouses and yards, criss-crossed with villages that still bustled even at the start of winter, all laid across a patchwork of undulating fields, much like the land around her family's estate in Surrey. She hadn't expected such emptiness.

The driver's door opened and the chauffeur slid silently behind the wheel once more. He eased the car through the gates, then stopped again a short way inside. This time, he didn't explain before getting out and Harry tried not to wince at the heavy clang of iron on iron as the gates were closed and chained. There was no going back now, she thought, although that had been true from the moment she'd alighted from the train at Ely; there were no return trains to London until the morning. A prickle of apprehension chased along her spine as the car resumed its journey. An overnight stay was undoubtedly required, in order to appreciate the terror that beset Philip St John, but now that Harry was here, she couldn't help wondering whether coming alone had been a mistake. Oliver had wanted to accompany her; Harry had stoutly refused, although she had accepted his offer to come and collect her the following day. She hoped refusing his company was not a decision she was going to regret.

The view from inside the walls did nothing to settle her disquiet. There was no avenue of trees lining the somewhat bumpy track to the house, nothing to offer protection from the biting November wind that whistled across the roof of the car. And when she looked to the manor house itself, she was struck by its stark isolation; its only neighbours were the birds circling high above. An almost palpable sense of loneliness hung over the landscape. Perhaps the solitude was what had first drawn Philip St John to live here, but it might also be contributing to the fear that was consuming him now, Harry thought. It was certainly affecting her and she hadn't even crossed the threshold of Thrumwell Manor yet. She gave herself a brisk mental shake. Holmes would not allow himself to be swayed by such fanciful notions and nor would she. Logic and deduction were the antidote to fear.

The house began to loom large, shaking off the dark shadows that had shrouded it from a distance. Harry turned a curious gaze upon it. The sun was low in the sky; the last of its rays lacing the clouds with delicate pink and orange, and Harry half-expected the fading light to reveal broken windows and a neglected roof. What she saw caused an involuntary gasp of shock to escape her. The walls of Thrumwell Manor were the colour of blood.

She blinked hard, cursing her overstimulated imagination, and looked again but the effect had not diminished. Crimson rippled across the stone, as though the building's lifeblood seeped from the wounds of its windows. Shaking the ridiculous notion away, Harry forced herself to study the scene. 'How extraordinary,' she said, striving to sound as though blood-drenched houses were an everyday experience. 'Does it always look like that?'

The driver nodded, his cap bobbing in the half-light. 'At this time of year, aye. It's the vines. They turn red just before winter.'

The vines, Harry thought, and almost laughed in relief. Of course that's what it was – a simple combination of leaves and the setting sun, fluttering in the wind. As the car drew to a halt, she could see the evidence with her own eyes; the walls of the house were indeed covered with thick scarlet leaves, from the ground floor all the way to the garret attic windows at the very top. She felt rather foolish as she got out of the car to stand on the gravel drive. Holmes would have deduced it in an instant, although she felt Dr Watson might have been more affected. But she had no time to dwell on her credulity. The large front door had opened and a tall, heavy-set, blond-haired man was hurrying down the stone steps to meet her.

'Miss Moss,' he said, throwing his arms wide in an expansive, theatrical greeting. 'I am John Archer. Welcome to Thrumwell Manor.'

5

His handshake was firm, although perhaps a little too enthusiastic to be entirely proper, but Harry did not hold that against him. The warmth of his smile was enough to dispel some of the apprehension that had enveloped her since passing through the iron gates of the manor, and she found she could not help smiling in return. 'Thank you, Mr Archer. Your home is very impressive.'

'My uncle's home,' he corrected without rancour, and turned to survey the vine-covered walls, now darkened to a deep burgundy by the dipping sun. 'But it is a splendid old pile. Was it wrong of me to hope that you might arrive in time to admire the effect of the leaves? They lend such a marvellously Gothic air to the place.'

'They do,' Harry agreed. A gust of icy wind caused her to shiver.

'But I am being a terrible host,' Archer cried, noticing her discomfort. 'You must come inside at once. Donaldson will bring your effects.'

Harry did not need any further encouragement. The temperature had dropped since she had alighted from the train at Ely and her breath was beginning to plume in the cold air. It would be below freezing before moonrise, she thought, and was glad she had heeded Mr Archer's warning and brought a thick coat. Not that she planned to spend much time outside during her brief visit to Thrumwell Manor. She followed Archer up the steps, hesitating only for a fraction of a second as she passed beneath the blood-red vines and through the ornately carved door frame to enter the house.

'How is your uncle today?' she asked as they arrived in a wood-panelled hallway with a heavy, grey flagstone floor. It was only marginally warmer than outside, Harry thought, but thankfully the whistling wind was shut out as soon as the door closed. Weak yellow light spilled feebly from several wall lamps, creating deep pockets of gloom where it did not reach. A wide stone staircase against one wall drew the eye, also lit with barely adequate wall lamps that did nothing to dispel the fall of night. It was a far cry from the entrance hall at Harry's family home, where a magnificent chandelier shimmered from the high ceiling, filling the room with light. Standing at the foot of the stairs was a woman of around thirty, dressed simply in black with her hands folded together. At her side was an enormous grey wolfhound. It eyed Harry with wary stillness and she wasn't altogether sure she blamed it.

'My uncle is in the library,' Archer said. 'As I told your associate, he rarely leaves that room, now. It is all I can do to get him to bed each evening. You can meet him presently, once you've settled into your room and recovered from your journey.' He took a few steps towards the woman. 'In the meantime, may I introduce Agnes, our housekeeper – I believe you have already spoken on the telephone. And beside her is Barrymore, my uncle's beloved wolfhound. He may look terrifying but I assure you he is a soft-hearted creature, especially if you happen to have a biscuit to offer him.'

The dog was large, even seated as he was now, and Harry guessed he must be twice the size of Tiggy and Winston, her beloved Labradors at Abinger Hall. He was covered in wiry grey fur and his head was cocked, his eyes alert as he assessed her. She would make friends with him later, she decided, once she'd had time to source a treat to allay his suspicions. Her gaze travelled to Agnes, who was watching her every bit as warily as Barrymore. 'Good afternoon, Agnes,' she said.

The woman nodded, her face pale in the dim light. She did not smile. 'Good afternoon, miss. I hope you had a pleasant journey.'

A soft country accent coloured her words, evident to Harry's ears now that her voice was not distorted by the crackle of the telephone. 'I did, thank you,' Harry replied. 'The train was punctual and not too crowded.'

John Archer rubbed his hands together in jovial approval. 'Excellent. Agnes, would you show Miss Moss to her room?' He turned to Harry. 'Once you've settled in, I thought perhaps tea in the drawing room. Unless you'd prefer something stronger?'

It could not be much past four o'clock, Harry thought, although dusk had fallen in earnest outside. 'Tea would be very welcome,' she said.

Archer nodded. 'And once you're refreshed, I thought I might show you the house. It might aid your investigations to understand the layout before – before I introduce you to my uncle.'

His good humour dimmed a little, as though this last task was something he was loath to undertake, and Harry could certainly understand why. Such a sudden deterioration in the health and behaviour of a loved one must be hard to accept and the instinct of any caring relative would be to shield them from outsiders. The fact that Harry was there expressly because of Philip St John's illness would not make the instinct to protect any easier to quell. 'Of course,' she said. 'That would be very helpful, thank you.'

Agnes stepped forward. 'This way, if you please.'

Harry followed her up the stairs, the steps of which were bare and worn in the centre with age and the passage of feet. She took care with her own footing in the dim light, keeping one hand on the smooth wooden balustrade as they climbed to the first floor. Tall leaded windows punctuated the landing and Harry felt a sharp burst of cold air radiate from the expanse of glass as she passed along the corridor. She made a mental note to wear a cardigan when she met Mr Archer for tea, and hurried to catch up to Agnes. 'Tell me, is it just you who sees to Mr Archer and his uncle?'

The housekeeper shook her head. 'No, miss. There's the cook, Mary. Mr Archer likes a hearty meal, as does the master, when he's in his right mind, and she's been here almost as long as I have. And then there's Donaldson, who drove you here. He's the groundskeeper as well as Mr Archer's driver.'

They must all be live-in staff, Harry thought, given the isolation of the house. Three was a reasonable number to cater for the needs of two gentlemen but she doubted it was enough to manage a property the size of Thrumwell Manor. Perhaps there were parts of the house that were unused. 'How long have you worked here?'

'Around fifteen years,' Agnes replied. 'Started as a maid for the old family what lived here, and stayed on when the master took the place on, after the war.'

Which meant this was very likely the only employment she had known, Harry thought. That spoke well of Philip St John, at least. 'And Donaldson?'

'He came not long after Mr Archer arrived, about a year ago.'

A little surprised, Harry considered this new information. Did it mean anything that John Archer had come to live with his uncle so recently? Where had he lived before? The housekeeper stopped beside a wooden door. 'I put you in the blue room. It's got good drapes to keep the wind out.'

Turning the handle, she pushed the door back and stood aside to allow Harry to enter. There could be no doubt how the room had got its name; the walls were covered in pale blue wallpaper and slightly faded cornflower blue velvet drapes shrouded the windows. A grand four-poster bed dominated the room, hung with the same cornflower blue velvet as the windows. The lighting was as weak here as elsewhere in the house, although Harry was glad to see a decent fire burned in the grate, beneath a white marble mantelpiece. Overall, the room was calm and welcoming, and Harry turned to smile her approval at Agnes. 'It's lovely. Thank you.'

The housekeeper nodded. 'There's a washbasin in the cabinet over there, and a pot under the bed, but the bathroom is just at the end of the corridor if you prefer.'

Harry very much did prefer; even her grandfather had stopped expecting the household staff to empty his chamber pot each morning. She cast her gaze around the room again and the pattern on the wallpaper caught her eye. Moving closer for a better look, she saw that what she'd taken from a distance to be stylised flowers and ferns was actually a line drawing of a man rowing a tiny boat, picked out in varying shades of blue and repeated over and over again across the paper. 'How unusual.'

'There's a lot of waterways round these parts,' Agnes said. 'The fens and the lodes that join them up to the rivers. People have been transporting goods on the water since long before the railway came.'

'Fascinating,' Harry said, studying the wallpaper again.

Agnes cleared her throat. 'Will there be anything else, miss? I can wait and take you to the drawing room, if you'd like.'

Harry shook her head. What she wanted was ten minutes alone, to gather her thoughts and consider what she had learned so far. But she had one last question for Agnes before she let her go. 'When we spoke on the telephone the first time I rang, you told me you thought Philip St John was cursed. What did you mean by that?'

The housekeeper started, glancing over her shoulder as though she feared someone might have overheard. 'I shouldn't have said that,' she said quickly. 'Mr Archer doesn't like us to talk about it.'

'But you believe it's true?'

Agnes hesitated, then took several steps closer. 'Not just me – the cook too. But she's a local, like me – she knows the stories. Mr Archer and William aren't from these parts; they've never heard about the *ferryman*.'

The final word was whispered in a tumbling, fearful rush, as though simply saying the name might invoke terrible consequences. 'I see,' Harry murmured. 'Who – or what – is the ferryman?'

Agnes flashed her a beseeching look and hurried to the window, twitching one of the drapes aside to peer out into the darkness. 'We try not to speak his name, especially not so near the fens. Some say it summons him.'

It was exactly as Oliver had predicted, Harry thought: a local myth that could be blamed for the unexplained. 'But you believe he is responsible for your master's condition? How?'

'He saw him,' Agnes said, with doleful certainty. 'Death always comes to those who see him. But I've said too much. Mr Archer won't like it.'

Damping down her frustration, Harry raised her eyebrows.

'Mr Archer has invited me here to discover what ails his uncle. How am I to do that if I can't explore all the possibilities?'

For a moment, Agnes looked torn. 'You'll have to ask him,' she said finally. After smoothing the curtain back into place, she crossed to the door. 'Will that be all?'

'Yes, thank you.' Harry decided to let her go. 'For now.'

The housekeeper nodded once and left, closing the door firmly behind her. Glancing around, Harry saw her case had been left at the foot of the bed and she set about unpacking the items she had brought with her. Given the nature of her visit, she had guessed she would not be expected to dress for dinner but she did want to change out of her travelling clothes and wash her hands and face. Once that was done, she perched on the end of the bed and took her notebook from her handbag to jot down what little new information she had gathered.

The cook was an unknown at present, but she had met three of the five people who lived at Thrumwell Manor and it was possible one of them knew more than they were telling about the illness of Philip St John. Getting to her feet, Harry crossed to the window and tugged the curtain aside to gaze out into the night. The room occupied the corner of the house and had windows in two of its walls; she assumed she would have excellent views across the front and north-eastern side of the estate. But for now, unbroken blackness met her gaze, and a low, whistling moan could be heard as the wind blew around the corner of the building. She was reminded with a shiver of unease that she truly was in the middle of nowhere. But it would not do to dwell on that, nor to be affected by the housekeeper's suggestion of mysterious ferrymen.

It was time to bring logic and common sense to bear, to eliminate the impossible and examine what was left. It was time to meet Philip St John.

The drawing room was just off the entrance hall. It was warmed by a roaring fire in the hearth, much to Harry's relief. Its windows were covered by heavy brocade curtains and its chairs faced towards the fire. Barrymore basked in the warmth of the flames; he raised his grey head when the door opened and then lowered it again when he observed Agnes, although Harry noticed he maintained a watchful eye on her as Archer ushered her towards the chairs. 'Tea?' Archer asked, waving a hand at a table laden with cups and saucers and a gently steaming teapot.

'Yes, please,' Harry said, settling into an armchair. 'With milk, thank you.'

He poured her a cup and balanced it deftly on a saucer to pass it to her, before filling a cup for himself. 'I thoroughly recommend the seed cake,' he said, indicating a delicious-looking, golden brown loaf topped with caraway seeds that sat invitingly at one end of the tray. 'The cook here is an excellent all-rounder but I believe her cakes are worthy of the finest London afternoon tea menu.'

Harry was about to regretfully decline, having learned from experience that juggling tea and cake did not go well when trying to take notes, when her stomach betrayed her with a perfectly timed rumble, reminding her that she had eaten nothing since her hurried lunch before boarding the train at Liverpool Street. 'Perhaps a small slice,' she allowed, putting her notebook to one side.

She sipped the tea, which was strong and hot and most welcome, and took the opportunity to study John Archer as he busied himself in cutting the cake. Oliver's estimate had been accurate, she thought – he was somewhere around his mid-thirties. Faint lines creased his forehead and the skin around his eyes, although his hair was as yet untouched by grey. He dressed well; his suit was expensively cut from a dark grey material but the waistcoat beneath his jacket was a glorious flash of claret and gold. His shoes were black and shiny – patent leather, if she was not mistaken, and made for style rather than comfort. He was, Harry guessed, something of a peacock but perhaps that wasn't such a surprise, given his profession.

'Your scrutiny does you credit, Miss Moss,' he said, without looking up. 'Do I meet with your expectations?'

It wasn't a rebuke – if anything, he seemed amused as he handed her a plate containing a generous slice of cake – but Harry still felt warmth rise in her cheeks. She fought to maintain her composure. 'You must forgive me. It's a peculiarity of the job – one never knows which tiny detail might help Mr Holmes to crack the case.'

'Indeed,' he said heartily and cleared his throat. '*You know my method. It is founded upon the observation of trifles.*'

'Exactly so,' Harry said, recognising the quote as one belonging to Holmes but unable to recall which of the many stories it had come from. 'Have you ever portrayed Mr Holmes on the stage?'

Archer shook his head. 'I am a great admirer of his work but I have not yet had the honour,' he said, and patted his gently rounded stomach. 'Sadly, I suspect I am more of a Watson.'

Harry could not help smiling. Oliver had been right about that too; it was difficult not to like John Archer. 'Is that what made you write to Holmes?'

'In a manner of speaking,' Archer said slowly, and some of his good humour slipped away. 'You must understand that my uncle is an intensely private man. He began writing as a way to occupy his mind while he recovered from the war, little dreaming his first book would propel him to such fame.' He sighed. 'He once told me that everyone he met seemed to demand something from him – an autograph, an endorsement, a recommendation. It overwhelmed him, forcing him to hide away for well over a decade. But the life of a recluse suited him, although he struggled frequently with writer's block.'

Harry nodded. She had visited the London Library the night before to investigate Philip St John's literary career and had discovered his output had been sporadic over the years since his startling first success in 1920. She had borrowed that novel, *The Blood-soaked Soil*, with every intention of reading it before bed but tiredness had overtaken her and she had fallen asleep. It now sat on the bedside table of the blue room upstairs and she hoped she might have some time to begin reading it later.

Archer fixed her with a look. 'You must be wondering what all this has to do with Sherlock Holmes but it is simply this: when my uncle fell ill, I rapidly came to suspect there was an identifiable cause for his sudden mental decline, although I was at a loss to discern what it might be. I could not approach the police for help, as they would undoubtedly fail to appreciate the complexity of our unhappy situation. I needed a remarkable intellect, a deductive genius who would see to the heart of the problem in an instant. In short, I needed Sherlock Holmes.'

Harry shifted uncomfortably in her armchair and took a mouthful of seed cake, wondering what Mr Archer would say if she revealed his confidence was entirely misplaced, that he did not have the brilliance of the great detective at his command, because such a man did not exist outside the imagination of Sir Arthur Conan Doyle. He only had her. The confession would meet with incredulity and denial and perhaps even anger, and the repercussions would resonate well beyond the grounds of Thrumwell Manor. No, she could not confront Archer with the truth, not when she had willingly entered into, and encouraged, the charade. She had come with the intention of discovering what she could in order to help Philip St John, fully aware that she did so under false pretences. All she could do was continue to play the game, and hope that her confidence in her own abilities was not misplaced.

'I understand your position completely,' she said. 'Has Mr St John given any clue about the source of his terror? Were his nightmares the first symptom?'

John Archer placed his cup and saucer on the tea tray and gazed pensively at the leaping flames in the fireplace. 'Tell me, Miss Moss. Do you believe in the supernatural?'

The question caught Harry by surprise. She had not expected him to raise the matter of the curse, given his housekeeper's repeated insistence that he would not hear of it. 'I do not,' she said, after a moment to recover her wits.

'Nor do I,' he said, with brusque approval. 'And yet there are circumstances at play here that defy logical explanation. That is why I sent for Holmes.'

Harry considered his words. It occurred to her that logic was something that might be beyond Philip St John. His mind must be entirely given over to emotion. 'Does your uncle believe there is a supernatural cause?'

Archer's gaze was resigned. 'He does. That is why he will not sleep, at least not without resistance, and dare not leave the library. He fears death stalks him, although he cannot say what form it takes.'

It sounded very much like a tragic case of paranoid delusion, Harry decided, but kept the observation to herself. She put her cup on the tea tray, along with her empty plate, and opened her notebook. 'And your doctor – what is his view?'

'A complete mental breakdown,' Archer said abruptly. 'He advises me to transfer my uncle to an asylum, so that he may receive proper treatment.'

Harry understood his unspoken reluctance. Care for the

mentally ill had endured a nightmarish reputation for centuries, with asylums leaving vulnerable patients at the mercy of neglect and abuse, often with no attempt at treatment or rehabilitation. Huge steps had been taken to modernise the way the medical profession treated psychological afflictions, and the inhumane conditions of the old lunatic asylums were long gone, but there was still much that was unknown and a dreadful stigma attached to being admitted to a psychiatric hospital. No wonder Archer was desperate to find the reason for his uncle's sudden illness. 'Perhaps it would help if you could describe what happened the day Mr St John's health took a turn for the worse,' she said. 'Did anything out of the ordinary occur?'

'Nothing,' Archer said. 'Believe me, I have gone over and over that day, and the days preceding it. All was as it usually was. My uncle is a creature of habit – he rarely leaves the grounds of the manor. He took Barrymore for his usual walk – as you can imagine, a hound of his size needs considerable exercise and they usually roam along the path that winds through Morden Fen, most of which is contained within the manor's estate. They are often gone for several hours.'

'I see,' Harry said. Her own family dogs also needed long walks, and enjoyed the run of the Abinger land that surrounded the hall. 'Do they take their walk in the morning or later in the day?'

Archer frowned. 'Generally mid-morning but on that particular day, they went first thing. He took an early breakfast and was gone before I came downstairs.'

A change in routine, she observed, scribbling furiously. 'Why was that?'

'It had been a particularly good sunrise,' Archer said, shrugging. 'My uncle was inspired to get as close to it as he could.'

'And when they returned, Mr St John seemed to be his usual self?'

'As far as I could tell. Barrymore had chased a heron into the fen and needed washing down, but Donaldson took care of that. I saw my uncle at lunch and he seemed as taciturn as ever. Asked me to run an errand to the village shop to collect some more tobacco for his pipe and said he had some business to attend to in the library.'

Harry had to admit it did not sound as though anything untoward had happened to trigger such terror in Philip St John. 'Did you notice any change in his behaviour that evening?'

'None at all.' Archer paused. 'I took Barrymore out for a short walk before it got dark, just as far as the gates and back, and met my uncle for a pre-dinner drink in this very room. We ate an excellent meal – venison, as I recall – and took leave of each other around ten o'clock.'

She made a note of the time. 'When did you become aware something was wrong?'

'When the screaming began,' he said. 'In my sleep-befuddled state, I assumed it must be Agnes, or perhaps Mary, but realised I was wrong the moment I stumbled from my room. It was coming from along the corridor, from my uncle's room, but that made no sense to me. The noise was a dreadful, high-pitched keening, not the kind of sound a man would make.' He shook his head at the memory. 'I've never heard anything like it.'

Harry grimaced in sympathy. 'What happened next?'

'The others arrived – Agnes and Mary in their nightclothes, Donaldson half-dressed, all of them just as bewildered and half-asleep as I. My uncle was in the habit of sleeping with a locked door, so Donaldson and I forced it open. We found him curled upright in the corner of the room, screaming and screaming as though burning alive, although there was no injury that I could see.' Archer glanced at Harry, his expression suddenly bleak. 'I'm ashamed to admit I struck him, although there was no other way to bring him to his senses.'

The fact that he was so clearly remorseful did him credit, Harry thought. 'Did it work?'

'It did, although it took some time for him to tell us what had prompted him to scream in the first place. A nightmare he said, of such unbearable horror that his mind had wiped all trace of it from his memory. He only remembered the fear – a paralysing terror, he called it. He did not remember the screaming.'

Harry thought back to the sequence of events Oliver had related to her. 'You managed to calm him and the household returned to bed. Is that correct?'

Archer nodded. 'We were all exhausted the next morning but otherwise none the worse. I had some business in Ely but told Agnes to keep an eye on her master. Upon my return, she reported that the day had been uneventful, although my uncle had been irritable and had not eaten. He was ill-tempered with me at dinner, and I saw he had no appetite for the splendid meal Mary had served. Under my instructions, Agnes prepared a mild sedative – a lavender and valerian root tea, which he grudgingly accepted. I suggested an early night and took myself to bed not long after nine o'clock.' He stood up then, and crossed to a polished cabinet against one wall. 'Forgive me, but I find I am in need of something stronger than tea. Can I offer you anything?'

Harry shook her head. Archer busied himself briefly with a glass and the whisky bottle, then returned to his seat. 'Where was I? Ah yes, the second night.' He stared broodingly into the fire. 'I confess that I had taken a heavy nightcap to bed with me and perhaps that made me sleep more soundly than I might otherwise have done, for it took longer for the screaming to wake me. When I arrived at my uncle's door, it was already open and he was surrounded by Agnes, Mary and Donaldson. He was not curled in the corner this time, but on his feet and brandishing an iron poker.'

The admission caused Harry a flicker of disquiet. 'I was under the impression he was not violent.'

Archer waved a hand. 'He isn't – not on that occasion, and never since. I quickly realised he was fending off some apparition or creature only he could see, but when I tried to take the poker from him, he pushed me aside and barrelled from the room. He was through the front door before any of us could stop him, vanishing into the pitch-black night.'

Into the freezing fen, Harry thought grimly. 'You followed.'

'We did,' Archer said, 'although we would not have found him had it not been for Barrymore. He sleeps downstairs and was out after his master before any of us had cleared the stairs, snarling and growling in a way I've never known before. It was his barking that led us to my uncle, half-drowned in amongst the sedge and reeds. Donaldson and I carried him back to the house, only semi-conscious, and Agnes and Mary dried him off. They did their best to warm him but it was clear from his shivering that he had caught a chill.'

'The doctor came the next morning,' Harry observed. 'Did he suggest admitting Mr St John to hospital then?'

'No. He prescribed medicine to reduce the fever, advised us to keep him calm and warm, and gave me a strong sleeping draught to administer at night.' Archer shook his head. 'In spite of being weakened by the fever, I do believe he was more himself during those few days. He slept, at least, which was a mercy for us all. But once the symptoms of the chill receded, the nightmares returned. Except now they were not confined to the night – the apparitions invaded his waking hours, and grew worse with every passing day.

Which is where you find us now, Miss Moss. Please tell me you can help.'

He looked so dispirited that Harry felt her own disquiet stir. 'It sounds like a terrible ordeal,' she said, even as the weight of the mystery he was expecting her to unravel settled across her shoulders. Could she uncover what was ailing his uncle? What if she failed? For a moment, she battled with the fear that she had undertaken a task that was far beyond her: she was not really a detective and certainly not as brilliant as Holmes. But she was also aware that this was a feeling she had encountered before, when she had gazed into the desperate eyes of Mildred Longstaff's family as they begged her to find their girl. She had been out of her depth then too, but it had not prevented her from solving the case and restoring Mildred to her family.

Straightening her spine, Harry met John Archer's beseeching gaze. 'I shall do everything in my power to help you.'

Archer got to his feet. 'Let me show you the layout of the house, so you can understand our movements better.' Lifting his glass, he swallowed the remainder of his whisky in one gulp. 'We will finish in the library, with my uncle. I can only hope I have done enough to prepare you for what he has become.'

6

As Harry had surmised, not all of Thrumwell Manor was in everyday use. The upper floors were closed off, apart from the attic rooms inhabited by Agnes, Donaldson and Mary. A servants' staircase allowed them to come and go freely without using the main stone stairs. To the right of the staircase, Archer opened and closed a succession of doors, giving Harry a brief glimpse of several other first-floor guest rooms; she had a jumbled impression of pink wallpaper and drapes, followed by yellow and then green. All were cold and dank through lack of use and she was relieved when they did not linger in any of them.

Archer's room was on the left of the stairs, three doors along from the blue room Harry occupied. It reminded her of her brothers' bedrooms at home – a little untidy but comfortable and lived-in. At the furthest end of the corridor was the room where Philip St John slept. It was warm in here too, with a banked fire in the hearth and a four-poster bed even grander than the one in Archer's room, but there was something in the stale air that reminded Harry of a sick room. A full set of iron tools sat beside the fire. No one had felt the need to confiscate the poker.

Once they had left Philip St John's room, its splintered lock patched up but not fitted with a replacement that could keep anyone out, Harry turned her attention to a discreet door set into the wood panelling of the end wall. 'Does this lead to the service staircase?'

'It does,' Archer said, and turned a small brass door handle. The door swung silently inward. 'They go from the basement all the way up to the attic rooms.'

Leaning into the inky darkness, Harry looked up and down the shadowy stairs. 'There are no lamps.'

Archer shook his head. 'They use oil lamps to light their way. The previous family didn't fit electric lights in there before they left and my uncle didn't see the need for so small a staff.'

It made sense, Harry supposed, but she didn't much like the idea of travelling up and down a dark, narrow staircase with only an oil lamp to guide her steps, and she couldn't imagine Chesterton, the butler at Abinger Hall, accepting such a thing. 'Of course,' she murmured.

The ground floor had unused rooms too. The ballroom had clearly not enjoyed any dancing for a very long time, which made Harry a little sad; it was filled with cloth-draped furniture and the parquet floor was thick with dust. A splendidly formal dining room had a similarly abandoned air, although Archer showed her a much smaller room containing a highly polished six-seater table that was much more suited to the modest needs of the manor's inhabitants. 'We'll dine around six-thirty this evening, if that suits you?' Archer said.

A quick glance at the carriage clock on the mantelpiece told Harry it was just past five-thirty now. 'Perfect,' she said.

The kitchens were exactly as Harry had expected them to be – warm, comforting and filled with delicious aromas that competed for her attention. Mary was a well-rounded woman in her fifties, with rosy cheeks and wisps of white hair that peeked beneath her cap. She was kneading a large slab of bread dough with the air of one who meant to pummel it into submission but she looked up and smiled when they entered. 'Agnes told me you'd arrived,' she said, when Archer introduced Harry. 'I hope you've brought a good appetite.'

Harry returned her smile. 'If the rest of your food is as delicious as your seed cake then I'm going to be leaving here half a stone heavier tomorrow.'

The cook beamed at her. 'Well, now, I aim to please.'

Archer rubbed his hands together. 'And you succeed very well, Mary. As I mentioned earlier, Miss Moss may want to ask you some questions about my uncle's illness. Please answer them as fully as you can.'

'I'm not sure what I can add but I'll do my best,' Mary said, and Harry thought she saw a shadow pass over the other woman's face.

'Nothing for now,' Harry reassured her. 'Perhaps after dinner, when you're not so busy.'

Mary nodded gratefully. 'Yes, miss. Thank you.'

Outside the kitchen, Archer waved a hand at a door at the far end of the corridor. 'That leads to the cellar, where we keep the wine. Do you need to see it?'

Harry made a mental adjustment to the map she was building in her mind and shook her head. 'Not at present.'

'Good. That just leaves the library.' Squaring his shoulders, he glanced at her. 'Now remember, his appearance might shock you but he is not in any way dangerous. You will be perfectly safe.'

'Please don't worry,' Harry said. 'I'm fully prepared.'

Archer looked as though he might add more but seemed to think better of it. Instead, he led her out of the domestic quarters and back into the main part of the house. He stopped at a heavy wooden door and gripped the brass handle with purpose. 'Ready?'

She nodded. 'Ready.'

The door opened with the faintest of sighs. Harry followed Archer into the room, which appeared at first glance to be a fairly typical country house library. Floor-to-ceiling bookshelves covered all four walls and were stacked with books of all shapes and sizes – tall atlases, leather-backed tomes, less expensive cloth-coated hardbacks. As with all the other regularly used rooms in the house, thick drapes hung at the windows – these ones in a deep burgundy silk, Harry noted, to complement the plush plum-coloured carpet. A fire burned in the hearth, stoked high with leaping yellow flames and bright orange coals; the smell of woodsmoke and soot mingled with the lighter aroma of pipe tobacco.

Two high-backed armchairs faced each other near the fire-place. From Harry's position at the door, neither seemed to be occupied, but then she saw a faint curl of smoke rising from the chair with its back to her. A low, fearful voice broke the silence. 'Who is it? Who's there?'

Archer strode forwards. 'It's me, Uncle. It's John.' He rounded the chair so that its occupant could see him. 'I've brought someone to see you.'

There was a sharp intake of breath, the suggestion of move-ment in the chair. 'Who is it? Who's there?' the voice repeated. This time its tone was querulous.

'A friend,' Archer said soothingly, and beckoned Harry nearer. 'Here she comes now. This is Miss Moss. She's staying with us this evening.'

Slowly, Harry made her way towards the centre of the room and turned towards the chair. She wasn't entirely sure what she expected to find – a skeletal figure, perhaps, with gaunt yellow skin and strands of grey hair, and claw-like hands that dug into the arms of the chair as if they were talons. What she actually saw was a sandy-haired man of around forty-five, wild-eyed but alert. That he had recently been ill was evident from the pallor of his complexion and the rapid rise and fall of his chest. One hand held a gently smouldering pipe, the other clutched at a sheaf of blankets tucked around him almost to chin height. 'Hello, Mr St John,' she said softly. 'How lovely to meet you.'

He surveyed her with sudden agitation. Twin spots of red burned in his cheeks, in stark contrast to the milk white of the rest of his face. 'You shouldn't be here.'

With a quick glance at Archer, Harry took the seat opposite Philip St John. 'Oh, but I've just arrived. I came especially to see you, after your nephew told me you'd caught a fever.'

At this, the older man glared at Archer. 'Is she a nurse? Another damned nurse to prod and poke at me?'

Harry smiled, hoping to disarm him. 'I'm not a nurse.' She held up her notebook and pen. 'See? No thermometer, no stethoscope and definitely no needles.'

His beady-eyed gaze came to rest on the notebook. 'A psychiatrist, then, come to take me away. Do they let women do that nowadays?'

'They do,' Harry said, 'but that isn't why I'm here, either. I'm – well, to be honest, I just wanted to meet you. I'm a great admirer of your writing, most especially *The Blood-soaked Soil*.'

Philip St John stilled. His eyes, which had been balefully fixed on Harry, flicked towards the bookshelves and then back again. The fingers clutching the blankets tightened, turning white with the pressure. 'My hand,' he moaned. 'We agreed on the hand.'

'Which one?' Archer asked sympathetically. 'The right again?'

'The right!' St John roared, spittle flying from his lips. 'It was ever my right.'

With sudden, spasmodic jerks, the arm nearest the fireplace began to convulse. The pipe fell from his hand, showering glowing tobacco across the layers in which he was wrapped. With a muttered oath, Archer sprang forward, seizing the uppermost blanket and shaking the wool towards the fire, so that the burning tobacco fell to the hearth. With a great effort of will, his uncle gripped his quivering right arm with his left. 'Be silent!' he bellowed, his gaze roving wildly to the bookshelves once more, eyes bulging at something only he could see. 'You shall not speak. It is mine as much as yours.'

He strained forward and, for a moment, Harry thought he meant to get up. But the impulse seemed to leave him almost as soon as it had arrived and he slumped back in his chair, lapsing into sullen, unintelligible muttering. Harry turned to Archer. 'Do you have any idea who he is talking to?'

The sound of her voice seemed to rouse St John again. His eyes came into focus as he dragged his gaze towards her. 'Who is it?' he demanded, and his peevish tone was a stark contrast to the fury of the minute before. 'Who's there?'

'None at all.' Archer finished refilling his uncle's pipe with tobacco from a box on the mantelpiece and laid it on a small table within his reach. 'It's always the same. I think his hands must pain him, although the right one seems the worst. The doctor thinks it might be from holding a pen for long periods of time when he is writing.'

Harry nodded. There was no typewriter in sight; Philip St John must draft his novels longhand. She studied him through lowered lashes, watching his fingers shake as he tried to grip the woollen blankets. 'Has it always convulsed that way?'

Archer shook his head. 'The doctor said it is a symptom of his mental distress.'

She frowned, her gaze travelling down to the carpet, where the puddle of wool twitched as St John moved. 'There must be some medication that can help. Has he prescribed anything other than the sedative?'

'A mild painkiller,' Archer said. 'To be blunt, he is a local doctor and not well versed in how to treat psychological illness, which is why he would prefer that my uncle be admitted to hospital. And while it may come to that eventually, I believe for the moment that he is better kept here, where I can observe him.'

Harry said nothing. Philip St John's gaze had wandered to the bookshelves again, although his eyes lacked focus. 'Be silent,' he muttered, drawing in a rattling breath. 'Your voice will not be heard.'

His chin sank slowly towards his chest. After a few seconds, he began to snore. 'Come,' Archer said softly. 'I imagine you've seen enough.'

She had. Wordlessly, she rose and followed him from the library. Archer closed the door behind them and stood for a long moment, before glancing at Harry with a bleak smile. 'Come now, Miss Moss. Surely now you feel the need of a drink?'

'Yes,' Harry said, resisting the urge to shiver in the colder air of the hallway. 'I rather think I do.'

* * *

John Archer had not exaggerated the excellence of Mary's cooking but, even so, Harry found she had little appetite for the food set before her at dinner. Philip St John did not join them to eat and Harry felt a little guilty at her relief when Archer said he would have a tray served in the library. Now that she had witnessed his illness for herself, she understood the strain his condition was placing on the house. Archer had been at pains to reassure her his uncle was not always so incoherent. 'His agitation comes and goes, although I fear he eats less each day.'

Archer was a good host, despite the unease that hung over the dining room like a cloud. He regaled Harry with tales of his acting career that were both interesting and amusing, and she might even have forgotten the reason she was at Thrumwell Manor had it not been for the occasional distant hoarse shout that drifted from the library. 'One of us sits with him most of the time,' Archer said, after a particularly lengthy disturbance had died away. 'Although there are occasions when he will not tolerate anyone being in the same room.'

Harry nodded. In other circumstances, she might have suggested he engage the services of a nurse but she suspected the presence of a stranger would only agitate Philip St John more. 'Your domestic staff are clearly devoted to him. I'm given to understand that Agnes is the longest serving. Is that correct?'

'It is,' Archer replied. 'She was scullery maid to the previous owner of the manor – a Mr Hobbs-Morton, I believe. My uncle bought the house in 1920 and Agnes chose to stay on as housekeeper, along with a groundsman and a cook.'

'She must have been very young,' Harry observed.

He raised his eyebrows. 'I suppose she must. I've never really thought about it – she's just always been here. I can't imagine the place without her.'

'I feel much the same about our family butler,' Harry said, and then remembered she was R. K. Moss, not Harry White. 'How long have you lived here?'

'About a year or so,' Archer said. 'I used to split my time between my mother in Essex and Uncle Philip, when acting jobs did not keep me in London, but she passed away and I came here.' He offered Harry a melancholy smile. 'There's nothing like the loss of a parent to make you value the family you have left.'

'Quite,' Harry said in sympathy. 'Do you find being so far from London interferes with your work? Evening performances must make it difficult to return home.'

'I tend to stay in town when I am in a production,' he explained. 'My uncle suffers my company but he doesn't seek it out. I rather think he prefers it when I'm not here, but I don't hold it against him. It's how he's always been.'

He launched cheerfully into another anecdote. They were like night and day, Harry observed as he talked, the nephew and his uncle. One garrulous and outgoing, unafraid to put himself forward and be admired or criticised by his audience, the other introverted and withdrawn, refusing to engage or even acknowledge those who read his work. It was astonishing they had anything in common, other than the bonds of family, but nothing she had seen or heard so far suggested their relationship was anything other than cordial. And yet she could not shake the certainty that not everything was as it seemed at Thrumwell Manor. In the world of crime fiction, a mysterious illness in a wealthy relative automatically cast suspicion on whoever was due to inherit their fortune, but Harry found it hard to believe that John Archer had anything to do with his uncle's sudden decline, and she could not fathom what anyone else at Thrumwell Manor had to gain from it. And once she had eliminated the four people who had any contact with Philip St John, who else was there? The malign ferryman Agnes had warned her about?

Weariness caught up with Harry shortly after they had finished the dessert course – an excellent steamed pudding – and she excused herself. She slowed as she approached the library door, seeing Barrymore curled up at its base as though standing guard against intruders. 'Hello, boy,' she said softly, digging into her pocket for the biscuit she had saved for exactly such an occasion. 'This is for you.'

The dog raised his head, sniffing the air. Harry offered the biscuit. He took it, despatching it with two decisive crunches, and eyed her as if hoping for more. She laughed. 'Maybe tomorrow.' She held out her hand for him to inspect, the way she always did when befriending a new dog. Cautious at first, he snuffled a wet nose against her fingers, then licked them once. Friendship accepted, he lowered his head to his paws once more. Harry bent down to ruffle his ears, and he closed his eyes in silent appreciation. 'Goodnight, Barrymore,' she said affectionately. 'Sleep well.'

* * *

It seemed to Harry that only minutes had passed since she had gone to bed before she jerked awake. She lay still, heart thudding, blinking in the darkness and trying to establish what had disturbed her. There had been a sound, she was sure – a crash somewhere nearby. Now she heard a muffled cry in the corridor outside her room, followed by the thudding of feet. Sitting up in alarm, Harry swung her legs out of bed and reached for her dressing gown. She pulled open the bedroom door and peered out, just in time to catch sight of Agnes flying past. 'What is it?' she called.

'The master,' Agnes cried over her shoulder. 'He's out of his mind!'

No sooner had she disappeared along the darkened corridor than Mary huffed into view, dressed in a voluminous white nightgown with an oil lantern in her hand. She tossed an agonised look Harry's way. 'Best if you stay in your room, miss,' she said, in between breaths. 'There's nothing you can do that we can't.'

Another desperate shout rang out, this one from downstairs. It was followed by a ferocious volley of barks. Harry stepped back into the bedroom and opened the wardrobe, pulling out the boots and warm coat Archer had advised her to bring. It did not take a detective like Holmes to deduce what had happened. Barrymore had not made a sound for the entire duration of her visit – that he was agitated now suggested something was happening outside the manor. She fumbled with the laces on her boots, forcing her impatient fingers to slow, and tugged her winter coat over her dressing gown. The corridor was empty but she could hear raised voices coming from below.

Harry hurried towards the stairs and was greeted on the ground floor by the sight of John Archer pulling on a coat, Donaldson standing by with a lantern in each hand. Mary and Agnes hovered nearby, anxiety and dread written large across their features. There was no sign of Philip St John or the Irish wolfhound.

Archer looked up as Harry approached. 'The worst has happened,' he said tersely. 'My uncle has been devoured by fear once again and has fled the safety of the house.'

Harry glanced between him and Donaldson, then tightened her coat more firmly around her. 'Let me help. Three pairs of eyes are better than two.'

Archer took one of the lanterns from his man. 'Thank you, but the fens are at their most treacherous in the dark. Donaldson and I will conduct the search.'

But Harry stood her ground. 'I have boots and a warm coat. Give me a lantern and I can help.'

He gave an impatient shake of his head. 'This is no place for a woman. Please, stay inside.'

It was exactly what Harry had expected to hear. She drew herself up and fixed him with a steely glare. 'Need I remind you of the reason you invited me here? Would Sherlock Holmes stand by while others risked their lives? Would he allow vital evidence to slip through his fingers?'

Archer stared at her.

'It is too dangerous,' Donaldson growled.

Harry ignored him and stretched out a hand to take the lamp Mary carried. 'Let me put it another way, Mr Archer. I am coming, whether you like it or not.'

He threw up his empty hand in frustration. 'Come, then. We are wasting precious time.'

The chill of the night bit at Harry's fingers as she hurried down the stone steps at the front of Thrumwell Manor. The moon glowed overhead, surrounded by stars, and she realised she had no idea what time it was. Frost glittered on the gravel beneath her boots and her breath plumed in clouds; the temperature must be well below freezing. It was no time to be outside, she thought with a shiver and quickened her pace. The last time Philip St John had fled his home in terror, he had contracted a fever that had weakened him. This time, the consequences could be fatal.

Archer and Donaldson had veered left. Harry followed the bobbing of their lanterns, breaking into a run to catch up to them. The crunch of gravel under her feet changed to spongy softness and she glanced down to see she was now running across grass. 'Any sign of him?' Archer's voice rang out in the darkness.

'Nothing,' Donaldson responded. 'Wait! Was that a bark?'

Harry cocked her head as she ran, listening. Above the sound of her own ragged breathing, all she heard was a strange sibilant sighing, the rustle of reeds that seemed to surround her, even though she knew that could not be true. 'Donaldson – turn south.' Archer's cry was commanding. 'Miss Moss – to me! You and I will search north.'

The weaving light from his lantern halted. Harry angled towards it, noticing the ground underfoot changing again, becoming wetter. Her boots sank into the grass, making it more difficult to run. With a burst of determination, she made for the stationary glow of Archer's lamp. His face loomed pale as she reached him. He held up a hand. 'Do you hear that? Splashing, up ahead.'

Harry listened. There was the unmistakable sound of something moving at speed through water but the darkness prevented her from identifying what it was, or where exactly it might be. 'Is it your uncle?'

'Or Barrymore,' Archer replied, peering into the night. 'No others would be out among the fens at this hour. But we must go carefully, for all our haste. There are deep waters here.'

Turning, he began to walk forward, his lantern held high. They had not gone far when Harry caught her first glimpse of the sedge that marked the edge of the fenland. The reedbed rose before them, its thin stalks huddling to resemble a ghost forest that stretched almost as tall as Harry herself. There was scarcely a breeze and yet the leaves shivered and swayed, so that it seemed to her that they hissed in warning. 'This way,' Archer advised her. 'Mark my footsteps and follow them as closely as you can.'

She did as he advised, straining her ears for any clue to the location of Philip St John. Icy water seeped inside her boots, which were not as sturdy as she had anticipated. Ahead of her, John Archer pushed the reeds aside as they made their way deeper into the fen. Faint sounds made themselves heard over the ever-present sighing: the squawk of a displaced bird, wings flapping as it took flight, the slap of water against boots. And then a long, mournful howl that sent a shudder of foreboding down the length of Harry's spine. 'Barrymore!' Archer exclaimed, his lantern swinging wildly as he tried to pinpoint the direction of the noise. 'Barrymore!'

The howl faded away, only to begin anew, louder and more desolate than before. 'This way,' Archer bellowed and plunged into the sedge.

Harry followed as best she could but the water sucked at her feet and slowed her progress. She kept her gaze fixed on Archer's light, dragging her boots free from the mire, her breath ever more ragged in her chest. Her woollen socks were soaked through, her toes numb. The cold weighed them down, making it harder to pull her feet clear of the water, and she stumbled more than once. If moving through the fen was this difficult for her, she could only imagine how deathly cold Philip St John must be, dressed only in nightclothes. He would not survive for long, she realised, and the thought spurred her on.

At last it seemed as though Barrymore's howls grew nearer. Ahead, Archer's light slowed. Harry pushed towards it, fearful she might lose sight of it if he lowered it to help his uncle. She had no idea where Donaldson might be, although she assumed he too was homing in on the wolfhound's distress call. And then she slipped, tumbling forwards into the brackish water, gasping as cold enveloped her arms. Her hands sank into the fen, reed stalks stabbing at her palms as she tried to break her fall. She landed almost flat, her face plunging beneath the water, filling her mouth and nostrils. Blessedly, her fingers made contact with the reedbed. She pushed with all her might and burst into the night once more, coughing and retching as she forced herself upright. Water cascaded from her sodden arms and chest; the cold gnawed at her skin. She blinked hard, not daring to wipe her eyes with mud-coated fingers, and cast around for her lantern. It lay half-submerged, its glow extinguished.

Desperately, she sought Archer and could have sobbed in relief when she saw his lamp in the distance. She plunged through the blackness towards it, hands outstretched and little caring about the water that splashed over her knees now; she was already drenched to the bone. Barrymore's howling stopped with a shocking abruptness that Harry could only pray meant he had been found. As she staggered on, she saw a second light bob into view, further away still. Donaldson, she thought with another burst of relief, and dragged her exhausted limbs onwards.

When at last she reached Archer's light, she was almost sent sprawling again, this time by an outstretched foot. Strong arms caught her before she met the water, and she looked up to see it was Donaldson pulling her to safety. 'Thank you,' she gasped, her teeth chattering around the words. 'Th-thank you.'

He said nothing as he released her, his grim gaze returning to the scene at their feet. They were in a small clearing, no wider than four feet. Barrymore stood guard over the body of his master, the shadows from the lantern lending him an almost supernatural size. Beside them, Archer crouched, clearing mud and decaying leaves from the face of Philip St John. Sharpness twisted in Harry's gut as she grasped the implications. 'Is he—'

'He lives,' Archer cut in, before she could finish the sentence. 'But barely. Take the lamp from Donaldson so that he can help me lift him. You will need to guide us back to the house.'

She did as she was told, curling her numbed fingers around the handle and willing herself not to let go. 'But where is Donaldson's lamp? I saw it bobbing and guessed he had found you.'

Donaldson shook his head. 'I dropped it almost as soon as I left you. It's no use now.'

Harry stared at him, uncomprehending. 'But—'

Archer stood up, radiating urgency. 'You take his feet, Donaldson. I'll take his arms.'

The water squelched as they lifted him, and poured from his thin nightclothes in a torrent. Barrymore padded around them and came to stand at Harry's side. She lowered her spare hand to rest upon his soaking-wet fur. 'Show me the way, Barrymore.'

It was the most difficult journey Harry had ever had to make. Her arm ached from holding the lantern aloft. Cold pulsed through her limbs; she could not feel her feet and would have tripped more than once had it not been for Barrymore's steadying presence. Behind her, soft grunts and muffled curses told her the men were fighting their own battles. She had no idea if she was leading them the right way. She could only blink up at the moon and hope the wolfhound at her side knew the way home.

At last, after what felt like hours, the ground became firmer under Harry's feet. The sedge began to thin; the water grew shallower. She stumbled out of the reeds and righted herself on the mossy grass. Up ahead, she saw the distant but unmistakable glow of Thrumwell Manor. An uneven sob caught in her throat. They were free of the fen. They were safe.

7

Agnes and Mary hurried down the steps to meet them as they crunched awkwardly across the gravel to the house. 'Oh no!' Agnes cried, when she took in the grey faces of the men, and saw the body they carried between them.

'Hot water and blankets,' Archer commanded, as he and Donaldson manoeuvred the stone stairs and burst into the hallway. 'And towels for the rest of us. Bring them to the drawing room.'

Harry hurried after them, pausing only to wrench the sodden boots and socks from her feet. The fire was still lit, although it had burned low. It glowed orange in the hearth as Archer and Donaldson lowered Philip St John to the floor in front of it. Ashen-faced, Archer pressed two fingers into his uncle's neck, searching for a pulse. When that did not help, he held a hand in front of the bluish lips and a faint flicker of relief crossed his features. 'Still breathing. But we must get him warm. Where is Agnes with the towels and blankets?'

As though summoned, the housekeeper burst into the room, her arms wrapped around a mound of folded blankets. Mary followed, carrying towels, which she deposited on an armchair. Archer looked up. 'Donaldson, a glass of brandy.'

The man did as instructed, returning from the drinks cabinet with a glass brimming with amber liquid. Gently, Archer raised his uncle's head until it rested in the crook of his shoulder and took the alcohol. He tilted the brandy to St John's lips, allowing a dribble to pass across the rim and seep into his mouth. The effect was almost instantaneous. Philip St John coughed and jerked forwards, a slew of fen water gushing down his chin. His eyes flew open and stared wildly at Archer. 'Steady, Uncle,' the younger man murmured. 'You're safe now; have no fear.'

St John's hands clutched at his nephew's chest. 'I am not safe! We are none of us safe.'

Archer held the brandy to his lips again. This time, more of the liquid passed his lips and he gasped as it burned its way down. Faint colour began to flow into his cheeks, although he shivered uncontrollably. 'We need to remove these wet clothes,' Archer said, and glanced across at Harry, who had also begun to shiver. 'Agnes, please run a bath for Miss Moss. Mary, perhaps you might provide us all with some tea.' He glanced up at Donaldson. 'I'd be grateful if you could dry Barrymore. Without him, we might all have drowned this night.'

Reluctantly, Harry allowed the housekeeper to lead her upstairs. The bath seemed to take an age to fill, during which Harry escaped to her bedroom to strip off her soaking coat and nightclothes, but at last it was ready. Agnes left Harry to it. She winced as she introduced her extremities to the gently steaming water, gritting her teeth at the tingle of increased blood flow and the sting of the many cuts and grazes on the palms of her hands. But once she was fully immersed, her aches and pains were soothed by the heat. She lay for a full fifteen minutes without moving, then set about washing the dirt from her hair.

Now that the adrenaline of the chase through the fens was wearing off, shock was numbing her reactions. Her thoughts were fragmented and hard to decipher, as though they were a radio signal coming from a great distance, and she found it hard to put events into sequence. Had Barrymore begun to howl before or after she had lost Archer? Donaldson must have been near – she had seen his lamp bobbing in the distance. Did he stumble over Philip St John or had Archer reached him first? And what had caused St John to run into the fens in the first place?

Warm at last, she dried herself on the soft white towels Agnes had provided and returned to her room. Sleep was out of the question – not without knowing how Philip St John fared. She dressed quickly, pulling on several pairs of socks and both the jumpers she had brought, and made her way back downstairs. Philip St John was now seated in the armchair, swaddled in blankets, his eyes drifting shut and jerking open suddenly in the manner of one fighting exhaustion but otherwise unmoving. Barrymore lay at his feet, his dark gaze fixing on Harry as she entered the drawing room. John Archer stood next to the fire, sipping a brandy of his own, still in the same clothes he had worn outside. Steam rose gently from the side nearest the flames. Agnes perched on the armchair opposite St John. She looked worn out too, Harry thought. There was no sign of Donaldson. She assumed he was restoring himself as she had done.

'I'm afraid the tea is stewed,' Archer said, indicating a tray on the table. 'Perhaps you'd prefer a brandy.'

'Thank you, but no,' Harry said. 'I am quite recovered. How is your uncle?'

'Still alive, despite his best efforts,' Archer said, without a trace of amusement. 'But the shock of his experience appears to have chased his demons away, at least temporarily. We may yet get some sleep.'

'Have you been able to establish why he ran from the house?'

Archer hesitated. 'Indirectly.' He glanced at the housekeeper. 'Agnes has discovered he did not take his sleeping draught. It appears he pretended to, and presented her with an empty glass as though he had, but instead he poured it into a fold of his chair in the library.'

'There's a sticky patch,' she said, sounding injured. 'I thought I could trust him to take it – I only turned my back for a moment.'

'No one blames you, Agnes,' Archer said soothingly. His gaze returned to Harry. 'But the exact reason for his departure is not clear. I can only assume it was another nightmare or hallucination.'

Harry shook her head. 'I didn't hear any screaming.'

'There was none,' Archer replied. 'He woke me when he threw a chair across the room. It hit the wall between his room and mine.'

The news made Harry pause. 'That sounds dangerous.'

Archer nodded, looking suddenly weary. 'He has taken a fresh dose of the sleeping draught now. That should ensure he sleeps well into the morning.'

Harry eyed the dozing man with a mixture of pity and concern. 'I hope there will be no ill effects from being out on such a cold night with so little protection from the elements. Was he unconscious when you discovered him?'

'He was,' Archer confirmed. 'Lying on his back, half in and half out of the water with Barrymore standing over him and snarling like a wolf, at least until he understood it was me who approached.'

Harry frowned, trying to piece together the sequence of events. 'When did Donaldson arrive? I saw his light among the fens and knew he must be near.'

'A few moments after me,' Archer said. 'I hadn't realised you'd fallen behind and was about to send him to look for you when we heard you splashing towards us.' He took a sip of brandy, his brow furrowing. 'But you must be mistaken about the lights. He'd lost his by the time he reached me. There was only one lantern.'

She cast her mind back, reliving the moment she had hauled herself upright after tumbling into the freezing fen. She had been panic-stricken, afraid she had lost Archer. Could she have thought she saw two lights when there had been only one? It was hard to be sure. 'But how else would I have known Donaldson had found you before I did?' she asked. 'I was not surprised that you were together. I expected him to be with you and he was.'

Archer eyed her sympathetically. 'Fear can play cruel tricks on the mind. There's no shame in thinking you saw something that wasn't there.'

Harry rubbed a hand across her eyes, the weight of the night's adventures suddenly taking their toll. 'Perhaps you're right.'

'Or perhaps there was someone else out there,' Agnes said, with brittle defiance. 'Someone... or something.'

'Agnes,' Archer snapped. 'Must I tell you again?'

The housekeeper folded her arms. 'It could have been him, although I pray for all our sakes it was not.'

Harry stared at her in blank incomprehension. 'Who? Who could it have been?'

Agnes closed her eyes for a fraction of a second. 'The ferryman,' she whispered, and put a hand to her mouth.

At the fireplace, Archer let out a growl. 'That's enough. I won't have this superstitious mumbo-jumbo raised again. There was no one else out there, Agnes – Miss Moss is confused.' He tossed back the rest of his drink and glowered at the housekeeper. 'I think it is time we all went back to bed. Please summon Donaldson to help me carry my uncle upstairs.'

For a moment, the other woman looked so mutinous that

Harry thought she would refuse. But Agnes got wordlessly to her feet and left the room, leaving Harry and Archer alone with the dozing Philip St John. 'My apologies, Miss Moss,' Archer said, after a heavy silence stretched between them. 'I did not invite you here to be regaled with old wives' tales and ghost stories. But nor did I anticipate you would risk your life chasing my uncle into the fens.'

'But you did invite me to fully observe his condition,' Harry said. 'At least I can lay claim to having done that.'

'True.' He eyed her broodingly. 'Have you reached any conclusions?'

'None that I am prepared to share at this stage,' she replied with total honesty. Many things troubled her about Philip St John's mysterious lapses into apparent madness, but very little of what she had seen made sense and she could not yet connect the dots to form a whole picture. What she needed was time to consider everything she had learned, but she had an unhappy suspicion that time was a luxury Philip St John did not have. 'I will return to London tomorrow and report back to you as soon as possible next week.'

Archer's gaze travelled to his slumbering uncle. 'Thank you. I know you appreciate the urgency of the situation.'

Harry took a breath. She did have a suggestion to make, although he would not thank her for it. 'Mr Archer, I strongly recommend that you consider removing your uncle to a place of safety, if only in the short term.' He began to object but she held up her hand. 'There is a malign influence on him here, something I have yet to identify, but you were right to suspect there is a reason for his condition. I do not mean Agnes's ferryman, or even anything supernatural, but I believe something in this house is affecting him. It might be better to get him out of harm's way.'

'But you have seen him, Miss Moss,' Archer exclaimed. 'An

asylum might ruin what little self-control he has left. I might not be able to get him out again.'

'That is a danger,' she conceded. 'But is there nowhere else? A discreet hotel or the home of a friend?'

Archer spread his hands. 'A hotel is out of the question – his illness would become public information within hours,' he said. 'And even though there are certain of my friends who could be trusted, I cannot be convinced that their employees would be similarly discreet. The risk is too great.'

Harry opened her mouth to point out that the risk of remaining far outweighed the chance that the public might discover Philip St John's ill health, but Donaldson chose that moment to appear in the doorway, dry and seemingly none the worse for their trudge through the night. Archer shook his head decisively. 'I'm afraid it is quite impossible to do as you suggest,' he said, as he put his glass down and moved nearer to St John. 'But for now, we would all do well to try and get some rest.'

Stifling a yawn, Harry decided not to argue further. Perhaps she would have better luck with Archer in the morning.

* * *

When Harry awoke, it took her several long seconds to remember where she was. The blue drapes around the bed confused her, as did the unfamiliar bumps in the mattress, and her head ached. Then she remembered she was at Thrumwell Manor, and the events of the night before came flooding back to her. How could she have forgotten?

Her hands stung as she pressed them against the sheets to lever herself out of bed, reminding her of the criss-crossed scratches that covered her palms. The hour felt late, she thought as she moved towards the window to pull the curtain aside. Had the rest of the household slept in too? Oliver was arriving to collect her at midday and there were many questions to be answered before Harry left Thrumwell Manor. In particular, she wanted to see the fens in the daylight, although she intended to keep to the paths this time.

The sky was a faded pale blue, dotted with wisps of white cloud that put her in mind of a watercolour painting. Her room was at the front of the house, overlooking the drive and the iron gates in the far distance. If she craned her head to the left, she could make out a faint yellow smudge on the horizon that she supposed must mark the start of Morden Fen. Archer had told her it surrounded the manor, and Agnes had suggested it linked to other waterways nearby, which made it unlikely that a boundary wall protected the estate on all sides. Harry's thoughts returned to the unexplained light she had seen the night before. Was it possible someone else might have been among the reeds in the darkness? To what end?

A soft knock at the bedroom door brought Harry from her musing. Letting the curtain fall back into place, she crossed the room and opened the door to find Agnes standing there, a laden coal scuttle in one hand. Her face was pale, with dark smudges beneath her eyes. 'Good morning, miss. Would you like me to make the fire up?'

'Yes, please,' Harry said, standing aside to let her in. 'Although I have no idea what time it is, other than it feels rather late.'

'Almost nine o'clock,' Agnes said as she made her way towards the fireplace. 'Mr Archer said not to disturb you.'

'I have only just woken up,' Harry confessed. She surveyed the remaining clothes she had brought and chose a blue day dress, which was impractical for exploring the fens but all she had that was clean and dry. What she wouldn't give for the practical men's trousers she had worn to disguise herself as she sought to solve the mystery of Mildred Longstaff's disappearance. 'How is Mr St John today? I hope he has not caught another chill.'

Agnes busied herself at the hearth. 'He hasn't woken yet. Mr Archer said not to disturb him either.'

That made sense, Harry thought as she dressed. 'It looks like a pleasant day,' she said. 'I thought I might take a walk around the grounds after breakfast.'

The housekeeper did not look up. 'It is a nice morning, although bitterly cold. Mary hung your coat in the kitchen and stuffed your boots with newspaper – they should be mostly dry.'

'Excellent,' Harry said, making a mental note to thank the cook when she saw her. 'You mentioned other waterways in the area yesterday – does Morden Fen join any of them?'

She nodded. 'Yes, although you couldn't pass anything bigger than a flat-bottomed skiff through. It flows into Morden lode, which is a small, manmade waterway meant for moving goods around. There are lots of them round these parts – they join the River Cam, where the big barges come back and forth from ports on the coast.'

Harry raised her eyebrows in surprise. She knew river transportation played a vital part for businesses across the country but she hadn't realised Thrumwell Manor was so close to such an important network. Perhaps it wasn't as isolated as it seemed. 'I see. And the villages around here, are they built around these lodes?'

'Some of them,' Agnes replied. 'Burwell village is probably the biggest, to the east of the manor. There's the brick company and fertiliser factory there, so they have their own lode that joins up with the Cam, as well as a place that builds and repairs barges. The villagers in Morden used to take a shortcut across the fen to reach Burwell lode, to avoid paying the tolls, but no one bothers now. Not since they stopped mining the fen.'

Harry felt her forehead crinkle as she tried to envisage the geography. 'But it's still possible?' she asked. 'To cut across the fen from Morden to Burwell, I mean.'

Agnes stopped sweeping the ashes then to give her a wary look. 'It's possible.'

Lowering her gaze to the buttons of the cardigan she had pulled over the thin dress, Harry considered the new information. The existence of a shortcut across the fen surrounding the manor increased the likelihood that she had not been confused over the lights. It could well be that someone had been trespassing in Morden Fen in the early hours of the morning. What she could not yet fathom was why. 'Thank you, Agnes, you've been most helpful.'

The housekeeper eyed her in silence for a moment, then returned her attention to the fireplace. 'Yes, miss. Breakfast will be served in the dining room, when you're ready.'

The thought succeeded in driving all thoughts of the fen from Harry's mind. She was starving and in dire need of a cup of tea. 'I'll go down now,' she said. 'Thanks.'

She was not surprised to find John Archer seated at the dining table, staring absently out of the window, an empty plate in front of him. He roused himself when she entered. 'Ah, Miss Moss. I trust you slept well?'

'I did,' Harry said. 'And you?'

'Like the proverbial log,' he replied. 'I fear that had my uncle awoken to another manic episode, I might very well have slept through it.'

She took a seat at the table and reached for the teapot, which appeared to be empty. 'I understand from Agnes that he is still asleep.'

Archer nodded. 'The sleeping draught,' he said, by way of explanation. 'I doubt he will rise before midday, which will give us all some respite. But let me ring for Mary, and some fresh tea.'

He rose to press a button near the door. Moments later, Mary appeared. 'Some fresh tea, please,' Archer said. 'And whatever Miss Moss would like to eat.'

Harry smiled at the cook, who had bustled forward to collect the teapot. 'Poached eggs on toast, if it's not too much trouble.'

'No trouble at all,' she said cheerfully.

Archer waited until she had left the room to fix Harry with a bleak look. 'It is a terrible thing but I fear we are all lighter of spirit when my uncle is sedated.'

'Understandably,' Harry said, with some sympathy. 'Caring for an invalid puts a strain on everyone, and Mr St John's condition seems particularly difficult to bear.'

He drummed his fingers on the table. 'And yet I am firm in my belief that Thrumwell Manor is the best place for him.' He raised one hand, as though to forestall her argument. 'I know you fear he is in danger here but I worry he would lose what little of his mind he had left if we were to move him.'

Harry could see there was no point in trying to change his mind. 'Whatever you think best.'

Archer nodded absently, then seemed to give himself a mental shake. 'But enough melancholy. What are your plans for this morning? Donaldson will be happy to return you to Ely station when you are ready.'

'Thank you, but I have arranged to be collected by Mr Fortescue, the gentleman you met last week,' Harry said. 'Before then, I thought I might take a walk around the estate. Agnes has been explaining the way the fen connects to the lodes and I wanted to see it for myself. Perhaps Barrymore might appreciate the exercise.'

If Archer thought her interest in the lodes peculiar, he did not say so. 'A capital idea. And it occurs to me that I shall be in London on Thursday – would that give you enough time to consult with Mr Holmes about the case? We could meet at my club.'

Harry smiled politely. 'The Garston Club does not admit women, sadly. But it may be possible to meet elsewhere. If Mr Holmes deems it necessary.'

'But of course, simply name the place,' Archer exclaimed, and dabbed at his mouth with a napkin. 'I'll leave you to your breakfast, if you don't mind, and tell Donaldson you'll be taking Barrymore out. Just ring the bell for Mary when you've finished eating.'

'Of course,' Harry said. 'Thank you.'

Nodding at her, he left the room. Harry helped herself to a glass of orange juice and sipped it thoughtfully. Archer's admission that the household was finding his uncle's illness a burden reinforced her suspicion that something was causing the man's condition to worsen, although she had no idea what that might be. She had not had time to examine the library in any great detail the night before, not with St John and Archer in attendance, but it would be empty now. Did she have time to sneak inside before Mary returned with her breakfast? She would need to be quick.

Moving decisively, Harry got to her feet and hurried to the door. She glanced out, checking both ways. The hallway was empty. Turning right, she walked as quickly as she dared. When she reached the closed door of the library, she hesitated. If it were locked, she would have to abandon the idea. Reaching down, she grasped the handle and turned. There was a loud click and the door opened. Checking she was not observed, Harry slipped inside.

The curtains were still drawn, giving the room a cold and gloomy aspect. Harry flicked a switch near the door and the wall lights flickered into life. They were as weak here as elsewhere in the house but a little light was better than none. She stood still for a moment, gathering her thoughts. Where to start? Hurrying forward, she approached the chair Philip St John had occupied the night before. Some effort had been made to clean it but there was an unmistakable dark stain where the brown leather seat cushion met the arm. Kneeling, Harry sniffed cautiously. The overriding odour was of stale pipe smoke and tobacco but she thought she detected a heavy, sweet scent that could have been medicinal. With some reluctance, Harry licked her finger and rubbed it across the stain. The taste was similar to that of cough medicine but with a faint bitter aftertaste that could certainly be the barbiturate commonly used in sleeping draughts.

What had prompted Philip St John to dispose of it instead of drinking it? Had it been the paranoia of his condition or something more? The drug it contained could certainly be dangerous – even lethal – if the wrong dosage were used. Had Philip St John suspected something?

Getting to her feet, Harry brushed fragments of charred tobacco from her knees, remnants of the spilled pipe the night before. She gazed around the room in search of further clues, anything that might inspire terror in an already troubled mind. Philip St John had seemed especially fixated with one of the bookshelves – which one had it been? She perched on the edge of the armchair, recreating his posture of the night before, then crossed the room to the tall rows of books. She ran her fingers along the spines until she reached a title she recognised: *The Blood-soaked Soil*. She'd made mention of it the night before but it appeared to mean little to the author. Harry supposed his mind was busy with other things – terrors she could not even guess at.

Conscious that she had been away from the dining room for some time, she crossed to the nearest window and peered behind the curtain. The view from here looked out across the fen. Anyone stood here in the early hours of the morning would have seen her stumbling from the reeds, with Archer and Donaldson carrying the unconscious Philip St John. Perhaps Mary and Agnes had watched from this room.

With a final look around, Harry made her way back to the door and switched the lights off. Glancing up and down the hallway, she slipped through the door and closed it carefully behind her. She was so intent on getting back to the dining room that she almost bumped into Mary, who was leaving the room. 'Oh!' the cook clucked, jumping backwards like a startled hen. 'I wondered where you'd got to.'

'The bathroom,' Harry managed, with a self-conscious laugh.

Mary relaxed a little. 'Your toast and eggs are ready, and there's fresh tea. Will you be wanting anything else?'

'No, thank you,' Harry said. 'I'm sure it's going to be delicious.'

Apparently mollified, the cook nodded. 'I'll leave you to it.'

The eggs were as good as anything Harry had tasted at Abinger Hall, poached to perfection on golden brown toast slathered with salty butter. She took her time over a cup of tea, reviewing what she had found in the library. There was no obvious evidence of anything untoward, other than the spilled medicine and that in itself proved nothing, except that Philip St John was wilier than any of them had thought. She was sure, if she asked, that John Archer would show her the bottle containing his uncle's sleeping draught and she would see the barbiturates listed as the active ingredient. It was, she suspected, simply another oddity that led nowhere. With a sigh, she finished her tea and piled up the used crockery on the silver tray Mary had left on the table. Since Harry needed to visit the kitchen to retrieve her boots and coat before her walk, she may as well return the tray at the same time.

The scent of freshly baked bread filled the air as Harry neared the kitchen. The cook had her hands in the sink and her back to the door when she entered the room. 'Is that you, Agnes? I could do with some help with these dishes.'

'I'm afraid not,' Harry said lightly. 'But I'm happy to dry if it helps.'

Mary spun around, her face a picture of consternation. 'Oh, I beg your pardon, miss. I wasn't expecting you.'

Harry slid the tray onto the ancient wooden table, taking care not to dislodge the rack of golden bread rolls that sat there cooling. 'I know. But I need my boots and I thought I would save you the job of clearing the dining room table.'

Mary shook her head. 'Mr Archer will have my guts if he finds out.'

'I won't tell him if you don't,' Harry said, smiling. She reached for one of the tea towels that hung from an overhead airer. 'But there is something I wanted to ask you about. Why don't I dry the dishes while we talk?'

For a moment, she thought Mary would refuse. 'Mr Archer won't like it,' she mumbled, but turned back to the sink and resumed her task.

Harry lifted a plate and set to work. 'Agnes tells me you're a local. Is that right?'

The cook nodded. 'Born and bred in Burwell,' she said. 'My pa worked at the fertiliser factory, back when they were mining the fens for dung, and my husband worked there too, until the accident that killed him.'

'Oh, I'm so sorry,' Harry said, lowering the plate to stare at the other woman.

'It was a long time ago,' she said. 'Nine years or more. That's why I came here. His job came with a worker's cottage and they wanted me out to give it to someone else. I needed somewhere quick and this job was live-in.'

Harry gazed at her with horrified sympathy. 'That must have been a dreadful time.'

Mary sighed. 'Like I said, it was a while ago. I'm not the first woman to lose her man to drowning round here, and I won't be the last.'

Perhaps it was an occupational hazard when so many men depended on the waterways for their livelihoods but Harry thought there was more to Mary's words than that. 'What do you mean?'

There was a silence, as though the cook was weighing her words carefully. 'I mean that you need to keep your wits about you in the fens. Anyone born round here knows it.'

Harry thought back to the night before. 'I wasn't born here and I can definitely vouch for that. I almost lost sight of Mr Archer and Donaldson and then I would have been in trouble.'

'I don't doubt it,' Mary said, placing the bowl she had washed on the draining board. She gave Harry a sideways look. 'Agnes says you saw a light.'

It was the last thing Harry expected her to say. 'I did,' she said, swallowing her surprise. 'Although Mr Archer tells me I must have been confused.'

Mary shrugged. 'Do you think you were?'

Harry hesitated. 'It was cold, and I'd just fallen into the water. But no, I don't think I was confused. I think I saw another light. At the time I assumed it was Donaldson but he says he dropped his lantern.' Now it was her turn to shrug. 'I suppose there must have been someone else out there.'

The cook did not look up. 'That's how he lures you in.'

'How who lures you in?' Harry asked, frowning.

'The ferryman,' Mary said. 'The stories say he was a boatman once, who was robbed and drowned by his passengers. Now he roams the fens at night, seeking souls to join him in the darkness. Once he's cast his light on you, death is sure to follow.'

It was the same story Agnes had spoken about, albeit with a little more ghoulish detail. 'Do you truly believe that?'

'I do,' Mary said in a matter-of-fact tone. 'It's how my Edward met his end. He saw a mysterious light one night, felt compelled to seek it out when darkness fell again but couldn't get close enough. On the third night, he never came home.'

Harry blinked at her in silent horror. 'There's those who claimed it was an accident,' Mary went on. 'That anyone who goes out into the fens at night risks drowning. But I knew my man and he changed the moment he saw that first light. It consumed him – he had to know more.' She glanced at Harry. 'You've been thinking about it too. I bet you're planning to take a walk in the fens, just to see how things lie. Am I right?'

'Well, yes, but—'

The cook nodded in satisfaction. 'You'll be safe enough during the day. It's night-time that's the danger and you'll be in London by the time darkness falls. But if you ever come back – that's when you'll feel the pull. Just like the master feels it.'

She should have guessed, Harry thought in dazed comprehension. Agnes had told her she blamed the ferryman for Philip St John's condition, although she had not explained the myth in full, and nor had John Archer. 'Are you suggesting that's why he ran into the fen last night? He was seeking the ferryman's light?'

'What other reason could it be?' Mary said. 'He's not been in his right mind since that first time. The sleeping draught prevents him from going out there most nights but yesterday he was too clever for his own good.' She shook her head. 'I fear for him. One more time and he'll be lost like all the others.'

Harry didn't know what to say. 'Surely you don't believe that.'

'It doesn't matter whether I do or I don't,' Mary replied. 'It's what will happen if the master stays here.'

Harry finished drying the last plate and placed her towel on the side. 'I'm afraid I don't agree. Mr St John is suffering from psychological distress, brought on by – well, I don't know what exactly but I mean to find out. He's not suffering from a curse or bewitched by a spell or anything of the kind. And nor am I.'

'That's what my husband said,' Mary said. 'He drowned all the same.'

The words hung in the air. Harry shook her head to clear the malaise. 'Thank you for drying my coat and my boots. I'll take them now.'

The cook met her gaze squarely. 'Take care on your walk. Don't go too deep.'

'I will,' Harry said, with more force than she intended. 'Thank you, Mary.'

She left the kitchen, and made for the entrance hall, where she was startled to see Donaldson waiting with Barrymore. 'Mr Archer said you'll be taking him for a walk.'

'That's right,' Harry said, wondering whether the groundsman was going to deliver another dire warning.

'Watch out for herons,' Donaldson said, as she bent to pull on her boots. 'He's a terror for chasing them.'

The words broke the gloom that had been cast by Mary's doom-laden prophesies. Harry laughed. 'Duly noted.' She took the lead from Donaldson. 'Come on, Barrymore. You can show me all your favourite birdwatching spots.'

8

Harry would not admit to being relieved that her visit to Thrumwell Manor was over, but her spirits definitely rose at the sight of Oliver's car slowing to a halt on the gravel a little after midday. John Archer hurried down the steps to greet him, much as he had done to Harry the day before. 'Mr Fortescue. Welcome, welcome. I trust you've had a good journey?'

Oliver shook his hand. 'Most agreeable,' he said. 'The Cambridgeshire countryside is quite lovely.'

'You will hear no argument from me,' Archer said. 'Will you take tea before you return to London?'

Oliver's gaze slid towards Harry, who gave the slightest possible shake of her head. 'Alas, we cannot. A prior commitment – I'm sure you understand.'

'Of course,' Archer said. 'But as I have mentioned to Miss Moss, I shall be in London myself on Thursday. Perhaps we can discuss matters then.'

'Perhaps,' Oliver said. 'Are you ready, Miss Moss?'

'I am,' she said, as Donaldson carried her case down the stairs and placed it beside Oliver's car. 'Thank you for your hospitality, Mr Archer. While I hope your uncle's condition improves, if that is not possible then I hope it does not get any worse.'

Archer sighed. 'I fear that is all any of us can hope.'

Barrymore appeared in the doorway, much to Harry's delight. She hurried over to ruffle his ears and offer him the biscuit she had kept especially. 'Goodbye, boy. Stay away from those herons, won't you?'

Oliver had loaded her case while she fussed over the dog, and he now stood by the driver's door, observing her. With a final farewell, Harry climbed into the passenger seat. Oliver handed her a folded Ordnance Survey map. 'You're in charge of getting us home. These tiny roads are a labyrinth – I got lost four times on the way here.'

Harry smiled as he started the engine. 'Seems easy enough to me. Go straight on until you reach the gate.'

He gave her a level look. 'Ha ha.'

He eased the car forward. Donaldson followed as far as the iron gates and then jumped out, hurrying ahead to open them. 'Were they chained when you arrived?' Harry asked Oliver as the groundsman waved them through.

'Yes,' Oliver murmured, nodding as Donaldson as they passed. 'They really don't want anyone to visit without an invitation, do they?'

'No,' she said, and offered him an apologetic look. 'Was it terribly bad of me to make you drive back to London without so much as a glass of water? The house is a peculiar place and I freely admit I was glad to leave.' She peered at the map. 'There's a village a few miles away, if you need a break. Turn right.'

'Yes, I think I know the one you mean.' He followed her instruction, then glanced across at her. 'I knew I should have come with you. Was Archer a problem?'

'Not him.' Harry took a deep breath, wondering where to begin. 'I should probably start with the curse.'

She launched into a description of everything she had experienced at Thrumwell Manor, from Agnes's first fearful warning about the ferryman, to Philip St John's terror and Mary's doom-laden predictions of death to come. Oliver listened intently, occasionally interrupting to ask a question but for the most part simply absorbing the story. When she finished, he was silent for several seconds. 'It appears I was wrong when I said you would be in no danger,' he said at length. 'I underestimated the situation quite badly, it seems.'

'We both did,' Harry said. 'But you also predicted I would get my feet wet. It might have turned out to be rather more than that but I lived to tell the tale.'

'Hmmm,' Oliver said, evidently unconvinced by her reassurances. 'I'm still not happy with Archer. What was he thinking, letting you run around the fen in the dark in winter?'

'He didn't *let* me do anything,' Harry retorted. 'Must I remind you that I am quite capable of making decisions for myself?'

'A decision that nearly got you drowned,' he said severely.

'Hardly drowned,' she objected. 'I admit it was a little terrifying in the moment, but Archer and his man were never actually very far away.'

'As well as an unidentified third party,' he pointed out. 'This ferryman, who I don't believe for a moment is some restless spirit out for revenge. He's far more likely to be a local criminal up to no good.'

Harry could hardly argue with that, since it had been the conclusion she had come to during her walk with Barrymore. There had been no obvious evidence of any criminal activity – no proverbial breadcrumb trail that led her to a stash of ill-gotten gains – but she had observed a trail of broken reeds that suggested a boat or skiff of some kind had forced its way through the fen recently. She had walked as far as the lode, which was a straight, water-filled ditch wide enough for a barge that stretched as far as she could see. There had not been another soul in sight, only the birds circling overhead. And she hadn't been able to entirely quell a whisper of disquiet deep in the pit of her stomach as the reeds rustled around her. The ferryman was nothing more than folklore, she had reminded herself, but the hairs on the back of her neck had still prickled as she made her way back to Thrumwell Manor.

'Were you able to establish whether anything within the house might have caused Philip St John's health to deteriorate so alarmingly?' Oliver asked.

'I'm afraid not,' Harry admitted. 'It would have to be something quite specific to him – perhaps something in his bedroom – and I didn't get more than a brief look at that.' She paused. 'Mr Archer said his uncle used to sleep with the door locked, although I'm sure that isn't true now.'

She stared out of the window at the passing countryside. Hadn't there been a Conan Doyle story in which a young woman had mysteriously died in a locked room? The culprit in that case had been a family member in the neighbouring bedroom, feeding a deadly snake through a hole in the wall. In another Holmes case, three siblings had been affected by a poisonous root thrown into the fireplace by their brother as he left the room. She very much doubted life was imitating art at Thrumwell Manor in so exact a manner but it was possible something in Philip St John's bedroom was causing him to hallucinate. Something that had only been recently introduced.

Oliver frowned when Harry voiced her thoughts. 'But what could cause such a startling breakdown? Archer said nothing out of the ordinary had occurred in the days before his uncle became ill.' He glanced across at her. 'Unless you're suggesting a more sinister explanation. That someone inside the house had reason to cause him harm.'

Harry bit her lip. Was she suggesting that? 'I don't know. It seems preposterously far-fetched to even think such a thing.' She rubbed her forehead. 'Maybe I've been reading too many stories.'

But Oliver's frown had deepened. 'Archer is certain it must be a psychological condition, despite the lack of any history of mental breakdown. But what if there's a physiological explanation?'

'Surely the doctor would have ruled that out,' Harry said doubtfully but, even as she spoke, she was recalling Archer's description of the night before. The doctor was a local, not especially experienced in unusual illnesses. It was quite possible he had misdiagnosed his patient.

'Not if he had already decided the problem was psychological,' Oliver replied. 'Think about it – a sudden bout of hallucinatory distress, accompanied by confusion and physical tremors. What could cause something like that?'

Harry thought back to the Holmes story in which two of the three siblings had been driven insane by breathing in toxic fumes. 'Poison,' she said quietly. 'He is being poisoned.'

'It certainly fits his symptoms,' Oliver said. 'The question is how.'

'It can't be something burned on the fire in St John's bedroom – the rest of the household would have been affected when they entered the room.' She shook her head. 'But if you're right, what I can't understand is why. There are only four people with access to him and I cannot fathom which of them would do such a thing.'

'That doesn't mean none of them would,' Oliver pointed out.

'I've tried plenty of cases where the perpetrator seemed entirely innocent, in spite of the mountain of evidence proving their guilt.'

Harry shook her head again. 'I don't understand what they're trying to achieve. An accidental overdose of his sleeping draught would be an easier death, if one of them wanted him dead. But who would benefit from it? Not the domestic staff – they run the risk of losing their jobs, and the roof over their heads. And not Archer – he positively dotes on his uncle.'

Oliver sighed and changed down a gear as he took on a particularly jagged corner. 'Although he is also an accomplished actor – perhaps his affection is just another act. No, don't argue with me; let's consider this logically. Who has the opportunity to poison Philip St John?'

'Any of them,' Harry said, after a moment's consideration. 'His bedroom is on the first floor, easily accessed without arousing suspicion. He eats separately from Archer, so it would be easy to add something to his food. The sleeping draught is usually dispensed by Agnes, the housekeeper, but I don't think it is kept under lock and key so any one of them could have doctored it with a little extra something to tip him over the edge. It's a shame I couldn't get a sample – we might have had it tested in London.'

Oliver glanced at her. 'You're stuck on the notion that the crime is the action of a single person – what if there is more than one person involved in poisoning him? What if it is a conspiracy?'

She reviewed what she knew of Agnes, Mary and Donaldson. 'If that is the case, they are all extremely talented actors. Slow down – you need to take this left.'

He braked, slowing the car and steering into the road she indicated. 'So that's opportunity settled,' he said, ignoring her objection. 'What about the means?'

'Hard to say when we don't know what's being used to poison him,' Harry said. 'But if it is the sleeping draught then it doesn't narrow things down. Any of them could have tampered with it at any time. And then there is the small matter of last night's hallucinations, which got worse when he *didn't* take the medicine.'

'Who served him his meal?'

'Agnes,' Harry said. 'Although Mary prepared it and Donaldson was inside the house. Archer was with me most of the time but not always. Again, if there's something in his food, anyone could have added it.'

Oliver frowned. 'Then we should consider motive, although you have suggested no one stands to gain by Philip St John's death, at least at first glance.'

'It's likely Archer would inherit Thrumwell Manor but he already lives there – why would he need to inherit the house sooner?'

'Who knows?' Oliver said. 'Perhaps he has gambling debts he needs to pay.'

Harry raised her eyebrows. 'Was there any evidence of that when you enquired about him at the Garston Club?'

'No,' Oliver admitted. 'He doesn't even play cards, from what I was told. What about the others?'

'Agnes has been at Thrumwell Manor longer than St John,' Harry said doubtfully. 'She was still very young when he bought the house. I suppose it's possible that his behaviour towards her has not always been proper, although she gave no sign of it, and I can't imagine why it has taken her so long to extract this rather convoluted revenge.'

'An excellent point,' he said. 'In the cases I've seen like that, the victims usually snap out of desperation or in self-defence. They lash out with whatever comes to hand; they don't often drive their abuser to the brink of insanity with a cunningly administered poison. What of the cook?'

Harry shrugged. 'Without her position at the house, she would have nowhere to live.'

'The groundsman, then,' Oliver said. 'He only joined the household recently. Maybe there's more to him than meets the eye.'

Harry thought of no-nonsense Donaldson, who had helped to carry Philip St John from the fen on two occasions. 'Wouldn't he have just let St John drown?'

Oliver grunted. 'So none of them have a motive,' he exclaimed in frustration. 'But someone is poisoning him. How can that be?'

Harry considered the problem thoughtfully. 'Whoever it is, they don't mean it to be the cause of his death, or he would be dead already. I think they mean to make it look as though he died by his own actions.' She paused to glance across at Oliver. 'And they don't care how much he suffers beforehand. That suggests revenge of some kind.'

'For an act we have yet to uncover,' he added, and groaned. 'This is making my head hurt. I'm not sure we're any further forward than we were before.'

'Mine too,' Harry said, sighing. 'And in the meantime, Philip St John's life hangs in the balance.' Realising she had not been concentrating on their route, she glanced down at the map. 'I think Morden village is up ahead, if you want to stretch your legs.'

Oliver winced. 'It's not my legs that are the problem, it's my back. I'm not sure I'm cut out to be a chauffeur.'

The village was as tiny as Harry remembered from her fleeting glance the day before – just a cluster of houses on either side of the main road. A shop overlooked a triangular village green, facing a pub on the other side, both of which were closed. Harry pointed to a wooden table and chairs outside the pub. 'It doesn't look like we're going to get a drink but we could sit over there.'

On impulse, she brought the map and spread it over the table.

'We're here,' she said, pointing to Morden village. Her finger slid across the paper. 'And there's Thrumwell Manor, right in between the villages of Burwell and Morden. Agnes said there's a shortcut across the fens but I can't see it marked on here.'

'Hardly a surprise, since she said it was an informal route,' Oliver observed.

Harry nodded and shifted her attention to the winding blue strip that represented the River Cam. 'See how the Cam joins up with this larger river – the Great Ouse, which goes all the way up to King's Lynn. I suppose the international barges come in there, through The Wash, and then travel down the river network, picking up and dropping off as required.'

Oliver studied the map. 'And look, these little strands must be the lodes she mentioned. There are quite a few of them.'

Harry squinted at the tiny print. 'A lot of them are still in use. But not the one here.' She looked up, wondering where the lode ran in relation to the houses, and saw a dark-haired young woman walking purposefully towards them from the direction of the shop. As she got nearer, Harry saw she carried two glasses of water.

'Hello,' she said, smiling. 'You look lost.'

'We are,' Harry said agreeably, seizing on the ready-made excuse. 'It's his fault for not following my directions.'

Oliver blinked, then caught on. 'Oh, rubbish. You just can't read a map.'

'I thought that must be it. We don't get many cars stopping here otherwise.' She held out the glasses of water. 'Here. Why don't you have these while I try to point you in the right direction?'

Both Oliver and Harry took a glass each. 'We're heading for Ely,' Harry lied. 'I hear the cathedral is wonderful.'

The young woman nodded. 'It certainly is.' She pointed at the map. 'You're not too far off course. Just follow this road for around a mile, then turn right at this fork here. You should be able to follow the signposts after that.'

Harry took a long sip of water. 'Thank you. Actually, you might be able to help with something else. We're planning a walking holiday along the River Cam once the weather warms up and I can see there are lots of little stream things to explore.' She traced a vague circle on the map. 'Are they worth looking at? There seems to be one in this very village.'

The woman's smile dimmed a little. 'You mean the lodes. They're used for goods transportation. Not what you'd call scenic – you'd be better off sticking to the river.'

'Oh, that's such a shame,' Harry twittered, ignoring the covert look Oliver was firing her way. 'I was hoping they might take us into the fens. We're keen birdwatchers, you see.'

'Really, I wouldn't bother,' the other woman said. 'Like I said, the lodes are mostly industrial and the fens themselves can be dangerous if you don't know them well. There are better places to go for birdwatching.' She held out a hand for the glasses. 'I expect you'll be wanting to get on your way. Just follow the road until you get to the fork. You can't go wrong.'

Oliver let out a long-suffering sigh and got to his feet. 'You haven't seen her map reading.'

Picking up the folded map, Harry used it to tap him on the arm. 'That's quite enough of that.' She smiled at the young woman. 'Cheerio, then. Thanks for taking the trouble to come over.'

'It's no trouble at all,' she replied. 'Goodbye. Safe travels.'

Oliver kept one eye on the rear-view mirror as they made their way out of the village. 'Is she still watching us?' Harry asked.

'Absolutely,' Oliver said. 'If I didn't know better, I'd say she was making sure we're actually leaving.'

Harry nodded. 'I got the impression she didn't entirely trust us.'

'Me too.' Oliver frowned as they rounded a corner and Morden village disappeared from sight. 'I wonder why.'

It was something Harry wondered about too, but perhaps they were both reading too much into it. People in small villages could often be mistrustful of strangers – it didn't have to mean anything. They drove in silence for a short while, punctuated only by Harry's directions. It was only when they reached the long, straight road that led to London that Harry was disagreeably reminded of a problem she had almost forgotten about while at Thrumwell Manor: the uninvited guest who had been in her office. 'There's something else I wanted your opinion on,' she said slowly to Oliver, unsure about the wisdom of telling him. 'Something worrying happened last week. I think someone broke into my office.'

His hands tightened on the wheel as he glanced over at her in shock. 'At the bank?'

She dipped her head. 'Yes.'

'Who? And to what end?'

'I don't know,' Harry admitted. 'Nothing was taken. I can only assume they were looking for information, perhaps about the telegrams Holmes has received or my own work.'

Oliver let out a doubtful huff. 'But who would be interested enough in those to break into your office?'

'Someone who wanted to know what the telegram was about,' Harry replied. 'But I won't know who that is until I catch them.'

'Catch them?' he echoed. 'That sounds foolhardy, Harry. What are you planning?'

'A trap. One that will hopefully make them easy to identify.'

'And then what?' he asked, with mounting alarm.

'I find out what they wanted,' she said simply.

Oliver shook his head. 'I don't know about this. Is it worth the risk?'

She'd known he would react like this, which was why she'd debated whether or not to tell him. 'You're a lawyer, Oliver. You're supposed to want justice.'

'Through the proper legal channels,' he countered. 'Not by confronting criminals and taking the law into your own hands.'

He meant their adventures in South London, she was sure, which had, admittedly, descended into a street fight. 'It has to be someone who works at the bank,' she said reasonably. 'Hardly a violent criminal.'

'That isn't the point and you know it.'

She swallowed her exasperation and tried again. 'Think of it this way. What would Holmes do?'

'Nothing, because he would have already deduced who the intruder was,' Oliver said, without missing a beat.

'He would not,' Harry said, rolling her eyes. 'He'd set a trap. And the guilty party would walk right into it.'

Oliver was quiet for a moment. 'But as I keep pointing out, this isn't a story. It's real life. And you are not—'

Harry exhaled. 'I'm not Sherlock Holmes. I know.'

'I was going to say invincible.' He eyed her with dawning resignation. 'Just promise me you'll be careful. No hiding in your office to confront them.'

She smiled at him. 'Don't be so silly. I have something much more elegant in mind. All it needs is a little preparation and they'll be caught red-handed.'

* * *

For all her bravado, Harry was on edge as the door of her office came into view the next morning. It was unlikely that the intruder had returned so soon after their first visit but not impossible. She paused before putting the key in the lock, her gaze travelling up to the top of the door, where she had carefully trapped a single strand of golden hair between the wood and the frame, barely visible unless someone was looking for it. Her tension eased a little. The hair was still in place. Either the door had not been opened or the intruder had grown considerably more sophisticated in his craft. She thought the former was more likely.

The room itself seemed similarly undisturbed. Harry stood in the doorway, breathing in and out, testing the air, but there was no telltale hint of cologne this time. As far as she could tell, no one had been inside since she had locked the door on Friday. Reassured, she crossed the threshold and began her day in earnest.

At lunchtime, she had a number of errands to run. The trap itself would not work without bait, and she suspected the telegram was what had triggered the search, so she took the Underground to the newly opened post office at Charing Cross and composed a telegram to Sherlock Holmes from a Mr Corby, requesting his assistance with the recovery of a stolen watch. After that, she visited a small chemist's shop on the Strand and made two purchases. Errands complete, she returned to Baker Street, the items she had bought hidden inside her handbag, and sat back to await Bobby's arrival. She did not have to wait long.

'Would you believe it, there's another telegram!' Bobby's breathless exclamation as he entered the office almost made Harry laugh. Digging her fingernails into her palms, she forced her features into what she hoped was an expression of surprise.

'Goodness me,' she said. 'It seems Mr Holmes is much in demand.'

Bobby did not put the message on the desk. Instead, he fixed Harry with a reproachful stare. 'Ain't you ever curious about whether any of these letters is true?'

'No,' she said.

'But what if—'

'No,' Harry repeated, more firmly. 'Is there anything else, Bobby?'

He pressed his mouth into a thin line, as though struggling to keep his thoughts to himself. Then he sighed and held the telegram towards her. She eyed him sympathetically as she took it. 'The letters are nowhere near as exciting as you imagine. Most of them are entirely unbelievable.'

His gaze remained fixed on the telegram. 'But not all of them.'

'Not all of them,' she conceded. 'But each writer seeks the help of one particular person – not me, and not Scotland Yard. Do you think they would thank me for sharing their private correspondence with the police?'

Bobby's mutinous expression shifted. 'No.'

She sat back in her chair. 'Well, then.'

'But that's three telegrams,' he said. 'It's got to mean something.'

'What it means is that the literary adventures of Sherlock Holmes are as popular as ever,' Harry said. She paused, wondering whether she had played the bait down a little too much. 'But I must confess there is something about the arrival of a telegram that creates a buzz of excitement.'

'You can say that again,' Bobby said. 'The whole post room stops when the delivery boy brings one addressed to Mr Holmes.'

It was exactly what Harry wanted to hear. 'I'm not surprised. It's the kind of thing that happens in the stories, after all.'

Bobby's eyes widened. 'Blimey, you're right. I hadn't thought of that.'

She placed the telegram on the desk. 'Unfortunately, the truth is almost certainly much less interesting. But there's no harm in dreaming sometimes.'

The post boy backed out of the room, his gaze far away, and Harry wondered whether she had said too much. But she could not take it back now. With luck, word of the telegram's arrival would reach the ears of the person who had broken into her office. All she could do now was set the trap at the end of the day and wait to see who, if anyone, sprang it.

9

Harry's hands shook for a full thirty minutes after she had left the bank for the day. Would the intruder be tempted back by the arrival of a third telegram? And, if they were, would Harry's carefully laid trap spring in the way she intended? Oliver was right – it was a risky strategy. The presence of the trap would make it apparent Harry knew someone had broken in. There could be unexpected consequences.

To distract herself, she detoured to St James' Square on the way home, and spent a calming twenty minutes browsing the stacks of the London Library. She left with a copy of *Mortlake's Common and Uncommon Poisons* under her arm. If she found herself unable to sleep, she could at least try to identify the cause of Philip St John's illness.

She awoke early, having fallen asleep over the chapter concerning garden poisons and dreamt of evil-looking potions she was expected to drink. Her face was pale in the mirror above the bathroom sink and she spent more time than usual trying to give her cheeks some colour. But at last it was time to leave for work. She did not want to draw attention to herself by arriving early.

Patrick nodded to her as she approached, pulling the door open wide to allow her through. 'Good morning, Miss White,' he said. 'How are you today?'

Harry smiled, although her gaze flew automatically to his right hand, which was resting on the brass door handle. She had left the handle of her office smeared with a thin layer of Vaseline, on top of which she had carefully painted a coating of the antiseptic tincture, Gentian Violet. Anyone who gripped the handle firmly, or even brushed against it, would find their skin indelibly stained a brilliant violet. The grooms at Abinger Hall used it to disinfect the horses' hooves and Harry had seen the results when they had not taken enough care to protect themselves, and no amount of scrubbing removed it. If anyone other than Harry had tried to enter the office, they would be obviously branded. But Patrick's fingers were clean and unstained. Not him, Harry thought to herself, unless he was left-handed. But a quick downward glance told her his other hand was unmarked too.

'I'm very well, thank you. Are you on your own today?'

'It appears so,' the doorman said, with a good-natured grimace. 'I'll be busy, if nothing else.'

It was on the tip of Harry's tongue to ask where Danny was, but she knew the question would seem improper. Instead, she adopted a sympathetic expression. 'I do hope Danny is not unwell.'

'I'll be sure to pass on your good wishes,' Patrick replied as she passed inside.

At the door to her office, Harry took a moment to study the handle. Was it her imagination or was the layer of Vaseline smudged? It was hard to tell. But she could not linger outside to examine it too closely. With a quick glance along the corridor to make sure she was not observed, she pulled a pair of gloves from her bag, and the damp muslin cloth she had brought from home. Taking great care, she wiped the handle clean of both the tincture and the jelly. When she was satisfied not a trace remained, she slotted the key into the lock. She was just about to turn it when she remembered the other precaution she had taken – the hair she had once again trapped between the door and the frame. Peering upwards, she searched for the single golden strand. She did not find it. The breath caught in her throat. There was only one way it could have been dislodged it. Someone had been in her office.

She did not imagine they were still there now but, even so, she opened the door with caution. As before, nothing looked out of place, apart from a silvery trace of Vaseline along the edge of the filing cabinet and a small purple smudge on the telegram she had deliberately left unopened on her desk. She was certain now that the intruder had fallen foul of the trap she had laid. The evidence was smeared all over her office.

Methodically, she set about wiping it away and then settled at her desk to start work. When Bobby arrived with the latest batch of letters, she surreptitiously studied his hands. They looked the same as always: pale, with fingernails bitten to the quick, and without even a hint of violet staining. 'What's the gossip from the post room today?' she asked him conversationally. 'Is there anything of note to report?'

Bobby scratched his chin. 'Nothing springs to mind,' he said, after examining the ceiling in thoughtful silence. 'It's Harold's birthday – he's forty-one today. And someone ate Mr Babbage's custard tart, which he isn't best pleased about.'

'I should imagine he's not,' Harry said, her lips quirking. 'But please wish Harold many happy returns from me.'

'I will,' Bobby said, looking a little surprised.

Harry took a breath, wondering how to ask whether anyone was afflicted by unusual violet stains. 'Is everyone quite well? I do hope no one has been taken unexpectedly ill.'

Now Bobby stared at her. 'Bernard says his bunion is playing up, but he's always complaining about that. Oh, and Jasper didn't turn up this morning. Mr Babbage says he's got toothache.'

She filed the name away, wondering as she did so whether the man's absence was genuinely down to toothache, or the fact that his hands were dyed purple. She had no idea what motive he might have for breaking into her office, not once but twice. It couldn't be simple inquisitiveness, surely. 'Have you delivered to the upper floors, yet?' she asked suddenly. 'Specifically to Mr Pemberton's office.'

'I did,' Bobby said, now frowning at her. 'And before you ask after his health, he's not at work today, either. I don't know why – I'm only the post boy.'

Harry beamed at him. 'Thank you, Bobby. That's very helpful.'

Once he had taken his trolley off to the next stop on his rounds, Harry jotted down the three absentees she had identified so far: Danny the doorman, Jasper from the post room, and Simeon Pemberton. Of the three, only Pemberton had what she considered to be a solid motive for prying into her business, but he was the kind of man she could not imagine doing his own dirty work, no matter how much she had enraged him. Jasper could be responsible, perhaps egged on by his colleagues to discover what crimes the telegrams were reporting; he would have been disappointed by what he read. And lastly, there was Danny, who was already under suspicion of spying for Pemberton. He was the one Harry suspected the most but she would have to wait until he returned to work to find out whether she was right.

It was a little after four o'clock when Harry left the bank. She smiled at Patrick, who wished her a pleasant evening, and set off for home. Dusk had already fallen and there was a dampness to the December air that made Harry tighten her scarf a little more closely around her neck. Some women wore furs to keep the cold at bay but the sight of them always made her melancholy, for as splendid and luxurious as the coats were, they had undoubtedly looked better on the animal. When she was not visiting the library, or meeting friends, it was her habit to take the Underground to Oxford Circus and walk the rest of the way to her apartment in Hamilton Square. Sometimes she detoured into the shops along the way, but Christmas shoppers had already begun to clog Oxford Street, eager to see the window displays at Selfridges, and Harry had no desire to get caught up in their midst.

She cut along Hanover Street and across the square, and from there she took Brook Street. But it wasn't until she paused to cross New Bond Street that she realised she was being followed. A man trailed some yards behind her, his trilby hat lowered and his face muffled by a scarf. His greatcoat was plain black, the collar turned up against the cold, but she had noticed him behind her in the queue at Baker Street. He hadn't caught her attention in the crowd, and she hadn't observed him near her on the train, but he had been there as she left Oxford Circus. And now he was here.

Heart thudding, Harry paused as though looking in the window of an expensive jewellery shop and used the reflection to observe her pursuer. If he carried on walking, she might be mistaken. But he did not continue on. He stopped, almost clumsily, and gazed into another shop window. Harry moved on at a leisurely pace, one eye on his movements, hoping she was wrong. Whoever he was, she could not allow him to follow her home.

She set off again, at pace this time, and led him briskly along Grosvenor Street. There was no doubt in her mind now; when she crossed the road, so did he. When she dawdled to window-shop, he did too. It occurred to her that she had two choices. Either she could try to lose him in the warren of cut-throughs and alleyways that made up Mayfair, or she could confront him and demand to know his business. And if she was going to attempt the latter, she needed to do it somewhere open and surrounded by people. She needed Berkeley Square.

She saw him hesitate as she entered by the northern gate but she kept going. There were not as many people there as she would have liked; it was almost fully dark and the streetlights created puddles of light in some parts and deep shadows in others. Harry took a seat on one of the benches and waited to see what he would do. He came idly along the path, as though out for an evening stroll, but could find no plausible reason to stop and was forced to continue past Harry. In a flash, she got to her feet and hurried after him. 'You there,' she said in a clear, distinct voice. 'Why have you been following me?'

He spun round, his face still obscured, both hands stuffed in his pockets. 'I want to know what you've done to me,' he growled.

Harry frowned. The voice was somewhat familiar but she couldn't quite place it. 'What on earth do you mean?'

With a rough gesture, he dragged the scarf away from his face with one gloved hand. A large violet stain covered his chin. 'How do I get it off?'

She understood everything then. He must have touched his face after he had turned the door handle. 'I'm afraid you can't, Danny,' she said, doing her best to sound calm. 'It's Gentian Violet – an antiseptic tincture. It won't do you any harm but it does take several months to fade.'

His hands balled into fists and she had to fight an urge to take a step backwards. 'You did this. I couldn't go to work today because of it.'

Harry held her head high. 'You have no one to blame but yourself. First thing tomorrow, I plan to tell Mr Babbage what you've done.' She glanced at his gloved hands. 'I daresay there's plenty more evidence.'

His demeanour changed, as though the full implications of his misfortune were only just becoming clear. 'It's your word against mine.'

'That might be true, if your guilt was not written all over your face.'

Danny looked as though he would argue, then dug his fists miserably into his pockets once again. 'Don't do that. They'll sack me.'

'Why shouldn't I?' she demanded. 'You broke into an office of the Abbey Road Building Society to read confidential correspondence not addressed to you. That is a criminal offence. You *should* lose your job.'

He threw her a wretched look. 'I admit it sounds bad when you put it like that. But I was just doing what Mr... what I was told to do. And I didn't even read the letters, not properly. All I had to find out was what those telegrams said.'

'Who told you to do it, Danny?' she asked, even though she already knew the answer.

Danny sighed. 'Mr Pemberton. He wasn't happy when I said I could only find one.'

The confirmation of her suspicion did not make Harry feel any better – in fact, the doorman's words caused her an even deeper moment of uneasiness. The existence of the second telegram was common knowledge; she would have to account for it if an official enquiry was ever made. Perhaps, once the case was over, she would file it with its sibling and deny, if asked, that she had gone to the Garston Club to meet with Archer. It would not be a lie, after all. 'But why should he care what the telegrams said?'

'I don't know.' Danny gave her a piteous look. 'I got nothing against you, Miss White. I was only doing what he said I should. It's no secret he's got it in for you, ever since you embarrassed him, but I've never done you wrong.'

Harry raised her eyebrows in disbelief. 'You don't consider spying on me as wrong? I know you've been reporting back to him about my timekeeping. You were the one who told him when I was late back from lunch, weren't you?'

There had been an occasion during Harry's investigation into Mildred Longstaff's disappearance when she had been unavoidably caught up and had returned late to the bank. Somehow, Mr Babbage had come to hear of it and he had strongly suggested that Simeon Pemberton had reported her indiscretion to him. Danny's gaze slid sideways, as though he was thinking about denying her accusation, then he shrugged. 'It didn't seem that bad at first. All I had to do was watch when you came and went. You don't know what it's like, being a doorman. Most people walk past like you're not even there. Then Mr Pemberton gave me this job and it seemed like he trusted me. I thought maybe if I did what he said, he might find me a better job somewhere else in the bank.'

She shook her head. 'And then you graduated to burglary. Congratulations, Danny. Lots of people are going to notice you now.'

The doorman's eyes widened in panic. 'Don't grass me up. I could help you.' He cast around for something to offer her. 'I could give you information – things you can use against him. That girl he forced to leave – I know where she lives. I bet she'd give you some good dirt, if you spoke to her.'

Thoughtfully, she considered the offer. Judging from their acrimonious encounter in the lift, Harry suspected there would come a time when Simeon Pemberton decided he wanted to remove her from the bank entirely. He'd told her she had no proof

– perhaps it would be useful to have solid evidence she could use to defend herself. 'What's her name?'

'Cecily,' he said eagerly. 'Cecily Earnshaw. She lives with her parents over Holland Park way. I could get you her address, if you promise not to tell Mr Babbage what I've done.'

Harry eyed his stained chin with something approaching pity. 'I don't know how you're going to explain that away.'

'I'll keep my scarf pulled up,' he said. 'It's cold enough to get away with it and, like I said, most people don't even look at me.'

She sighed. Could she really trust someone who had already betrayed her? 'I'll think about your offer. If I decide to accept, I'll let you know.'

Danny opened his mouth as if to argue, then thought better of it. 'Thank you. And I'm sorry if I scared you. I didn't know what else to do.'

'I'm not that easily scared,' she said, and it was almost true. 'But all the same, don't ever do it again.'

'No, Miss White,' he said fervently. 'I won't.'

She watched him all the way out of the gate, and then gave it a further ten minutes before she left and set off once more for Hamilton Square. Was the address of Cecily Earnshaw something she needed? The story she would offer must be depressingly predictable. And yet Danny had a point – it would give Harry something to hold over Simeon Pemberton when he eventually came for her. It was worthy of consideration, at least.

10

Harry had very few memories of what life had been like during the Great War. She knew her father had served, could remember long periods of time when he was not at home, but her brothers had been too young to join up and the worst of the horror had passed her by. Plenty of her friends had been touched by the tragedy, however, and Harry was well aware how lucky she was. And never was she more conscious of her privilege than when she read Philip St John's first novel, the one that had made his literary fortune.

The *Blood-soaked Soil* was set in 1917, and chronicled the life of a young man in the trenches, from his patriotic pride at signing up, to his horror as the reality of war stripped his romantic notions away. It was every bit as searing as the poetry of Wilfred Owen, and Harry was frequently moved to tears as she read. Even the dedication – *To Rupert Templeton, who died that I might live* – caused an ache in her chest. It took her two nights to read it, staying up far later than she should, and when she had finished, she understood why its author was considered such a prodigious talent. It made her all the more determined to solve the mystery of his illness.

All too conscious that John Archer was expecting an update on Thursday, Harry spent much of Tuesday evening poring over the book of poisons she had borrowed from the London Library. Many of the toxins described had symptoms that did not fit with what she had observed; often, they were instantly debilitating, making death an inevitability. There were only a handful that caused a gradual onset of symptoms, and she could not imagine how anyone at Thrumwell Manor could have acquired them. Her initial suspicion was lead poisoning from old pipes, but long-term exposure caused anaemia and a blue tinge around the lips and gums that she felt sure a doctor would have noticed. Short-term exposure in high doses presented itself as tiredness, appetite loss and hallucinations – all of which got Harry's attention – but were also accompanied by nausea, vomiting and diarrhoea, which were thankfully not symptoms Philip St John suffered from. It was a conundrum Harry would have given a great deal to solve but as yet no solution presented itself.

Her research was interrupted around eight-thirty by the telephone. She answered to hear Oliver's voice on the line. 'Hello. I thought I'd check in and see how you were faring with setting the trap for your bank burglar.'

'Very well,' she said, with some satisfaction. 'In fact, I caught him. He confessed to the whole thing – it turns out he's been working for Pemberton but now he wants to be some kind of double agent. Can you believe it?'

'Yes, unfortunately,' Oliver said, sounding disapproving. 'It's the kind of thing I hear a lot, working in the court system. Some of the more hardened criminals will say anything they think you want to hear. I hope you turned him down.'

'Not yet,' Harry said. 'He says he can give me the address of the young secretary Mr Pemberton seduced. I thought that might be information worth having.'

'Maybe,' Oliver said doubtfully. 'But I'd be surprised if he can be trusted.'

'I thought it might be worth a visit,' Harry said. 'It wouldn't hurt to hear her story.'

'Be careful. I know you can look after yourself but Pemberton strikes me as the kind of man who gets vicious when cornered.'

'All the more reason to talk to the poor girl,' Harry replied. 'She might be in need of a friend.'

'Perhaps,' Oliver said, although Harry thought he still sounded unconvinced. 'Speaking of friends, I got a rather odd letter today. It was addressed to a Sarah Smith, care of Oliver Fortescue Esq, from someone called Beth Chamberlain, and it claimed Mildred Longstaff was a mutual friend. Does that mean anything to you?'

Harry felt her jaw drop in astonishment. Sarah Smith was the alias she had adopted when she'd been investigating Mildred's disappearance. She had met Beth while undercover at a shady employment bureau and the young woman had helped her to establish who the true criminals in the case had been. 'Yes, but I can't imagine why she's writing to you.'

'I suppose she saw my name in the newspaper and put two and two together. She says she has information about Polly Spender.' Oliver paused. 'Isn't that the name of the maid who used to work for Lady Finchem?'

'The same,' Harry said, feeling a surge of excitement. 'She's the one who helped to frame Mildred, but she disappeared before I could question her. What does Beth say about her?'

'Not much,' Oliver replied. 'She says she'll be at the Mother Red Cap pub in Camden tomorrow evening at seven o'clock if you want to know more.'

Harry digested the unexpected news. Mildred had been cleared of the crime she had been accused of, and released from Holloway prison, but Harry was sure Polly knew something that might lead to the arrest of the gang leaders behind the robbery. Had Beth found something that would help Harry to discover their identities?

'Are you going to go?' Oliver asked, when she didn't speak. 'It sounds—'

'Dangerous,' Harry cut in. 'Yes, I know.'

'I was going to say interesting,' Oliver said. 'It goes without saying that it's probably dangerous.'

'Beth is smart and she might have found something we can pass along to Scotland Yard,' Harry said firmly. 'She won't put either of us in harm's way.'

Shortly after that, she rang off and sat staring into space for a few moments. Then she roused herself and went to find the bag of serviceable but old clothes she wore when she became Sarah Smith. It looked very much as though another trip to Camden was on the cards.

* * *

Harry found Beth sitting at the same table they'd shared the last time she had visited the Mother Red Cap public house, nursing a half-drunk pint of mild. She squinted up when Harry arrived, then smiled. 'Well, well, if it ain't my mate Sarah Smith.'

'Hello, Beth,' Harry said, attempting to copy the young woman's perfect Cockney accent and trying not to cringe at the result. She really needed to practise her vowel sounds. 'Can I get you a drink?'

'Don't mind if you do,' Beth said. 'I'll have the usual.'

Harry made her way to the bar, easing her way through the

crowd and returning with two pints. 'So,' Beth said as she joined her on the hard wooden bench. 'How've you been? I saw your friend Mildred got out.'

'She did,' Harry said, pretending to sip her drink. 'Nothing to do with me, of course. It was all her lawyer that done it.'

Beth gave her an innocent look. 'Oh, of course.'

'How's things with you?' Harry asked. 'Have you managed to find a job yet?'

Beth sighed. 'No. I've been round Mrs Haverford's a few times but there's not much going.' She paused. 'Not for someone that knows right from wrong, at any rate.'

Harry nodded. Mrs Haverford's Bureau of Excellence provided domestic staff to wealthy families and Harry suspected it had been involved in the robbery that had put Mildred in prison. She hadn't been able to uncover any proof but she knew Polly Spender had been placed at Lady Finchem's house by Mrs Haverford. It was not necessarily a bad thing that Beth was not directly involved with the agency, Harry thought, but she kept that to herself. 'Something will turn up. You'll see.'

Beth grunted. 'Anyway, I didn't invite you here to be a little ray of sunshine.' She glanced quickly around, then lowered her voice. 'I've found out where Polly Spender is. It turns out she ain't working either – not since leaving her last place. She's back with her old mum and dad in Southwark.'

'That is interesting,' Harry said. 'I wonder why Mrs Haverford hasn't found her a new job.'

Beth leaned closer. 'The word is she's not looking. Between you and me, I reckon little Polly Spender is scared of something. If someone were to make it worth her while, she might have some interesting things to say.'

Harry eyed her. 'You've got her address?'

'I have,' Beth replied, 'but it's not the sort of area the likes of you should visit.'

She raised her eyebrows meaningfully and Harry knew exactly what she was getting at. The last time they had met, Beth had guessed Harry was not who she was pretending to be and had warned her to take more care over her disguise. 'So what are you suggesting?' she said.

'I'm not suggesting anything,' Beth countered. 'I'm reminding you to have a care. Polly Spender comes from a bad family. They don't take kindly to outsiders.'

Harry wanted to throw up her hands in frustration. 'Yes, I understand. So how am I supposed to find out what Polly knows?'

Beth squinted at the ceiling. 'I could find out for you. For a small fee.'

And there it was, Harry thought, although she couldn't really blame Beth. No job meant no money and she had younger sisters at home. 'How small a fee?' she asked.

'Nothing outrageous,' Beth said. 'Enough to make it worth my while. I might need a bit extra to persuade Polly to talk. And I'll pass on everything she tells me. Can't say fairer than that.'

Harry considered the offer. She did not have time to visit Polly herself – would it actually be more effective to allow Beth to do the job on her behalf? 'Name your price.'

Beth did. It was more than Harry had expected but not by much. And perhaps Beth thought she might haggle but Harry had no taste for that. 'Deal,' she said, and rummaged in her bag for the cloth purse she imagined Sarah Smith might use. She pushed three shillings across the table. 'Here's half now; you'll get the rest once you've talked to Polly. If you keep your train tickets, I'll pay for those too.'

'Blimey,' Beth said taking the money before Harry could change her mind, and perhaps before any of their fellow drinkers could observe her newfound wealth. 'I should have asked for twice as much.'

Harry gave her a speculative look. 'Do a good job and there might be more work for you. Let's see what you can get out of Polly first.'

Beth raised her glass and held it out towards Harry. 'I'll drink to that, Sarah Smith. Cheers!'

* * *

Harry did not see Danny at the entrance to the bank when she arrived at her usual time on Thursday morning, but that was not a surprise. She hadn't seen him on Wednesday yet Patrick had assured he was fully recovered when she'd asked after him, which made her think he was avoiding her. The rudimentary burglar alarm Harry placed on the top of her office door each evening had been undisturbed for two nights now but a folded square of paper had been pushed under the door that morning. She looked at it for a moment, then bent to pick it up.

44 Norland Square
Holland Park
W11

Harry considered the untidy handwriting. Holmes would be able to tell everything about the author in a trice: which hand they used to write, where they had been to school and what they had eaten for breakfast. Harry knew none of these things but it was obvious who had written it. She had not yet accepted the doorman's desperate attempt to stave off the consequences of his actions but she had to admit the thought of discovering more about Cecily Earnshaw intrigued her.

Was it worth a visit to Norland Square? She need not admit that they shared a similarly unhappy experience and it would give her comfort to know she had something she could use against Simeon Pemberton if he ever came for her again. And Holland Park was no great distance – a mere six stops on the Underground from Oxford Circus. If she went directly from work, she would still be back in time to meet with John Archer and Oliver in the Winter Garden of the Landmark Hotel in Marylebone. She could even telephone Oliver in advance to warn him she might be a little delayed, to allow for an extended conversation with Cecily, if the young woman was at home. And then there was the small matter of offering a plausible enough reason to ask to see her, something that would not arouse suspicion in such a delicate situation. Harry would have to give it some thought.

* * *

Norland Square was a pleasant collection of Victorian terraced houses overlooking a private garden. Their white stucco-fronted walls stretched along all four sides, rising up over four storeys with cast-iron balconies punctuating the first floor over columned porches and identical black front doors. Harry rang the bell of number 44 and prepared a brisk smile. 'Good afternoon,' she said to the maid who opened the front door. 'Is Miss Cecily Earnshaw at home? I am Miss Foster, from the Abbey Road Building Society. I have some paperwork for her to sign.'

The girl stared at her, then glanced over her shoulder, as though hoping to consult someone else. Finally, she stepped back and opened the door wider. 'You'd better come in.'

Harry did so and glanced around the airy hallway, taking in the fresh flowers on the gilt console table and the hushed air. 'I assure you I won't take up too much of Miss Earnshaw's time.'

Once again, the maid looked uncertain. 'Wait here.'

She disappeared along a narrow passageway to one side of the staircase and Harry presumed she was going to consult the housekeeper; the residents of Norland Square were clearly wealthy but she did not think any of them would employ a butler. Moments later, the maid returned but she was not in the company of another servant. Unless Harry was very much mistaken, the woman who was eyeing her with cold mistrust was the lady of the house – Mrs Earnshaw herself. 'Can I help you?'

Her tone was chilly, giving Harry the impression that help was the last thing she intended to offer. She adopted an efficient tone. 'As I explained to your maid, my name is Miss Foster, from the Abbey Road Building Society. I'm looking for Cecily Earnshaw, who was until recently employed by the bank. Are you her mother?'

Mrs Earnshaw continued to regard Harry without warmth. 'She left the bank months ago. What is this about?'

Harry patted the folder she carried under one arm. 'It appears the bank did not complete all the paperwork to sever her employment – a regrettable oversight on our part, for which I wholeheartedly apologise. I have the papers with me now. It should not take very long.'

The older woman held out her hand. 'Cecily is not here. But you may leave the papers. I will see to it that she signs them.'

Harry did not move. 'Unfortunately, they are of a confidential nature. I cannot share them with anyone other than Miss Earnshaw herself.'

'I am her mother,' Mrs Earnshaw said, drawing herself up and favouring Harry with a haughty glower. 'You may entrust them to me.'

'Even so, I cannot leave them,' Harry said, with polite determination. 'Perhaps there is another, more suitable time I might return to see her.'

'There is not,' she snapped. 'My daughter no longer lives here, Miss Foster. If you cannot leave the papers with me for her to sign at a later date, then the matter must remain unresolved.'

Harry blinked and tried to cover her surprise. 'But the... the papers. The outstanding signature—'

'Must remain outstanding,' Mrs Earnshaw cut in. 'Now, I must ask that you leave. Do not call here again – you will not be admitted.'

Turning on her heel, she crossed the hallway and disappeared down the same passageway from which she had come. Harry stared after her, shocked by both the coldness with which the woman had uttered her daughter's name and the rudeness she had displayed. The maid hovered anxiously at Harry's side. 'Shall I show you out, miss?'

'Yes,' Harry said, recovering her composure enough to nod at the girl. 'Thank you.'

She made her way slowly along the street, replaying the interview in her mind. Was Mrs Earnshaw telling the truth when she said Cecily did not live there any longer? It was possible she was lying to protect her daughter from an inquisitive stranger, which was perfectly understandable in the circumstances. But if that were the case, Harry would find it almost impossible to speak to Cecily alone, if at all. Sighing, she turned the corner and made for the Underground station. At least she would not be late to meet Mr Archer. But she had not taken more than a few steps when she became aware of running feet behind her and a breathless voice calling her name. 'Miss Foster!'

Harry turned to see the Earnshaws' maid hurrying towards her, a coat thrown over her uniform. When the girl was near enough, she thrust out a hand. 'Here. This is Cecily's address.'

'Her address?' Harry repeated, taking the small square of paper. 'Where is she?'

'In Brighton,' the maid said. 'With her aunt. No surprise after how she was treated.'

She almost spat the words, leaving Harry in no doubt over what must have followed Cecily's disgrace at the bank. 'Her parents sent her away?'

The maid nodded. 'Said she was an embarrassment to them, a stain on their good name. Can you believe it? Their own flesh and blood!'

Having met Mrs Earnshaw, Harry found it all too easy to believe. Unfolding the paper, she read the address: '11 Circus Street, Brighton.'

'It never sat right with me, what they done. Just sending her off like that, with no thought for how she might support herself.' The maid flashed a rebellious look at Harry. 'If you do see her, tell her Susanna sends her best.'

'I will,' Harry said, and smiled. 'I'm sure it will mean a lot to her.'

Susanna bobbed, then glanced over her shoulder. 'I'd better get back, before they miss me.'

Harry nodded. 'Go. And thank you. I'll see what may be done to help Cecily.'

She watched as the girl made her way back towards the corner and disappeared into Norland Square once more, then resumed her journey towards Holland Park station, deep in thought. It seemed a trip to Brighton was on the horizon. There might be more to Cecily Earnshaw's story than she had realised.

11

John Archer seemed to have aged ten years in the few days since Harry had last seen him, and the splendid, palm tree bedecked elegance of the Landmark's Winter Garden courtyard only made the change in his appearance more conspicuous. He looked tired; dark circles hung beneath his eyes and his skin had lost some of its ruddy good health. She thought he had lost weight too, although he could afford to lose some of the padding around his midriff. It was clear his uncle's illness was taking a toll on him and Harry could only guess how it was affecting the others at Thrumwell Manor. What was clear was that the situation could not go on for much longer. John Archer was coming to the end of his strength just as certainly as his uncle was.

She watched as he ran a tired hand over his face. 'At least I can say he is no worse, even if he seems no better,' he said, when she enquired after Philip St John. 'There have been no more incidents in the fen, for which we are all grateful.'

Harry felt Oliver's eyes upon her. 'Have you considered my suggestion of removing him from Thrumwell Manor?' She paused, weighing up how much to tell him. 'I am starting to feel most strongly that it is the best course of action for both you and your uncle.'

'It may come to that,' Archer admitted, with a wretched sigh. 'I have even considered a specialist institution. But I fear he may be beyond even their help now.'

Harry exchanged a long look with Oliver. Did either of them really believe Archer was a suspect? She did not think so. It was time to reveal her suspicions.

'Poison?' He gaped, when she laid her thoughts before him. 'But how? Who? There are but four of us.'

'I don't know the how yet,' Harry admitted. 'I need to identify the poison first and that is taking some time, since I have no sample to send to a laboratory. As for who in your household is responsible, that is also unclear. I have not been able to determine why anyone might want to injure your uncle.'

'Because none of us would!' Archer cried, in a voice loud enough to attract attention from those seated at the tables around them and cause a brief lull in the genteel murmur of conversation and chink of cutlery. 'Surely you must be mistaken. What does Mr Holmes say?'

Harry hesitated, avoiding Oliver's gaze. 'He is attempting to identify the poison,' she said, after a moment. 'But he also feels that the safest course of action is to remove Mr St John from Thrumwell Manor. To put him beyond the reach of the immediate danger.'

Archer shook his head, unwilling to accept her words. 'It cannot be. None of them would harm him – aside from anything else, their livelihoods depend on him.'

'And yet it appears one of them *is* harming him,' Harry said, with quiet determination. 'If he were being inadvertently affected by something in your household environment – lead pipes, for example – then you would all be unwell with the same symptoms.

But it is only your uncle who suffers, and it seems to me that his symptoms could logically be explained by something more than a sudden psychological affliction.' She met his tormented gaze with much sympathy and fell back on the principles of Sherlock Holmes. 'If we rule out all other possibilities, then what remains, however improbable, must be the truth.'

He was silent for a long moment, then turned brooding eyes upon Oliver. 'Do you agree?'

'I trust what Miss Moss tells me,' he said simply. 'Given all she has described, I think it possible, perhaps even probable, that her suggestion fits, although I don't think we have all the pieces yet.'

'Then we must find them,' Archer rumbled. 'If it is poison then we must establish which of the household is responsible for such a monstrous act and we must confront them.'

Harry exchanged a look with Oliver. 'There may be more than one involved,' she warned. 'It might be a partnership, or perhaps even all.'

Archer's brows furrowed in consternation. 'I cannot believe that,' he exclaimed, once again garnering curious looks from their fellow diners. 'Agnes is devoted to my uncle – Mary too. And Donaldson has helped me carry him from the fens when it would surely have been easier to let him perish if he meant him ill.'

'And yet someone is responsible,' Harry pointed out as gently as she could.

'But not all,' Archer held. 'I cannot believe they are all three bent on harm. However, I agree we must resolve this matter soon, before it is too late.' He looked from Harry to Oliver. 'Will you come this weekend? Commit to catching whoever is responsible before my uncle succumbs to their wickedness?'

His anguish was so palpable that Harry could not refuse him, even though she was not at all sure she could bring matters to a head so quickly. 'Of course,' she said. 'I will come.'

'As will I,' Oliver said. 'But if we cannot establish who is to blame, perhaps you should consider taking Mr St John away.'

'As you wish,' Archer said, and checked his pocket watch. 'I should certainly hurry back to Cambridgeshire. My head is still spinning from all you have said but it may be that my presence will protect my uncle, although I admit it has not helped much so far.'

His words prompted Harry to make another suggestion. 'Try to act normally if you can,' she said. 'If the poisoner thinks they are discovered, they might be tempted to take more risks, which could put you and your uncle in terrible danger.'

Archer's smile was bleak. 'Acting is perhaps the only thing I can manage, Miss Moss.'

After he had gone, Oliver fixed Harry with a curious stare. 'You said Holmes was trying to identify the poison used. Does that mean you have been looking into the possibilities?'

She nodded. 'With the aid of a book I borrowed from the library. *Mortlake's Common and Uncommon Poisons*.'

He raised an eyebrow. 'I see. And has Mortlake been of much help?'

'He has,' she said. 'If nothing else, I'm now well-versed in all the ways one human being might poison another. It seems a lot of these substances are far too easy to get hold of.'

'Believe me, I know,' Oliver said. 'Cases of poison are all too common in court, in spite of the authorities' efforts to make them harder to obtain.'

'Whatever it is, it's not one of the usual suspects,' Harry said. 'We can rule out arsenic, strychnine, hemlock and a whole host of other Agatha Christie favourites. The symptoms don't fit.'

Oliver drank the remainder of his tea and dabbed at his mouth with a napkin. 'You'd better get back to your research, then. What time shall I pick you up tomorrow? Five o'clock?'

Harry bit her lip, wondering whether to tell him she planned a trip to Brighton before they could leave for Thrumwell Manor. 'Better make it six,' she said, deciding to keep the day trip to herself for now. 'I've got a few things to take care of first.'

He shook his head. 'I can't believe you've roped me into another of your Holmesian escapades.'

Harry smiled. 'Oh, admit it, Oliver. You're enjoying yourself.'

He sighed as he signalled for the waiter. 'That's half the trouble. I rather think I am.'

* * *

Mr Babbage took Harry's request for a day's holiday well, even though it was, as she pointed out, terribly last minute. 'Sometimes we just have to seize the moment, Miss White,' he said jovially down the telephone. 'A trip to the seaside sounds like a capital idea. It's not as though you have anything urgent awaiting your attention here, is it?'

'No,' Harry agreed. 'Mr Holmes is hardly going to investigate any of the letters he receives behind my back, is he?'

Her employer chuckled and she could picture his jowls wobbling with amusement. 'Exactly so,' he said. 'I'll trust you to fill in the relevant paperwork on Monday when you're back. Have a nice time.'

He was, Harry reflected as she waited at Victoria station for the Brighton train, a good man. All things considered, she had been very fortunate after her encounter with Simeon Pemberton. It seemed the same could not be said of Cecily Earnshaw.

Circus Street was a good ten-minute walk from Brighton railway station. She took directions from a confectioner's stand beside the entrance and tried not to let his horrified expression trouble her when she told him her destination. 'Begging your pardon, miss, but that's no place for a young lady like you.'

'Isn't it?' she said, a little taken aback. 'A friend of mine is staying there.'

The man shook his head. 'It's a slum,' he said darkly. 'None but pickpockets and head thumpers and – and other bawdy types live there. Take my advice and steer clear of it.'

When it became clear Harry was not going to take his advice, he supplied her with grudging directions and watched her go as though he expected to read about her grisly murder in the evening newspaper. As she approached the area he had described, Harry's optimism that he had been mistaken began to waver. Circus Street was tucked away behind Victoria Gardens, only a short way from the Royal Pavilion, with its Indian-inspired turrets and minarets. But it was apparent even as Harry rounded the corner of Sussex Street that the confectioner's assessment had not been far wrong. Several of the squat terraced houses were boarded up and some had large gaps where the roof tiles should be. A derelict pub stood on the corner, its windows smashed and the door kicked loose so that it swung lazily in the wind. The smell of decay hung in the air.

An assortment of ragged-clothed children were playing outside, their faces pinched and hollow-cheeked beneath the grime as they chased a wooden ball along the filthy gutter. They stopped their game when they saw Harry. The eldest nudged one of the younger boys and she watched as he scurried along the street and disappeared into one of the nearby houses. They ought to be in school, she thought, and indeed there did seem to be a school at the very end of Circus Street, or at least a tall, red-bricked building that looked like an educational establishment. Either that or a prison. Harry pressed her lips together. The stark evidence of poverty was not at all what she had imagined when the Earnshaws' maid had revealed Cecily had gone to stay with her aunt.

Glancing to the right and the left, Harry tried to make out door numbers but they seemed to be few and far between. Drawing herself up, she addressed the children. 'I'm looking for number 11. Do any of you know which house that is?'

They eyed her with mute incomprehension, as though she had spoken in another language. 'Number 11,' she repeated patiently. 'Which is it?'

A woman appeared from the doorway through which the boy had disappeared, wiping her hands on her apron. 'Whatever you're peddling, we don't want it.'

Harry took a few steps closer. 'I'm not selling anything. I just—'

'And we don't want to be saved, thank you all the same,' the woman went on, as though Harry had not spoken. 'You should spare us all the trouble and clear off.'

Harry took a deep breath. If she'd known the area she was visiting was so squalid, she might have come as Sarah Smith. A second woman materialised in the door of a neighbouring house, smaller and thinner faced but equally suspicious. 'What's going on, Joan?'

'Another do-gooder, come to save us all from ourselves,' the first woman scoffed.

The newcomer folded her arms. 'The only good she can do for me is by slinging her hook.'

Joan laughed. 'Hear that? Sling your hook, she says.'

Gritting her teeth, Harry approached them. 'I'm looking for someone – Cecily Earnshaw. I have her address as 11 Circus Street. Is that correct?'

Was it her imagination or did Joan's eyes narrow. 'No one of that name here,' she said, her tone flat. 'I reckon you've got the wrong address.'

Harry eyed her more closely. She was tall and thin, with grey hair and dark eyes that missed nothing and strong forearms that looked like they knew what hard work was. And she reminded Harry of someone, although she was certain they had never met before. 'You're Cecily's aunt,' she declared. 'Susanna told me she came here to stay with you. Please, I just want to talk to her.'

Joan's eyes flashed. 'I don't know what you're on about.'

But it was too late. Harry had seen the flicker of recognition when she had mentioned the maid's name. 'I know she's in trouble, through no fault of her own. And I know the man responsible, although I wish I didn't.'

'What do you want with her?' Joan asked, after staring hard at Harry for several seconds.

'To talk to her,' Harry said. 'That's all.'

Time seemed to stand still as Joan considered her request and Harry got the impression she was weighing up the best way to get rid of her. Pursing her lips, she stood to one side. 'Come in, then.'

Every one of Harry's senses was screaming at her not to go into the house. She pushed them aside and slowly approached the door. Beyond it was a gloomy single room, thick with steam and the stinging aroma of bleach. A narrow bare-wood staircase led upwards but it was the large wooden tub in the centre of the room that caught Harry's eye, filled with wet clothes. 'You're a laundress,' she said.

'The cheapest this side of the Pavilion,' Joan said, with more than a hint of pride. 'Most of the hotels use professional laundries these days but there's still plenty of work if you know who to ask.'

That explained the strong arms, Harry thought, and peered through the steam to the room beyond. 'Is Cecily in there?'

Joan nodded. 'Don't keep her long. She has to earn her keep.'

Already feeling her clothes begin to stick to her back, Harry pushed through the steam to the back room, which turned out to be a kitchen. A young woman was bent over a smaller wooden tub, scrubbing what looked like towels against a long, ribbed board. Her brown hair was coiled into a bun at the nape of her neck but tendrils had escaped to stick damply to her skin. She turned as Harry came in, a startled look on her flushed face, and Harry saw with a dismayed rush of comprehension that she was heavily pregnant. 'Cecily?' she asked.

Warily, the other woman nodded. 'That's right. Who are you?'

'My name is Harriet. I work at the Abbey Road Building Society.'

Instantly, Cecily's hand curled around her belly and Harry caught a flash of fear in her dark eyes. 'I left there months ago. What do you want?'

'Nothing, except to ask you a few questions,' Harry reassured her. 'I think we have an acquaintance in common. Or should I say, an enemy in common.'

For a moment, Cecily simply stared at her, then understanding dawned on her face. She let the sopping towel drop into the tub and straightened up with a wince. 'Not here,' she said, in a low voice, rubbing the small of her back. 'My aunt doesn't know the truth and I'd rather she didn't find out.'

She dried her hands and reached behind to untie her apron. 'I'm going for a walk, Aunt Joan,' she called. 'I won't be long.'

Joan appeared from the other room, scowling. 'Those towels won't wash themselves. There's another load arriving this afternoon.'

Cecily inclined her head. 'I know. But my back is aching and I need some fresh air. This lady and I can take a stroll along the promenade while we talk.'

From the mulish expression on the older woman's face, Harry

knew she wanted to refuse. But then she relented. 'Thirty minutes, no more.'

'Yes, Aunt,' Cecily said, and took a shapeless coat from behind the door.

It was a relief to be back outside, Harry thought as she took deep lungfuls of bracing salt-laced air, despite the foul odour that hung over Circus Street. The gaggle of children were still there, watching them. 'This way,' Cecily said, turning left and making for the end of the road. 'It's much nicer when you can see the sea.'

The wind was biting when they reached the seafront, whipping the grey-blue waves into prancing white horses. Harry wrapped her coat around herself more tightly as they made their way along the promenade, dodging other walkers and the few hardy tourists who had chosen December to sample what Brighton had to offer. She glanced across at Cecily, filled with wretchedness for her unfortunate situation. 'Does your aunt work you very hard?'

The other woman glanced down at her hands, which were red and rough-skinned. 'She has a living to make,' she said. 'I'm happy to help. It's the least I can do after she took me in.'

'She's your mother's sister – is that right?'

Cecily eyed her with surprise that bordered on alarm. 'Yes, that's right. But how could you know that? I thought you worked at the bank.'

'I do,' Harry said. 'But I went to find you at your family home in Norland Square. Your mother told me you no longer lived there and your maid, Susanna, came after me to give me your address here. She sends her best wishes, incidentally.'

That coaxed a smile from Cecily. 'She was always my favourite. I miss her sometimes, and the life I used to have.'

Harry pictured the smart rows of Norland Square, overlooking

the private garden, and compared it to Circus Street. 'I can imagine. How long is it since you left?'

She gazed out at the waves. 'Around four months. It was
August when I first arrived here and the weather was better. I
liked being by the sea when the beaches were busy and the sun
was shining.'

'Did you know your aunt particularly well before you came?'

Cecily shook her head. 'No, not well. I remember she used to
visit us in London, when I was a child, but as you can tell, she and
my mother have ended up with wildly different lives. Mother
chose practicality over romance and married a banker, who did
very well for himself. Whereas Joan fell in love with a sailor, who
was killed in a U-boat attack during the war.' She threw Harry a
pensive look. 'Mother used to say she never really recovered,
although she did eventually marry a fisherman. We didn't see her
after that.'

Harry nodded. A fisherman's wife would not fit in Norland
Square. 'But you knew where to find her.'

'She used to write to my mother sometimes,' Cecily said. 'Usually asking for money. Mother hid the letters in a secret drawer in
her bureau – Father would have been angry if he'd known she was
still in touch with Joan and I don't imagine she wanted him to
know that she sent any money.'

The revelation surprised Harry. She'd been of the opinion that
Mrs Earnshaw was a cold-hearted harridan who had thrown her
only child from the house in her time of direst need. The fact that
she had supported her sister financially softened her opinion,
although only a little. 'Why don't you tell me what happened with
Simeon Pemberton? I assume he is responsible for your
condition.'

The mention of his name caused the other woman to glance

sharply at Harry. 'Do you really work at the bank? You're not a private detective or a reporter for a newspaper, are you?'

The question gave Harry a moment's pause, because if she was really honest, there were times when she *was* a private detective. But she was not labouring on behalf of Sherlock Holmes now. 'Yes, I really do work at the bank. I used to be Mr Pemberton's personal assistant and now—' She stopped speaking to decide how much information she wanted to share. 'And now I work in another department.'

Cecily was not deceived. 'You too,' she said softly.

'In a manner of speaking,' Harry said. 'But tell me what happened to you.'

She let out a laugh then, strange and harsh. 'What happened to me is that I was a fool. I said yes when I should have said no and this—' she waved a hand at her swollen belly '—is what it got me.'

Harry eyed her compassionately. 'You're not the first to make that mistake and you most certainly won't be the last.'

'No,' Cecily said, glancing away in humiliation. 'I'm sure you can imagine how it went. At first, it was just praise for my work – a well-typed letter, that kind of thing. I was flattered – he was such an important man; it meant a lot that he noticed. The other women used to say he had his eye on me, but I didn't pay them any attention. I was only a lowly secretary, after all, and he had a whole department to manage, not to mention being a married man.'

Harry said nothing. It had occurred to her to wonder what the other secretaries had known about Simeon Pemberton, after he had attempted to seduce her. They had at least tried to warn Cecily, it seemed.

'Anyway, soon he was saying nice things about my appearance too,' the young woman went on. 'He said my hair was like burnished copper, which I didn't believe for a moment but I liked hearing him say it. The first time he kissed me was a shock – I think I pushed him away. But he said he couldn't help himself, that he couldn't stop thinking about me and he'd never seen anyone more beautiful.' She fixed her gaze on the ground, shame burning in her cheeks. 'I didn't push him away after that.'

Harry turned to watch the sea, observing the rise and fall of the swell and the seagulls that swooped overhead with detached interest. Simeon Pemberton had said nothing the first time he'd tried to kiss her. He'd said nothing afterwards, either, but that was because she had kneed him so sharply in the groin that he had not been capable of speech.

'After a while, he confessed that his wife didn't care for him but he could tell I was different. He – he told me he loved me.' Cecily looked beseechingly at Harry. 'I knew it was wrong but no one had ever talked to me like that. He said he would leave his wife, when the time was right, and we'd set up home together. I knew Father would approve, even if he was a divorced man, and it made it easier, somehow, to forget that we were doing something wrong. And then I missed a month, and another. Simeon was furious – he accused me of trying to trap him, even went so far as to say the baby could not be his.'

She stopped talking, visibly upset. Harry seethed inwardly at Pemberton's ugly yet predictable reaction to the awful fate he had inflicted on Cecily. She was not blameless but his refusal to take responsibility only infuriated Harry more. One day, she would find a way to hold him accountable, she vowed. They walked in silence for a few minutes until Cecily had herself under control again. 'I didn't know what to do. He was so different. He told me I'd have to leave the bank and if I tried to claim my situation was anything to do with him, he'd deny everything. I didn't dare tell my father – for weeks, I pretended to go to work each day. Then my mother noticed my belly and the game was up. She turned white as a sheet, didn't say a word. She just walked out of the room.'

Harry's hands clenched into fists by her sides. Her own mother could be a bit overbearing and occasionally infuriating, but her actions came from a place of love and Harry knew that if she ever found herself in so desperate a situation, she would not be abandoned with such heartlessness. 'I'm sorry,' she said quietly, as Cecily wiped a tear from her cheek.

The other woman looked at her. 'Why should you be sorry? It's not your fault.'

Harry made a helpless gesture. 'No, but even so. It must have been very difficult for you.'

Cecily shrugged. 'For days she didn't speak to me, then one morning about a week later, she gave me some pills. She'd got them from America, she said, and told me to take one each day.'

An awful suspicion began to dawn on Harry. She turned sharply to Cecily, who let out a barely muffled sob. 'I didn't know what it would do! I thought it must be vitamins of some kind, a supplement to keep us both healthy. It was only when I became ill that I realised the truth.'

Harry was aghast as her worst fear was confirmed. Abortion was not only illegal but terribly risky – the newspapers were full of stories about women who had tried to end an unwanted pregnancy and had lost their own lives in the process. For once, she had no words to offer. Cecily did not meet her gaze. 'I don't think I've ever been so unwell as I was then. The convulsions. The hallucinations. For days, I was confined to my bed, but I remember trying to run from the house more than once. When I slept, I was haunted by nightmares. And when at last I got better and I could think clearly again, it became obvious that it had been for nothing. I was still with child.' She paused, her expression bleak. 'That was when my mother told my father.'

It was, Harry thought, almost too horrific to contemplate. That a mother would risk her own child's life in such a way... But something else was nagging at her, something about the list of symptoms Cecily had described. They bore a chilling similarity to those endured by Philip St John, although she doubted he had been fed the same pills Cecily had. 'The medicine your mother got from America,' she said slowly. 'Did you ever learn its name?'

Cecily frowned. 'The brand name was on the box. What was it, now? Mylex? Morlex? Mother said it was an ancient herbal medicine, distilled from some kind of grain.' She shook her head. 'Argot? I'm sorry, I can't remember exactly.'

Harry frowned. Argot. Where had she heard that name before? Had it been one of the poisons listed in the book that was sitting on her bedside table? 'Don't distress yourself,' she told Cecily. 'It doesn't matter.'

They walked in silence for a moment, then Cecily spoke again. 'Once I understood what Mother had tried to do, I could not bear to even look at her. But worse was to come. When my father learned that I was to be an unmarried mother, he told me I had brought shame on his good name and cast me out of the house.'

Again, Harry was appalled by the callousness of the Earnshaws. 'So you came here.'

'It was the only place I could think of,' Cecily said. 'Joan was understandably a little taken aback to see me, after so many years, but she soon realised what the situation was. She said I could stay, if I earned my keep. I've been here ever since.'

It was, Harry thought, one of the saddest stories she had ever heard. And she could not see how things were going to improve for Cecily. Once the baby arrived, she would not be able to work. Would Joan be so accommodating when her niece was unable to scrub laundry? The house appeared to be no more than a two-up, two-down construction, hardly big enough for Joan and her family, let alone Cecily and her child. And then there was Circus Street itself, squalid and derelict, falling down around the ears of those who sheltered there. It was no place to raise a child. But she did not know how to help Cecily. Until an hour ago, they had been strangers.

'I am glad the pills did not work,' Cecily said, suddenly breaking the silence in a clear, determined tone. She raised her chin. 'I know you pity me and my situation but at least I will have my baby and we will find a way to manage somehow.'

Harry gave her an earnest look. 'I don't pity you, Cecily. I admire you for having the strength and initiative to find some-where to go. But I do admit to being concerned for you both.' She paused, remembering the sneering comments of Joan and her neighbour back at Circus Street. 'There are charities that can help—'

Vehemently, Cecily shook her head. 'I know about those. They take the baby away the moment it's born.' Her hand curved around her stomach. 'I'd never see my child again.'

There were such places, Harry had to admit, but they were not what she had meant. 'What if I was able to secure some money – enough to give you a fresh start somewhere better than this. Would you take it?'

Cecily stared at her. 'But where would it come from?'

'Perhaps one of the charities I mentioned, but not the ones you mean. My grandmother is involved with a number of them, many of which are quite successful in terms of fundraising. I might be able to persuade one of them to support you, in the short term, to allow you to get back on your feet.'

The other woman did not answer immediately. 'You are very kind,' she said at last. 'But the shame of being an unmarried mother... I would be a pariah, no matter where I settled, and my child would be forever tarred by the same brush. At least here I am not alone.'

Harry was tempted to point out that being alone in relative comfort might be preferable to the filth of a slum but she held back, recognising it was not her decision to make. 'Perhaps you might agree to think about it,' she said. 'The offer will still be there if you change your mind, and you can always reach me at the bank.'

Cecily sighed and rubbed her back once more. 'You are very kind,' she said again, 'but I really should be getting back. I have been much longer than thirty minutes.'

Harry eyed her weary expression and wished she could do more to help. But she could not force the young woman to accept her assistance. 'I wish you well, Cecily. Both of you.'

'Thank you,' she said, and let out a strange, puzzled laugh. 'Although I'm not sure I really understand what brought you here. You said we had a common enemy, and I realise that must be Mr Pemberton, but I'm not sure hearing my tale of woe was enough to bring you all the way from London.' She studied Harry in bewilderment. 'Have I helped you in some way?'

The question gave Harry a moment's pause, because discovering the unhappy depths of Simeon Pemberton's cruelty could not be said to have helped in any practical terms. But knowing the severity of his secret had given her something to use against him in the future, although she would not make the details public if it meant ruining Cecily's reputation even further. Impulsively, Harry reached out to squeeze the younger woman's arm. 'You've given me more than you will ever know.'

12

If the man at the confectioner's stand was surprised to see Harry had escaped Circus Street with her life, he did not show it as she hurried past him and into Brighton station to catch the train back to London. Perhaps he had already forgotten her, she thought as she checked she had the correct platform. She had to concede his warning had not been entirely without merit.

She was relieved to find she had the compartment to herself for the journey home and, since she had managed to catch the non-stop train, that happy state of affairs continued all the way to Victoria. It gave her a much-needed opportunity to jot down all she had learned in her notebook. The fury she felt on Cecily Earnshaw's behalf drove her pen across the page. Simeon Pemberton had used and discarded her in such a morally bereft manner that it made Harry's blood boil and the actions of the Earnshaws were equally reprehensible: one had administered a potentially life-threatening drug without seeming to care that it might cost Cecily her life, and the other seemed to value his good name more than the safety and wellbeing of his only child. She could not help feeling that Cecily was safer away from the clutches of all three, although she feared the young woman had put herself into even greater danger by taking up residence in Circus Street. She could only hope Cecily's aunt truly felt some warmth towards her unfortunate niece, and would not turn her out as readily as her parents had.

The train pulled into Victoria station a little after four o'clock, leaving Harry with just enough time to get home to Mayfair to prepare for her trip to Morden Fen. She also wanted to consult *Mortlake's Common and Uncommon Poisons*. Cecily's description of the symptoms invoked by the drug she had taken sounded so much like those suffered by Philip St John that Harry was certain it could not be coincidence. Medicine was often a balancing act using substances that were deadly in other circumstances. Could it be the ingredient in the pills Cecily had unwittingly taken might contain the poison that had been used against John Archer's uncle?

She packed quickly, rummaging under her bed for a pair of dusty wellington boots she had rarely needed since moving to London and adding the men's trousers and cap she had used as a disguise during the last case she had investigated. The trousers were an ugly brown and too large, not in any way stylish like the ones being worn more and more frequently by fashionable women, but she hoped they might provide some warmth in case of another midnight chase among the fens. More than her night-clothes, certainly. The final item she packed was a torch. It might not do much to pierce the darkness but it would be better than nothing.

Once she had gathered everything she needed, she made a pot of tea and sat down with her copy of Mortlake. Her attention skimmed from page to page, skipping the poisons she had already discounted. Many listed hallucinations as a symptom – even the more deadly substances affected the mind when given in small doses – but there were other effects that did not match with those Harry had observed in Philip St John. She was also looking for something else – a poison that was known to affect pregnancy. And after a time, she found it. Cecily had not been far off with her jumbled recollections. It was Ergot she had been given by her mother, not Argot.

According to Mortlake, it was a fungal spore that infected grain crops. If accidentally ingested – usually in bread – its symptoms included hallucinations, loss of appetite, tremors, fatigue and, if left untreated, death. Mortlake also observed its effect on pregnant women, although he made no mention of any pills that might be taken on purpose. Those had come from America, Cecily had said, and Harry considered it unlikely they had come from a legal source. Slowly, she closed the book. Bread. There was only one person at Thrumwell Manor responsible for the household baking and the fact that no one but Philip St John had been poisoned told Harry that any contamination could not be an accident. She did not know why Mary was exacting such a terrible punishment on her employer but, before the weekend was over, she intended to find out.

Harry was waiting by the side of the road with her case when Oliver arrived. She got in and fixed him with a resolute gaze. 'I think I know who the poisoner is.'

As he drove, she told him about the trap she had laid for Danny, the address he had supplied for Cecily and the journey she had made to Brighton. She finished with her suspicion about the poison used and how she supposed it had been administered.

'Flour?' Oliver repeated incredulously as they left London behind and entered Hertfordshire. 'Whoever heard of poisoned flour?'

'Mortlake mentions a tragedy in France where thousands of people died from eating contaminated grain,' Harry said.

'Although those deaths were accidental, not murder. But the sooner we get to Thrumwell Manor, the better.'

He glanced across at her, his expression pensive. 'Are you sure about this?'

'Nothing else fits,' she said. 'Ergot poisoning occurs from eating infected grain. As the cook, Mary bakes every day, but only Philip St John has been poisoned. It's hard to see how it could be anything but intentional. So that's means and opportunity. I don't know why yet.'

Oliver puffed out his cheeks. 'We're going to need evidence.'

'One of us can sneak into the kitchen.' She paused. 'Although it might not be easy to find the flour she's been using. I don't suppose she keeps it in a jar with a skull and crossbones on it.'

'Probably not,' he agreed ruefully. 'How much of this are you going to share with Archer?'

It was a question that made Harry frown. 'Nothing for now. I want to make sure I'm right first.'

He nodded his approval. 'We could have things wrapped up by tomorrow. Where's the police station? We're going to have to call them in.'

Harry hadn't thought that far ahead. A serious crime had been committed – of course the police would need to be summoned. And it made sense that Oliver's first thought was to involve them – he was a lawyer, after all. But Harry's investigative instincts had been moulded by Agatha Christie and Sir Arthur Conan Doyle, whose detectives preferred to solve the case themselves and often only involved the police at the last. Once again she was reminded that things worked differently in real life. 'The nearest must be in Ely, I expect. But let's be certain of the facts before we accuse anyone.'

Night did not make navigation of the unlit country roads easy. More than once, Oliver was obliged to brake and reverse the car to correct after a missed signpost. Harry did her best with the map but the roads were still unfamiliar and the experience only served to remind her how remote Thrumwell Manor was. Eventually, they passed through Morden village, where the occasional window winked at them but all was otherwise quiet. A single street lamp on the village green was the only light, although the pub did appear to be open. They did not stop and Harry was relieved when she recognised the boundary wall that ran along the narrow road to the manor. The sweep of Oliver's headlights picked out Donaldson on the other side of the gates, waiting inside the car that had collected Harry from Ely station. Had that only been a week ago, she mused as she watched him grapple with the chains. It felt like longer.

Oliver waited until the gates were open, then eased the car through. 'Thanks, Donaldson,' he said, winding down the window. 'We'll drive on up to the house. Don't worry about bringing the cases in. I'll take them.'

The man nodded. 'As you wish.'

Harry's impression of Thrumwell Manor as they drew nearer was markedly different to her previous visit. Now the house was dressed in almost total darkness, its windows shrouded by curtains so no light escaped. Two wall lamps illuminated the front door, fixed on either side to light the top step of the stone stairs that led up to it. Oliver drew the car to a halt on the gravel and both he and Harry got out. He took their cases from the back seat and surveyed the house with a frown. 'I've had warmer welcomes. Should we ring the bell, do you think?'

Harry was not looking at the door. She was gazing back the way they had come, towards the gate, where she had expected to see the headlights of Donaldson's car sweeping up the drive. But there were no lights. 'That's odd,' she said. 'I expected Donaldson to follow us.'

Oliver turned to look. 'Perhaps he was waiting to let us in before going out somewhere. Why, did you want him for something?'

'No,' Harry said, and realised she couldn't explain why the groundsman's absence made her uneasy. Her gaze traversed the darkness, skimming the inky black that shrouded the fen, and Mary's prediction of the previous weekend floated into her mind. *It's night-time that's the danger... if you ever come back – that's when you'll feel the pull.* It was all nonsense, she reminded herself. She'd come back to Thrumwell Manor of her own volition, not because the mysterious ferryman had summoned her. And there were certainly no lights to be seen now – nothing broke the gloom, not even the moon. She pulled her coat tight against the wind and shivered. 'It doesn't matter. Come on, let's get inside.'

It took longer than Harry expected for the door to open. Agnes peered out through the crack, her expression pinched and anxious. 'Oh,' she said, and the tension on her face eased slightly. 'Good evening, Miss Moss. Mr Fortescue. Welcome back.'

With a creak, the door opened wider to allow them to enter and closed again once they stood in the weak yellow light in the hall. She turned a heavy iron key in the lock and removed it, tucking it into her apron pocket. Harry supposed it was an effort to prevent Philip St John from using the door to escape, but it was still a little disconcerting to know they were locked inside the house. 'Mr Archer has asked me to show you to your rooms,' Agnes said, turning to them. 'He's with his uncle now and will join you for drinks in the drawing room shortly.'

Perhaps it was the strain of St John's illness but Harry thought the housekeeper moved with less vigour than she had on her last visit. There was a weariness about her shoulders that seemed to weigh her down as she trudged up the stairs. Was it guilt that caused her lethargy, or the helplessness of watching her master decline? Harry did not know but it made her more determined to resolve the darkness hanging over Thrumwell Manor. One way or another, it would end this weekend.

She turned right at the top of the stairs, showing Oliver to the green room Harry had briefly visited on her tour of the house. It had clearly been aired since then; it smelled much fresher and was now warmed by a fire. 'I've put you in the blue room again, miss,' Agnes said to Harry, once Oliver was settled. 'I hope that suits you.'

'Very much so,' Harry said. 'Thank you.'

The bedroom was just as it had been for Harry's last visit, although the counterpane on the bed was now a patchwork of cornflower blue and white rather than the royal blue one that had matched the curtains. She was glad to see the drapes themselves were firmly closed, shutting out the night. After crossing to the hearth, the housekeeper added some coal to the flames. Harry opened her case and began to unpack. 'How are you, Agnes?'

The housekeeper did not look up. 'I can't complain, miss, although I wish the master would get better. We try not to leave him unattended now and it makes life harder for us all.'

'Of course,' Harry said sympathetically. The not quite concealed tremble in the other woman's tone made it hard to believe she had anything to do with Philip St John's affliction. 'Mary told me that according to the curse, his third sighting of the ferryman will be his last. Is that why you locked the front door?'

The other woman stilled briefly, then resumed tending the fire. 'It seems like a sensible precaution.'

'I assume Donaldson will use the trade entrance when he comes back,' Harry said, watching her. 'I notice he did not return to the house after opening the gate for us.'

Agnes got to her feet. 'He has business in the village,' she said, brushing specks of coal dust from her fingers. 'If there's nothing else, I'll go and relieve Mr Archer so he can join you in the drawing room.'

Harry studied her, observing the guarded set to her face. She wanted to ask her about Mary, whether she had noticed anything strange about her behaviour, but she could not think of a way to do so without sounding clumsy. She inclined her head. 'Thank you, Agnes.'

Once she had unpacked, Harry made her way along the landing to knock at Oliver's door. After a few seconds he opened it. 'How's your room?' she asked.

'Green,' he replied. 'But not uncomfortable. Yours?'

'Blue,' she said. 'Shall we go down? The drawing room is just off the hall.'

Oliver waved a hand. 'Lead on.'

Archer was standing beside the fireplace when they entered the drawing room, the grey wolfhound at his feet. 'Welcome,' he said, hurrying forward to shake their hands with his usual enthusiasm, for all he looked even more fatigued than he had on Thursday. 'Thank you for coming.'

'Not at all,' Harry said, bending to ruffle Barrymore's wiry coat. 'How is your uncle?'

He sighed. 'Much the same. I know your suspicions must be correct, Miss Moss, but I must confess I simply cannot fathom how he is being poisoned, much less who is doing it. They all appear to be as devoted to him as ever.'

Harry exchanged a glance with Oliver, who had reached out a hand for Barrymore to sniff. Archer seemed tired but he was otherwise in good health. It appeared he had not set any alarm bells ringing that might result in desperate measures by the poisoner. 'That is why we are here,' she said. 'I intend to answer both questions this weekend.'

'And I have every faith you will,' Archer said. He crossed

towards the drinks cabinet. 'But I am being a neglectful host. What can I offer you to drink?'

'A gin and tonic, please,' Harry said.

'I'll have the same, if it's not too much trouble,' Oliver said, then leaned nearer to Harry. 'Are you sure it's safe for us to eat the food Mary prepares? What if she realises we suspect her and decides to poison us too?'

'She can't have any idea we know,' she murmured back. 'And mass poisoning would rather give the game away, don't you think? So much harder to explain than a single case.'

Oliver raised a sardonic eyebrow. 'I'm not entirely reassured by that.'

Harry scratched Barrymore's grizzled chin and dug into her pocket for a biscuit. 'I think we're safe,' she whispered. 'Just steer clear of the bread.'

Whatever he was about to say next was forestalled by a knock at the door. Barrymore's ears cocked and he let out a low rumbling growl. Archer looked up, gin bottle in hand. 'Yes?'

The door opened to reveal Donaldson. Barrymore subsided, although Harry noticed he kept his eyes fixed on the groundsman. 'I'm sorry, Mr Archer. I wasn't able to get it. The shop was closed up for the night and there was no sign of Eliza.'

Archer let out a tsk of annoyance. 'It is my fault for failing to realise supplies were low. But there's nothing to be done now.' He nodded at the man. 'Thank you for trying. I'll go to the village myself in the morning.'

'Very good, sir,' Donaldson said, and withdrew.

Aware that both Harry and Oliver were eyeing him with polite curiosity, Archer cleared his throat. 'No great mystery. My uncle's pipe tobacco has run out. I sent Donaldson to get some more but, as you heard, he did not succeed.'

So that was where he had gone after opening the gate, Harry

thought. Oliver had been correct; there was a reasonable explanation for his disappearance. 'Is your uncle a regular smoker?' she asked.

'He likes a pipe after meals, although not first thing in the morning.' Archer grimaced. 'Awful stuff – I can't bear it myself. It won't hurt him to have a break from it. His chest isn't fully recovered from the chill he caught, you know.'

Harry imagined the doctor might have recommended a rest from smoking after St John's initial fever but perhaps he had been ignored. 'I expect it will do him good,' she agreed. 'I read *The Blood-soaked Soil*, incidentally. It's quite an extraordinary achievement.'

At that, Archer's expression relaxed somewhat. 'I think so too,' he said, handing out their drinks. 'He wrote it in the trenches, you know, while serving as an infantryman on the Western Front.'

She had not known but the revelation made perfect sense. The descriptions of the horrific conditions could only have been written by someone who had experienced them first hand. 'Then it is even more remarkable. Where did he get the paper?'

'I believe he traded it for chocolate sent from home,' Archer replied. 'And occasionally cigarettes.'

Chocolate and cigarettes had been high-value commodities then, Harry thought, worth more than money to the soldiers. Philip St John must have been desperate to get his story out. 'I'd like to read more of his work,' she said. 'Do you have any of his other books I might borrow?'

'Of course,' Archer said. 'There are copies of them all in the library. I'll get you a selection now.'

'Oh, please don't trouble yourself,' she protested. 'Some point over the weekend would be fine.'

'There's no time like the present,' he said jovially. 'Agnes is with him now but it gives me an excuse to check on them.' He glanced at Oliver. 'I hope you don't mind not meeting my uncle this evening. He's often more unsettled at this time of day and I thought tomorrow might be better.'

'Not at all,' Oliver said. 'You know best.'

Archer gave a short laugh. 'Do I? I sometimes wonder if I know anything at all. But I'll get the books, Miss Moss.'

Once he had left the room, Oliver took a sip of his drink. 'Well, it seems we almost have a full house. Donaldson is just back from the village and Agnes is in the library with St John. That just leaves the cook to be accounted for.'

'She'll be in the kitchen, I expect, preparing the evening meal,' Harry said. 'It makes sense to investigate the pantry later, once everyone has gone to bed. I'm not sure what I'm looking for, but I'll see if I can find any evidence of Ergot.'

'Not on your own,' he said firmly. 'If you're snooping around in the dark, I'm coming with you.'

She was about to object – one person was less likely to make a noise than two – but decided it was an argument they did not need to have. All she needed to do was wait until he had fallen asleep to sneak downstairs to the kitchen. He raised an eyebrow. 'And don't go thinking you'll wait until I'm asleep to do it. I'm coming with you and that's that.'

Harry sipped her drink, half amused and half irritated that he had guessed her plan. But she felt the atmosphere at Thrumwell Manor weighing on her more heavily than it had during her last visit, and while she didn't need Oliver watching over her as she searched the kitchen for poison, she had to admit she was glad he had accompanied her this time. 'Fine,' she huffed.

Archer bustled back into the room, carrying four leather-bound books. 'Here you are,' he said, handing the pile to Harry. 'These should keep you busy.'

He had brought a copy of *The Blood-soaked Soil*, as well as three

more recent novels. She passed the first book to Oliver, who
opened the cover with some curiosity. '*To Rupert Templeton, who
died that I might live,*' he read aloud, running a finger across the
dedication. 'Who is Rupert Templeton? Do you know?'

'Ah,' Archer said, bending to prod at the fire with an iron
poker. 'That's rather a tragic tale. He and my uncle served together
on the front line – brothers in arms, I suppose you might say.
Rupert was a writer too – I imagine they used it as a form of
escape. Anyway, it didn't end well for Rupert and Uncle Philip was
devastated. My mother said he never wanted to talk about the war
but he once told her that Rupert had saved his life.'

'How?' Harry asked softly.

'He refused to elaborate,' Archer said, straightening up.
'Which makes it all the more remarkable that he wrote *The Blood-
soaked Soil* but I suppose the writing process can be cathartic. I
still remember seeing him scribbling away, night after night,
when I was a child. I used to think it helped him come to terms
with it all, until I moved back here and discovered he won't touch
a penny of the royalties from it. I once heard him call it blood
money.'

Harry could understand St John's reluctance to revisit such
painful memories but his aversion to the money earned by his
first novel was surprising. It had been in print since publication in
1920 and, as far as she could tell, remained a well-read book.
'What does he do with it?'

Archer shrugged. 'All I know is that it goes into a separate
account and is not to be touched under any circumstances.
Thankfully, he earns a good income from his subsequent novels
and he lives a relatively modest lifestyle.'

She nodded absently. Perhaps it was not so strange that Philip
St John viewed his earnings from a book about the horror of the
war as blood money. It did not appear that any of his other work

had touched on so terrible a subject. Opening the cover of another of his novels, she began to read but she had not got much further than the first page when the door opened again and Mary appeared. 'Dinner is served.'

Oliver cocked his head, asking if this was the cook, and she gave the faintest of nods. 'Excellent,' Archer said, and beamed at them both. 'I don't know about you but I'm famished. Let's tuck in.'

13

Harry did her best to forget her suspicions about Mary as they ate but it was hard not to wonder whether the chicken pie had been laced with something more than tarragon and white wine. Across the table, she sensed Oliver had the same reservations and reminded herself that she had no hard proof the cook was responsible for poisoning anyone. The cook's mouth had tightened when she had entered the dining room and caught sight of Harry but she thought that had more to do with the reckless disregard of her warning about what might happen if she saw the ferryman again than a suspicion that Harry might be onto her. And the pie smelled delicious.

As during her previous visit, Archer was an entertaining host, even though his manner was more subdued. He made no complaint when, shortly before ten o'clock, she gathered up the books he had brought from the library and claimed an early night. 'Would you like me to ask Mary to make you some warm milk?' he offered, when she made her excuses.

'Please don't trouble her,' Harry said. 'I'm sure I shall still be awake at midnight, reading your uncle's excellent books.' She glanced at Oliver, and saw her message had been received. 'Good-night to you both.'

The first thing Harry noticed, once she had settled herself against the plump pillows of the bed, was that Philip St John's later novels were shorter than *The Blood-soaked Soil*. That wasn't so unusual, she supposed – it had been so successful that perhaps his publisher had asked for more books to supply public demand rather more quickly than St John had expected. The subject matter was markedly different too; *The Jungle* was about a teacher at a public school, struggling to deal with a secret alcohol addiction. *Paris By Night* told the story of two friends who became enemies after their business fell apart. Harry read the opening chapters of both and was struck by the change of tone and style in the post-war novels. She supposed that had been a commercial decision too – the Roaring Twenties had been about gaiety and hedonism and putting the awfulness of war behind them – but *The Blood-soaked Soil* had an aching depth to it that she found to be lacking in the books that had followed. And having heard from Archer that his uncle refused to touch the money it brought in, Harry could only assume Philip St John's aversion to his painful memories had affected the way he wrote his subsequent novels too. There were no further dedications to Rupert Templeton; St John had dedicated his other books to his mother, his sister and his beloved nephew.

Sounds on the landing around eleven o'clock told her the rest of the household had retired. She continued to read, refusing to let her heavy eyelids beat her. Just after midnight, she heard a soft tapping at her door. She slipped out of bed and stooped to pull on her shoes. Picking up the torch from the bedside table, she inched the door open a crack. 'Ready?' Oliver asked, when she peered out at him.

She was glad to observe he was still wearing day clothes, just as she was; she feared the sight of him in pyjamas would have stirred up some inconvenient thoughts she had no time to deal with. 'Of course,' she whispered, easing through the gap to stand beside him. 'We'll use the servants' staircase. It leads directly to the kitchen.'

The hidden stairs were even darker than Harry remembered. Pressing the button to switch the torch on, she cast its pale beam around. 'We'd better go slowly. Stay close.'

The air was still as they navigated a series of narrow stairways. Harry kept the torch trained on the steps as they descended, her other hand holding the thin metal rail that served as a banister. She was aware of Oliver close behind, could hear his breath in her ear, and felt a quiver of something that was most definitely not going to help with the task in hand. Forcing herself to ignore his proximity, she concentrated on lighting the way. It would not do to get distracted and drop the torch.

The stairs ended in a door that opened just outside the kitchen. Holding up one hand, Harry listened intently. Most domestic staff rose early in the morning, and so went to bed at a sensible time, but this was a strange household, in more ways than one. After a few seconds, she was satisfied the room was empty. Praying the hinges would not creak, she lifted the latch and entered the shadowy room.

The weak electric light that seemed so feeble elsewhere in the house felt bright when Harry first flicked the switch on the wall, but her eyes quickly adjusted. The kitchen was warm, its fire still glowing red in the wide hearth. A large bowl stood in the centre of the table, covered by a white tea towel. 'Dough,' Harry murmured, lifting the corner of the cloth. She gazed around the room. 'You take the cupboards; I'll check the pantry.'

'Do you have any idea what we're looking for?' he asked.

Harry hesitated. Mortlake had listed several ways Ergot

poisoning occurred in humans; these included a tincture that had been distilled from infected grain, an overdose of prescribed medication for a variety of health conditions, and the ingestion of fungal spores through contaminated flour. 'If Mary is administering the poison through bread she only gives to Philip St John, she'll be careful to keep the infected flour separate. Look for a sealed bag or a stoppered jar of some kind. Maybe even a small bottle. It could be marked *Rye*.'

He began to open the cupboards, methodically searching the shelves. Harry made for the pantry. It was well organised and stocked with everything she might expect in a working kitchen. A large sack of plain flour sat in one corner, securely tied. Another contained strong flour, which Harry assumed the cook used to bake bread, but it seemed unlikely that would be the source of Ergot; it would be too easy to make a mistake and poison everyone. She kept an eye out for unlabelled bottles that might contain a tincture. She assumed only a few drops would be enough to poison St John's food, but she found nothing that seemed suspicious. Before she knew it, almost half an hour had passed and she had not discovered anything that proved Mary's guilt.

Oliver was similarly empty-handed. 'Is there somewhere else it might be kept?' he asked, when he had searched the last cupboard. 'An outdoor storeroom?'

It was worth exploring, Harry decided. They might not get another chance. There was only one other exit from the kitchen: a solid oak door with two black iron bolts and a hefty key in the lock just below the door handle. Steadily, Oliver drew the bolts back. Harry held her breath, praying they were well oiled. The key turned with a clunk that sounded too loud. They both froze, listening. Barrymore could not be far away; if they woke him, his barking would rouse the entire household. But all remained quiet.

Turning the handle with care, Oliver opened the door and they slipped out into the freezing night air.

The first door Harry tried led to an outside toilet. It was clearly in regular use. She flashed her torch around to reveal a neat pile of torn paper resting on an upturned bucket and a candle on the windowsill beside a box of matches. Cobwebs dangled from the overhead cistern but there was no sign of any spiders. A jumble of wellington boots was piled up in one corner. Closing the door, Harry glanced around to locate Oliver. He was peering into an outbuilding on the far side of the yard, his hands cupped against the window as he tried to make out what was inside. 'Looks like a garage,' he said. 'The car Donaldson drives is in there.'

Harry nodded and made for another small building. But as she approached the door, a flash caught her eye in the black night beyond the building. She stopped, switching off the torch to stare past the rough stone wall. The kitchen was in the rear corner of the house, and she supposed its windows would look towards the fen during the day. Was her imagination playing tricks on her? There was nothing to see now. She strained into the shadows and was about to switch the torch back on when another flash bloomed and died in the darkness. 'Oliver,' she whispered urgently. 'Did you see that? A light over there.'

He was at her side in a moment. 'Where?'

'Past the buildings. Wait – there it is again.' There could be no mistake this time. Harry was sure of what she'd seen – a light bobbing in the fen. Her heart thudded as Mary's words echoed around her head. 'Someone is out there.'

'But who?' Oliver asked. 'Someone from the house?'

Harry shook her head and cast around, trying to get her bearings. 'I don't think so. Let's see, the lode is that way.' She turned to point at what she hoped was north. 'And the edge of the fen nearest the house is over there.'

'In that case whoever it is must be in a boat,' Oliver said.

'They must be,' she replied, and fought hard against a mental image of a lone ferryman sculling through the reeds. Holmes would have no truck with such fancies and nor should she. 'I think this is what Agnes mentioned last week, even though she said no one did it any more. Someone is cutting across the fen from Morden village to Burwell, in the dead of night.' She fired a determined look his way. 'We need to find out who.'

She expected him to argue, to try and talk her out of it, but he simply nodded. 'We can try.'

'I'll keep the torch angled down so they don't see the light,' she said, then stopped. 'Wait! There were some boots in the outside toilet. Let's see if any of them fit.'

Oliver was in luck – he found a pair that fitted almost immediately. Harry was less fortunate and was forced to settle for one that was the right size and one that was at least one size too large. They would have to do, she decided. She had no time to go and get her own boots from upstairs. 'Okay,' she said, clenching her toes to keep the larger boot from slipping. 'Follow me and stay very close.'

Bending low, she half-hobbled, half-scurried to the edge of the outbuildings and stopped to take stock. The light was easier to spot now, bobbing in and out of sight as though hidden by the reeds. 'We need to be quick,' she murmured, pushing her fear to one side. 'If they get too far out we'll lose them.'

The endless sighing of the sedge grew louder. All too soon the ground changed consistency and became marshy. The reedbed loomed up, causing Harry to murmur in surprise, and she edged sideways, seeking a way in. Now that they were nearer, she could hear the loose slosh of the water being displaced by the boat, a faint snatch of murmured words. Whoever it was, they were moving very slowly, in no apparent hurry. Harry waded through the whispering reeds, hoping her borrowed boots were tall enough to prevent water from slopping onto her feet. She was cold enough already. Some distance ahead, the lantern swung back and forth, filling Harry with a dreadful anticipation that made her shiver.

Without stopping to think, she reached back with her spare hand and grabbed Oliver's fingers, needing reassurance that she was not alone. Nothing could happen to her as long as they stuck together.

They crept on, the sound of their movements masked by the slap of the water against the boat. The murmuring carried further now, and Harry realised with a start that she could make out two voices over the constant shivering of the sedge.

'We... before tomorrow...'

'Package... final... barge.'

The words were snatched away by the breeze but the implications were not lost on Harry. The voices were male and perfectly ordinary, quietly discussing the job they were undertaking. The light they carried did not represent a restless spirit in search of the lost. Feeling more than a little foolish, she grasped the logical explanation close to her chest and pushed on, straining to catch more of the conversation. They were perhaps only ten or twelve feet behind now; she could make out muffled figures in the lamplight, confirming her belief that this could not be the ferryman.

She glanced back at Oliver, wondering whether he had reached the same conclusion. But of course he had, she thought as she caught sight of his set features. Oliver believed in facts and evidence. He was not as foolish as she was. Grateful she had not embarrassed herself by revealing her fears, Harry turned forwards again and cocked her head. The wind died a little, making it easier to pick out the words over the reeds and the slosh of the water. This voice was deeper, perhaps older. 'Last delivery... King's Lynn... collect payment.'

'I am glad.' The other voice seemed suddenly louder, as though raised in passion. 'It's... risky. What if we get caught?'

Deep Voice rumbled. 'No... suspects...'

More words followed, too low for Harry to make out. Now that her irrational fears had been vanquished, she was impatient to discover what was being transported, and by whom. She edged closer. '...Philip St John.'

The familiar name almost made Harry gasp. There was a word for those who moved goods around in secret: smugglers. Could it be that Philip St John was somehow involved?

'He's out...' Deep Voice said, '...no... sense...'

'...dangerous.' The second voice rose in tone, as though agitated, and the words were clear over the hiss of the reeds. 'What if... wrong?'

'...so far...' He seemed to be trying to soothe his companion. 'Over... soon...'

Harry pushed forward again. If she could just get a clear view of the boat, she might be able to see what it was they carried. But in her haste, she trod on something thin and hard protruding from the water. It cracked sharply beneath her foot. There was a loud curse. The lamp swung wildly. The gentle slosh of the boat stopped. 'What was that?'

Harry felt Oliver duck low. Instinctively, she did the same, turning the light of the torch against her body and hoping the reeds would hide them. Her heart hammered against her ribs. She did not dare draw breath. Those they were pursuing might not be the fabled ferryman but they were still almost certainly dangerous men. If they came looking for the source of the snapped twig, they would stumble right into Harry and Oliver.

'It's nothing. A bird.'

A soft splash suggested the boat had begun to move again. 'Let's get... done,' the second voice said, sounding fretful once more. 'The sooner... Burwell... better.'

Harry's racing pulse began to slow. She stayed still, listening. When she judged the boat had moved far enough away, she turned to Oliver. 'Did you hear any of that?'

He nodded. 'Enough to know they are up to no good.'

'Should we follow them? Find out what they're doing?'

'No. Let's get back on dry land. We can talk back at the house.'

In other circumstances, Harry might have argued but she was cold and wet and unwilling to risk another broken twig. With care, they retraced their steps. Harry's mind whirled as she considered the implications of what they had overheard. She did not understand everything – not yet – but one thing was clear. There was something infinitely more dangerous than the supernatural out on the fens that night.

* * *

Abandoning their borrowed boots in the outhouse once more, Harry and Oliver made their way back into the kitchen and locked the door behind them. By unspoken agreement, Harry made a pot of tea. Neither of them said much as they waited for the kettle to whistle. It was only when they were seated opposite each other at the kitchen table, two steaming cups in front of them, that they broke their silence.

'Well,' Harry said, in a flat murmur that still sounded too loud in the hush. 'That changes things.'

Oliver inclined his head. 'It's clear this isn't the first time they've made that journey.'

Harry wrapped her hands around her cup. 'Agnes said the locals used the shortcut across the fen to avoid tolls on the barges, but what if they also used it to move things in secret. Illegal things.'

'Smugglers.'

'Yes.' She leaned forward. 'Let's say you've hidden something on one of the big barges that come along the river from the coast but you don't want it to be examined at the tolls. So you offload it before then and transfer it to another barge on a different waterway. One that has already been through the tolls and passed the checks.'

Oliver frowned. 'Why not just drive it there?'

Harry hesitated. 'I don't know. Maybe it's easier to get it back on the boat from the water. Loading something from a car might attract more attention.'

'Fine,' he allowed. 'So they get the contraband past the tolls. Then what?'

'I suppose it gets distributed to wherever it needs to go. I don't really know that either, or what it is they are moving. But it's risky – they said so. Which makes me suspect it's not legal.' She fixed him with a meaningful stare. 'And that's not all. Did you hear one of them mention Philip St John? Does that mean he's involved somehow?'

He nodded, his expression sombre. 'I did hear that, yes. But if he was part of a smuggling ring, why would Archer invite Sherlock Holmes to investigate?'

'Archer doesn't know,' Harry suggested. 'But I can't help feeling that's not it. The second voice sounded fearful when he mentioned St John. Almost like he thought he would give the game away. That doesn't sound like he's part of the operation.'

'I picked up on that too,' Oliver said. 'The other one was less concerned. He didn't seem to think St John was a threat.'

Harry brooded into her cup. 'He certainly isn't at the moment.'

Replaying the snatches of conversation in her mind, she looked up sharply. 'Unless—'

'Unless what?'

She gnawed at her lip as her thoughts tumbled over one another. 'What if that's what Philip St John's illness is really about? What if he saw something he wasn't supposed to – something similar to us – and needed to be silenced?' A frown dug into her forehead as she considered the possibilities. 'Not silenced – they're not killers, whatever else they might be. But kept quiet. What if they're making sure no one listens to a word he says?'

Oliver's expression transformed into grim understanding. 'Then we need to work out how they're doing it.'

'Give me a minute, Oliver,' Harry said, puffing out her cheeks. 'An hour ago we thought Mary was poisoning him.'

Oliver did not smile. 'She could be. This doesn't rule her out – she might be working with them. Any of the domestic staff might be in league with the smugglers.'

Harry couldn't argue. It was Mary who'd filled her head with nonsense about the ferryman – had that been a smokescreen to keep her from venturing out on the fens in the dark? 'It definitely wasn't Mary or Agnes out there tonight.'

'No,' Oliver conceded. 'It could have been Donaldson, though.'

'I suppose so. I couldn't hear clearly enough.' She rubbed her eyes wearily and gazed bleakly across the table. 'What a mess. Just when I think we've worked out who the poisoner is, everything gets thrown up in the air again. I hadn't even considered the possibility of an enemy outside the walls.'

'Because it wasn't likely. There was no reason to suspect anyone might want to keep St John quiet,' Oliver said. 'You couldn't have known any of this from the story Archer told.'

The fact that it was true did not make Harry feel any better. At least Oliver did not know the worst of her shame: that she'd almost believed the ferryman might be the one wielding the lantern that night. 'Holmes would have known.'

Oliver reached across the table to take her hand. 'Only because Sir Arthur Conan Doyle wrote it that way. If I've learned anything from observing Scotland Yard's investigations, it's that real-life detective work involves dedication, determination and a large helping of luck.' He squeezed her fingers. 'It's not all flashes of brilliance and playing the violin.'

Harry smiled at his kindly reassurance. She liked the way her hand felt in his, warm and cocooned. 'That's a very good thing because I can't play the violin.' She yawned. 'Do you think it might be time to get some sleep?'

He gathered up the cups and took them to the sink to wash. 'Now that is a brilliant piece of reasoning. Things will look clearer in the morning.'

Harry hoped he was right. The myth of the ferryman might have been dispelled but she was beginning to suspect that very little was as it seemed at Thrumwell Manor.

14

John Archer met Harry in the dining room the following morning with the kind of ebullient cheer that suggested he, at least, had rested well. 'Miss Moss!' he said, abandoning the newspaper he was reading and getting up from the table to usher her towards an empty chair. 'How good to see you. Did you sleep soundly?'

'I did,' Harry said, and crossed her fingers. She had fallen asleep the moment she got into bed but her dreams had been haunted by a cowled figure that floated in and out of sight, reaching for her with long thin arms but never quite catching her. She had woken in a cold sweat just after dawn and had only dozed since; as a result, her head felt thick and woolly. 'Did you?'

'Very well,' he said. 'And I awoke to excellent news. It appears my uncle has turned a corner. Agnes reports that he asked her quite distinctly for a kipper this morning.'

Harry was not sure whether she had heard correctly. 'I'm sorry, did you say a kipper?'

'I did,' he said, beaming. 'And the significance of that is that kippers were his usual breakfast. Before he became ill. It has been some time since he was well enough to request anything for breakfast, much less a kipper.'

'Ah,' Harry said. 'I see.' The implications of what he was saying pierced her tiredness. 'Oh, I *see*.'

'I did think he was a little less erratic when I escorted him upstairs last night but I assumed it was just exhaustion,' Archer said. 'Dare I dream our long nightmare may be coming to an end?'

'Let us hope so,' Harry said, and reached for the teapot. The change in Philip St John was unexpected, especially considering what she and Oliver had overheard. What had altered that might bring about such an improvement? 'But I am very glad to hear he is better. I wonder – do you think he might be well enough for me to visit him briefly? I'd like to observe his condition.'

'Of course,' Archer said. 'I plan to see him myself, after breakfast. We shall go together.'

She was halfway through her poached eggs on toast when Oliver appeared in the doorway of the dining room. Archer leapt up and made a show of ushering him to the seat opposite Harry, then rang the bell for Mary. 'I thoroughly recommend the bacon and eggs,' he said, when the cook appeared.

Oliver smiled. 'I shall take your recommendation. I find myself with the appetite of your wolfhound this morning.'

Archer nodded. 'I feel like that most mornings,' he said, with a rueful glance at his middle. He tapped the folded newspaper on the table. 'Would you think me terribly rude if I read while you eat? Breakfast is when I generally catch up with the news.'

'Not at all,' Harry said. Her father had been known to hide behind the newspaper for the entire duration of the meal.

'I say catch up, we are usually a day or two behind,' he said as he shook the pages out, and Harry recognised Friday's headlines about a tragic train crash in Switzerland, and the new record set by Amy Johnson flying solo from London to Africa. 'But the news reaches us eventually.'

He lapsed into an absorbed silence as he perused the print. Oliver poured himself a cup of coffee and eyed Harry across the table. 'How are you this morning?'

'No worse than I should be,' she said dryly. 'But Mr Archer has just been telling me his uncle seems more lucid today.'

The faintest of perplexed frowns crossed Oliver's face. 'I'm very glad to hear it,' he replied cautiously. 'Is there any indication why?'

'Good Lord, such a small world.' Archer did not look up from the paper as he interrupted. 'I know the chap mentioned here, Ishmael Bloom. He took a house near the village for a month or so last summer, drove a very fast car that almost ran me off the road once or twice.'

'Ishmael Bloom,' Oliver echoed slowly. 'Why do I recognise that name?'

Archer peered at the newsprint. 'It says here he was arrested in Southampton, straight off the boat from New York, on suspicion of being the leader of an international narcotics ring. The authorities were forced to release him without charge but he remains a person of interest to Scotland Yard.' He paused. 'It must be the same man, surely. There can't be two Americans called Ishmael Bloom.'

'It's possible, I suppose,' Oliver said. 'Did he strike you as the kind of character who might be up to no good?'

'He was certainly a devil behind the wheel,' Archer said, after a moment's thought. 'And no one seemed to know what he was actually doing here. But that's often the way of things these days and I must confess I forgot all about him once he'd left.'

Harry stared down at her plate. It could not be a coincidence and yet the whole idea of an international drug smuggler at large in the Cambridgeshire fens seemed laughable. She could not imagine anywhere less likely than the village of Morden to be caught up in anything more criminal than a spot of poaching. But the more she considered it, the less ridiculous it seemed. Agnes had observed more than once how important the nearby river network was, with connections that spread all over the country, and it was that observation that made Harry wonder. The drugs could come in from Europe by boat, be transported along the rivers via barges and moved across the fens to avoid tolls and perhaps even customs officers. And the kind of people involved in a drug smuggling ring might go to extreme lengths to prevent anyone discovering what they were doing. They might even turn to poison.

Harry looked up to see Oliver watching her and she knew without asking that he had made the same connection. 'Your uncle never met Bloom, did he?'

Archer lowered the paper in surprise. 'I can't imagine how he would have. I mean, I spotted Bloom's car outside the pub a few times but Uncle Philip rarely leaves the manor grounds. Why do you ask?'

She shook her head. 'No reason. Bloom sounds like the sort of character a writer might find interesting, that's all.'

'Ah, I see what you mean,' Archer said. 'Yes, I must admit to tucking one or two of his mannerisms away myself, in case I'm ever required to play a brash American gentleman, although he's rather less of a gentleman than I realised, if Scotland Yard is to be believed. It just goes to show you never can tell.'

He returned to the newspaper, leaving Harry to turn her suspicions over and over in her mind. She wanted to discuss them with Oliver, to confirm that he had reached the same conclusion she had, but that was impossible within earshot of John Archer. She was about to excuse herself when Mary appeared with Oliver's breakfast. He took the plate with enthusiasm and Harry forced herself to wait patiently as he ate, studying the articles on the back of the newspaper to pass the time. When at last he had finished eating, Archer folded the paper and cleared his throat. 'I thought I might pay a brief visit to my uncle now, if you wanted to see how he fares for yourselves.'

As much as Harry longed to talk to Oliver, she was also curious about Philip St John's turn for the better. 'That would be helpful,' she said. 'Thank you.'

'Follow me.'

They encountered Agnes as she was leaving the library, a tray laden with breakfast crockery in her hand. She nodded at Archer as he stood back to allow her into the corridor but said nothing. Inside the room, the drapes had been drawn back, dispelling some of the gloom Harry had observed on her last visit. She glanced outside at the faint smudge on the horizon that marked the edge of the fen and frowned. Splashing after the boat and listening to the snatches of conversation felt like part of a bad dream now, but the sense of peril the experience had invoked lingered in her thoughts. She did not know what Philip St John had done to incur the smugglers' wrath but she was certain it had resulted in his sudden ill health. If he was able, she hoped he might add those pieces to the puzzle now.

Archer strode towards the armchairs that flanked the fireplace. 'Good morning, Uncle Philip,' he said, his voice hearty above the crackle of the fire. 'How was your kipper?'

'Most enjoyable,' Philip St John said, his voice frail but clear. 'I told Agnes I may even manage another later.'

He certainly sounded better, Harry thought as she followed Archer. Philip St John was seated in the same chair as before, with a blanket tucked around his lap, and still bore the hallmarks of a man who was far from well. His skin had a greyish tinge and his eyes were underscored by dark circles, but Harry thought she detected improvements in his appearance as well as his mental clarity. He sat upright and the tremors that had plagued him were noticeably weaker. His expression sharpened as he observed her and she had the impression he was not pleased by her presence. 'Who's this?' he asked, and the words were an echo of his peevish questions the last time Harry had met him.

Archer smiled in reassurance. 'This is Miss Moss, Uncle. She's a friend, staying for the weekend with the excellent Mr Fortescue here.'

'Good morning, Mr St John,' Harry said with a polite smile, as Oliver hung discreetly back. 'It is an honour to meet you again, although I must apologise for intruding on your hospitality at a time like this.'

Philip St John did not smile. 'As my nephew will attest, I am a poor host even when well.'

'I would say reluctant, rather than poor,' Archer put in hastily. 'But we are not here to exhaust you and will keep our visit brief. Is there anything you need?'

The older man turned an irritated gaze from Harry to Archer. 'I have had no tobacco since yesterday. Where is Donaldson?'

'I'm afraid the shop had closed by the time I sent him to the village,' Archer said apologetically. 'I will go this morning.'

Philip St John's hand twitched and shook. He glared at it. 'Why does this damnable hand of mine shake so?'

'It is a symptom of your illness,' Archer reminded him. 'I'm sure it will ease as you recover your strength.'

The older man grunted. 'It will ease sooner if I am brought my tobacco.'

Harry cleared her throat. 'I may be able to help with that. Mr Fortescue and I are going to the village shortly – would you like us to collect your tobacco while we are there?'

'I don't care who collects it, as long as I have it,' he grumbled, but she thought he sounded very slightly less antagonistic.

'You really don't have to,' Archer told Harry.

'But we are going anyway,' she pointed out. 'It's no trouble.'

'In which case, it would be churlish of me not to accept your kind offer,' he said. 'Thank you.'

In the hallway outside the library, Harry eyed Oliver with triumph. 'You look like you've lost a penny and found a pound,' he observed. 'What have I missed?'

'I think I know how Philip St John is being poisoned,' she said. 'Apart from the sleeping draught, prescribed by the family doctor, there's only one thing that comes into the house solely for Philip St John, and that is his tobacco.'

Light dawned in Oliver's eyes. 'Which comes from the village shop.'

'Exactly.' Harry shook her head, remembering once more the Holmes story about the brother who had murdered his siblings by throwing poison into the fireplace. 'It cannot be a coincidence that St John's health improves dramatically when he cannot smoke. The tobacco has to be responsible – either something is added at the village, or here at the house.'

Oliver shifted uneasily. 'It's usually brought by Donaldson. Does that mean we should suspect him rather than Mary now?'

'No one is above suspicion,' Harry said. 'Apart from Archer, who I still cannot believe would harm his uncle. But we need proof and there's only one place to get that.' She fixed Oliver with a determined stare. 'Let's take another trip to Morden village.'

* * *

The shop was small but appeared to be well stocked, in the way village stores often were. A wooden counter ran along one wall, behind which stood a dark-haired woman. She looked up as the bell above the counter rang and Harry recognised her as the good Samaritan they had met the weekend before, outside the pub. 'Hello again,' she said, her gaze roving from Harry to Oliver in surprise. 'Don't tell me you're still lost.'

Harry laughed. 'No, we found our way to Ely in the end, thanks to your directions.'

The woman cocked her head. 'I'm glad to hear that. And yet here you are again.'

'Yes, we're staying at Thrumwell Manor,' Harry explained.

The woman frowned. 'At the manor?' Her eyes flicked between them. 'Mr St John isn't usually one for taking guests.'

'My cousin, John, invited us,' Harry said. 'Poor Uncle Philip has been so under the weather and John thought a visit might perk him up a bit.'

She nodded, although Harry was not sure she believed her. 'I did hear he was unwell. Agnes was beside herself with worry last time I saw her, said she thought he'd taken leave of his senses.' Her gaze narrowed a little. 'I'm surprised at Mr Archer, inviting you to stay at such a difficult time.'

Harry adopted a tone of carefree jollity. 'Happily, my uncle is much improved,' she said. 'Anyway, we've come to collect his tobacco. John told us to ask for Eliza – that's you, isn't it?'

The woman did not return her cheeriness. 'That's right. But Donaldson usually gets the tobacco. Where is he?'

'He came down last night but left it too late and you were closed,' Harry replied. 'We were coming out for a drive and thought we'd save him a job.'

Eliza pursed her lips. 'You won't mind if I call the manor, just to check? We've had some strange folk around here lately – you can't be too careful.'

'Of course,' Harry said, waving her hand with blithe uncon-
cern. 'Call away – they'll vouch for us.'

She disappeared through a door at the far end of the counter.
Moments later, Harry heard the soft murmur of her voice and
presumed she was speaking on the telephone. She turned to
Oliver. 'Buy some tobacco,' she whispered. 'I want to see if she
takes it from the same place as St John's.'

When Eliza returned, her expression was still guarded but she
seemed to have accepted their story. 'Agnes says it's fine to give it
to you. She also says Mary needs some cornflour, if you wouldn't
mind taking that too.'

'Not at all,' Harry said. 'Anything to help out.'

Eliza took a box of cornflour from the shelf behind her, then
reached under the counter for a small, paper-wrapped package.
She pushed both across the counter. 'I'll add them to the manor
bill. Make sure you don't open the tobacco. Mr St John is very
particular about it, so Agnes says.'

Harry let out a little laugh. 'Oh, believe me, I know. He's quite
the tyrant.' She turned to Oliver. 'Didn't you want some tobacco
too? For your pipe.'

The sudden, unbidden image of him puffing at a pipe almost
undid her; she had to dig her nails into her palms to stop a wild
giggle from escaping. 'I do,' Oliver said, with a commendably
straight face. 'How clever of you to remember I've run out. I'll take
an ounce of the stuff, if you don't mind.'

Nodding, Eliza measured the tobacco out and wrapped it.
'That's two shillings.'

Oliver handed over the coins and thanked her. 'I'm very
pleased to hear Mr St John is feeling better,' the woman said.
'Please do pass on my regards.'

'I'll be delighted to,' Harry replied. 'He's still a little frail at the moment but we're hoping he'll be back to his old self by the morning.'

Eliza patted the tobacco. 'This should help, at least.'

'Thanks,' Harry said, gathering up the cornflour and packet and leaving Oliver to pick up the tobacco he had bought. 'Maybe we'll see you again before we leave.'

'Maybe,' Eliza said, with a smile that Harry saw did not quite reach her eyes. 'If you get lost again.'

They were almost at the car when Harry spoke next. 'Is she still watching?'

Oliver passed around the bonnet and inserted the key in the door before he glanced casually up. 'Yes. I can see her at the window.'

Harry did not look round as she got into the car. 'I don't think she trusted us.'

'No,' Oliver agreed, 'but the feeling is mutual.' He glanced across from the driver's seat. 'What now?'

'We take Philip St John his tobacco,' Harry said. 'And then we wait. If my suspicions are correct, we have a very interesting night ahead of us.'

15

It was a little after lunch when Harry went to the library. Philip St John sat dozing in his armchair, an upturned paperback resting on his lap. Reluctant to disturb him, she sat in the chair opposite and took the opportunity to study him. The grey pallor that hung over him appeared to have receded still further since the morning; she noted faint colour creeping into his cheeks. He was not in good health – not yet – but she judged he would be in a day or two. As long as he was not poisoned further.

He had probably been handsome as a young man, she thought, although age was beginning to catch up with him now. She imagined his sandy hair had been strawberry blond then, his bearing proud with the easy arrogance of youth, his head filled with dreams of becoming a writer. He would have been in his twenties when the Great War had broken out; had he gone to the Western Front in glad anticipation of serving his country? How quickly that eagerness must have turned to despair when he understood the reality of life in the trenches. The fact that he had never spoken about his experience told its own story. Or perhaps, as Archer had suggested, he had poured all he needed to say into his writing.

Leaving the tobacco on the side table, Harry got to her feet and crossed quietly to the bookshelves. The range of titles was impressive – just as good as that of the library at Abinger Hall. But there was a noticeable gap on one shelf. She presumed this was where the books Archer had given her had sat. The titles to either side leaned against each other, lopsided and unsupported. She reached out to straighten them and, as she did so, she saw there was another book hidden behind them. Frowning, she removed some of the volumes in front and pulled it free. It was a hardback copy of *The Blood-soaked Soil*.

She opened the cover. It was a first edition, published in 1920. Harry stared at it reverently, suspecting it must be worth much more now than it had been on the day it was published. Turning the page, she expected to see the now-familiar dedication and blinked in surprise. It had been scored out, eviscerated so that the words did not exist. With a huff of dismay, Harry flipped to the opening chapter. That too had been slashed, three vicious lines slicing diagonally across the page, cutting into the paper beneath. In stunned silence, she leafed through the rest of the pages. All had been carved into tatters, an act of violence that both shocked and saddened her. Who could have done such a thing? And why?

'Are you a spirit?'

The question made Harry jump. The book tumbled from her fingers, sending a flurry of lacerated paper fluttering like sycamore seeds. The spine landed with a heavy thud at her feet. Harry did not bend to pick it up. Instead, she turned to eye Philip St John, who was watching her without apparent emotion. 'No,' she said, gathering her wits. 'I am Miss Moss. We met this morning.'

His gaze focused more keenly on her. 'Yes,' he said slowly. 'Yes, I remember now. You were going to bring me some tobacco.'

Harry smiled in spite of herself. 'I did bring you some. It's on the table there. Would you like me to fill your pipe?'

'No, I would not,' he snapped. 'I am not an invalid, despite what my nephew may claim.'

He reached for the package she had left on the table. Kneeling, Harry began to gather the shredded paper together, determined not to let Philip St John see the mutilation. But the fall had dislodged the binding. The book would not close. Getting to her feet, Harry slid it unobtrusively back into the gap on the bookshelf. She would ask Archer about it later, find out if he knew how it had come to be damaged.

'Why did you ask if I was a spirit?' she said, crossing back to the armchair to sit across from St John.

'Because I often see someone standing in that exact spot,' he said. 'But when I look again, they are not truly there.'

Part of the hallucinations he had endured, Harry guessed, and offered a reassuring smile. 'I assure you I am most definitely here.'

Lighting the pipe, he puffed several times to draw the tobacco, and studied Harry through the cloud of smoke. 'A fact I am well aware of,' he said dryly.

Harry weighed her options. Now that his mind seemed to be clearer, she could tell he was no fool. She decided brutal honesty was the best way to deal with him. 'Mr St John, I must tell you that I don't believe your illness is a natural one. I believe you have been poisoned.'

He gaped at her and, for a moment, she regretted her candidness. 'Poisoned?' he echoed. 'Are you mad?'

'Not at all,' she said, and leaned forward. 'It appears there are criminals at large in Morden Fen – desperate men who will go to any length to protect their identities. I can't be sure exactly what happened to make them target you, but I am certain they did, with the intention of keeping you quiet until they had finished their work.' Harry sat back. 'And they used the tobacco you smoke to do it.'

St John lowered the pipe. 'My tobacco? How?'

'I don't know exactly,' she admitted. 'Tests should tell us more. But the tobacco you are smoking now is uncontaminated. You may be sure of that.'

He stared at her. 'You must be mistaken. Who would do such a thing?'

'I don't know that, either,' Harry said, 'but I have my suspicions. If I'm right, you are in more danger now than you have ever been.'

St John eyed her mutely, the pipe smoking gently in his hand. Harry held his gaze. 'I fear there is a very real danger the perpetrators may try to silence you forever,' she said. 'Your unexpected recovery may force their hand but please rest assured we plan to apprehend them before any harm befalls you.'

'We?' Philip St John said in irritated bewilderment. 'Who the devil do you mean by we?'

Harry took a deep breath. 'Myself, Mr Fortescue and your nephew. No one else can know what we intend. And we will need your help to catch them.'

He sat in silence for a moment, his pipe smouldering in his hand. 'Poison. I can scarcely believe it. And yet...' His gaze slid towards the bookshelves once more, then he seemed to reach a decision. He narrowed his eyes. 'What do you want me to do?'

* * *

The bedroom was warm, stuffy, and dark, the ideal environment for sleep. And indeed, one person in the room was in the realm of dreams: his gentle snore both reassuring and grating on Harry's already frayed nerves. Her senses told her it must be after midnight; the tick of the clock on the mantelpiece marked each passing second with maddening precision. They had been waiting this way for more than an hour: Harry behind the drapes, with Barrymore at her feet and the icy chill of the window at her back, Oliver in the shadow of the wardrobe to the left of the bedroom door, Archer crouched behind a vast armchair. Peering round the edge of the curtain, Harry could see nothing of the others, but she knew they were there. She really hoped they were not waiting in vain.

Philip St John had played his part to perfection; it was obvious to Harry that acting ability ran in the family. A short while after dinner, he had begun to bellow in the library, proclaiming he had seen lights on the fen. The household staff had come running when the shouting began, dismayed at his sudden relapse, and Mary had begged Archer not to venture into the night. 'He's out there, sir,' she had exclaimed, her face dreadful. 'Waiting to take you.'

Archer had not listened; he and Donaldson had rushed outside with Barrymore to search among the reeds. Agnes had set about comforting her master, filling his pipe and offering him brandy. Mary had hovered by the window, wringing her hands and uttering dire predictions. When the two men returned, empty-handed but certain someone had been out on the fen, St John announced it was not the first time he had seen the lights. 'There are sinister forces at work,' he declared with some imperiousness. 'I insist the police are summoned first thing in the morning so I can tell them all I know.'

'The police?' Mary cried. 'What good will they be against the supernatural? Oh, we are doomed!'

Harry had seen Archer's expression tighten but, for once, he did not reprimand the cook. 'That will do, Mary,' was all he said.

She had subsided then, exchanging mutinous glances with the housekeeper, who had looked apprehensive. 'Must we call the police?' she asked. 'I fear it will make it more difficult to keep the master's illness to ourselves.'

'I'm afraid we must take that risk,' Archer said solemnly. 'My uncle is adamant that he tells them everything he knows. We cannot deny him that.'

It was perhaps a little overdone but Harry took the opportunity to observe each of them, searching their demeanour for clues about which of them might be uneasy over what Philip St John had seen. Donaldson said nothing, his expression taciturn and closed. Agnes cast the occasional anxious glance towards the windows but seemed more concerned with tending to her master. It was Mary who was the most disturbed and Harry couldn't help wondering whether it was the fear of discovery that was making her jumpy. At length, Archer instructed Agnes to prepare the sleeping draught for his uncle. Harry waited until Philip St John had raised the dose to his lips, then leapt to her feet, pointing at the window. 'What's that?'

Mary let out a cry as everyone turned to look. Oliver strode forward to peer out. 'There's nothing there.'

'Oh,' Harry said, subsiding. 'But I was sure I saw something.'

Archer took the empty glass from his uncle and frowned. 'This is not helping anyone's nerves. I suggest we retire to bed.'

With uneasy acquiescence, they had done as he instructed. Or at least, some of them had. Harry, Oliver and Archer had gone to their rooms, only to sneak along the corridor once the house had settled into silence. They had taken up their posts in St John's bedroom without speaking, waiting to see who, if anyone, would take the bait.

The minutes ticked past, stretching into another hour. Someone – Oliver or Archer – coughed, a hurriedly stifled sound that felt as loud as a gunshot. Harry shifted behind the drapes and massaged the small of her back. She wished she had worn another jumper, the cold was stiffening her muscles. At her feet, Barrymore twitched in his sleep. Had she been wrong in her suspicions? How much longer should they wait before giving up? And then she felt Barrymore tense. He raised his head, brushing against her knee, then rose. A low growl rumbled in the darkness. Harry dropped a warning hand to rest upon his head. 'Sssshhh, boy. I know.'

The dog fell silent, although he continued to radiate tension. Somewhere nearby, a floorboard creaked. Harry held her breath. Her companions must have heard it too – were they poised and ready? A faint rattle. Another creak. The unmistakable sound of the door handle turning.

Harry moved to peer through the gap in the curtain. Her eyes had grown well used to the dark; she picked out the four-poster bed, its drapes left open to reveal the hump of a sleeping body. The wardrobe loomed behind the door – she could not make out Oliver. The armchair that hid Archer was a hunched monster, waiting to attack. For a moment, nothing moved. Then, with the faintest whisper, the door edged from its frame and slowly opened.

The figure that entered was nothing more than a smudge. They carried no light. Harry tensed as they stopped in the entrance of the room. She pressed her hand against Barrymore's skull, hoping the dog understood. *Not yet, boy*, she willed him in silence. *Wait.*

Apparently satisfied, the figure started to move towards the bed. Harry heard the rustle of cotton, saw a blur of white as one of the pillows was raised. Every sinew burned with the desire to burst out of her hiding place, to stop what was about to happen, but she held back. Whoever the intruder was must be caught in the act of trying to silence Philip St John forever. She watched, eyes stinging with the strain of picking out the movements in the dark. When she saw the pillow being lowered, she snatched her hand from Barrymore's head and hauled back the curtain. 'Now!' she cried.

The wolfhound leapt forward, snarling and snapping in the dark. Across the room, Harry heard Oliver and Archer move. Bounding from her hiding place, she switched on the torch she held in her other hand, training its beam on the face of the would-be attacker. Raising a hand, they tried to ward off the light. Archer and Oliver advanced, grim-faced, just as Philip St John sat up in bed. He rubbed his eyes, blinking at the brightness of the torch, and turned his head to stare at the figure cowering before Barrymore's bared teeth. 'What the blazes are you doing?' he said, gaping in astonishment.

'Eliza has come to kill you before you give her up to the police,' Harry said, her tone flat. 'Isn't that right?'

The other woman lowered her arm, the pillow dropping to the bed. Her eyes flickered wildly from side to side, searching for an escape. But Barrymore stood between her and the door, his rumbling snarl full of menace. She drew a ragged breath and glared at Philip St John. 'If you hadn't been poking about in things that don't concern you, I wouldn't have had to.'

'But...' St John shook his head in bewilderment. 'I don't know what you're talking about.'

'Don't give me that,' she scoffed. 'You came across our skiff that morning, returning to Morden from Burwell. You saw us.'

He blinked at her, open-mouthed. Then understanding slowly dawned in his eyes as a memory floated through the fog of the past weeks. 'I remember. I did see you – you and—' He ran a hand across his eyes. 'And someone else – I don't know who. I asked what you were doing.'

Eliza's lip curled. 'I knew you didn't believe the story we gave you – why would anyone risk the fens to move honest goods when they could go by road? But it was so early and we'd missed our rendezvous the night before – we didn't think anyone would be out.'

St John still appeared to be adjusting to the sudden recollection. 'I was suspicious. I was going to tell the police. And then – and then—'

'And then you were poisoned,' Harry supplied. 'I know you put something in the tobacco, Eliza – tincture of Ergot, if I'm not mistaken.'

The other woman's expression slackened in surprise. 'How did you know that?'

'An educated guess,' Harry said. 'But I'm impressed by the speed at which you administered the poison. Did you have it already prepared?'

'I had the tincture,' Eliza admitted. 'It's used for—' She broke off and seemed to recollect herself. 'Never you mind what it's used for. I had it, all the same. And I knew Archer was coming to collect the tobacco, so I took the chance.'

Beside her, Harry saw Archer clench his fists. 'I only wanted to shut him up,' Eliza defended herself, as if the admission made her actions less terrible. 'I could have killed him any time.'

'But what were you moving that was important enough to poison a man?' Archer burst out.

Eliza glanced at him scornfully. 'Don't you know?'

'He may not,' Oliver said, stepping forwards. 'But we do. You're working with Ishmael Bloom and you were moving narcotics.' He offered a cool smile. 'The game is up, Eliza. One call to Scotland Yard and they'll be able to round up your whole gang. In fact—'

He was interrupted by a hoarse bellow from the hallway. 'I told you not to come!'

For a moment, they all stood frozen, staring at the figure in the doorway. 'How could I not come?' Eliza snapped. 'I could hardly leave it to you.'

Harry turned the torch towards the door. 'Mr Donaldson,' she said coolly. 'How good of you to incriminate yourself.'

He jerked his head to glower at her but said nothing.

'Don't just stand there, you fool!' Eliza cried. 'Help me!'

The command seemed to jolt Donaldson into action. With a snarl, he barrelled into the room, crashing into Oliver and knocking him into the wall. Harry gasped as his head snapped against the wood panels. At the same time, Eliza snatched up the counterpane and hurled it at Barrymore, smothering the dog in the heavy fabric. Archer roared in fury and leapt towards her, but stumbled over the writhing animal. Before Harry could move, Eliza was bounding across the room, making for the door.

Staggering to his feet, Donaldson vanished after her. Heart racing, Harry stared after them, unsure whether to give chase or go to Oliver, who lay in a crumpled heap. But there was really only one choice. With a muttered oath, she hurried to his side and played the torch over his pale face. 'Oliver?'

Behind her, Archer had succeeded in releasing Barrymore. With a volley of ferocious barks, the dog hurtled from the room. 'I'll follow them!' Archer cried, running from the room.

Oliver let out a groan. His eyes fluttered open. 'Harry?'

She wanted to sob with relief. 'You're alive.'

'Of course he's alive.' Philip St John was clambering out of the bed, his expression fierce. 'He's a lawyer – they're made of stone. But I'll stay with him. You go and help my nephew.'

This time, Harry felt no hesitation. Snatching up her torch, she hurtled from the room and made for the servants' staircase.

As she yanked open the door, she almost collided with Agnes, who gasped and shrank back. 'What's happening?' the house-keeper cried. 'I heard shouting.'

Mary peered over her shoulder. 'It's the master, isn't it? He's lost his senses again.'

'He's in his room,' Harry said, stepping back to allow them onto the landing. 'But Mr Fortescue is injured. Please tend to his head.'

She did not wait to answer their startled questions, but hurried down the stairs as fast as she dared. In the kitchen, no one was in sight but the window was shattered and the door leading outside was wide open. Cursing, she ran through it and into the freezing night.

There were no lights to guide her this time. Straining her ears, Harry listened for the telltale splashing that would give away the direction the flight had taken. A shout rang out in the darkness, followed by the sound of something heavy hitting the water. A woman screamed – Harry guessed that must be Eliza and made for the source of the noise. The beam of her torch picked out the ground directly before her but even so she stumbled. She'd had the foresight to wear her boots when she had dressed for the night's adventures but she had not anticipated she would need a coat. By the time she reached the fen, her feet were already drenched and she was shivering. But she did not stop.

The sound of fighting increased. Following the crashing and furious cries, Harry splashed onwards, burst through a clump of reeds to see Archer and Donaldson locked in battle. Eliza was watching, kept at bay by a snarling, terrifying Barrymore. With a yell, Harry thrust towards the men. Donaldson saw her first. He swung at Archer, knocking him backwards into her. Harry tumbled, sprawling on her back in the fen. Razor-sharp reeds sliced at her skin as she landed in the ice-cold water. The impact sent the breath gushing from her lungs. She lay still for a moment, wheezing, then scrambled to her feet. The torch lay a short distance away, lodged half in, half out of the sedge, its light extinguished. With an oath, Harry snatched it up and stabbed at the switch. Dead. She dropped it in the water and turned to the brawl once more.

It was immediately clear Donaldson was the better fighter. He laid punch after punch on Archer, who did his best to weave out of the way but was hampered by the water sloshing against his thighs. Rallying, Archer landed a punch of his own. Donaldson staggered backwards, shaking his head. Sensing his advantage, Archer pressed forward but Donaldson was ready. With a howl, he threw himself into the other man, bearing him through the air and landing them both flat in the water. With mounting horror, Harry watched as Donaldson forced Archer's head beneath the surface. Archer fought back, spluttering and coughing, but his assailant was too strong. Once more, Donaldson plunged him under the water. 'Stop!' Harry cried. 'You're going to kill him!'

But it was clear from the demented grimace on Donaldson's face that he did not intend to stop. Wildly, Harry looked around for a branch or a tree stump she could use as a weapon. She found nothing. And then she remembered the torch. Where had it been? Scrambling sideways, she clutched desperately among the waterlogged vegetation until at last her fingers closed around it. She hauled it from the water and launched herself towards the struggling men, praying she was not too late. Archer's feet were thrashing now as Donaldson tried to finish the job. Eliza let out a cry of warning. Donaldson's head jerked up, presenting Harry with a target. Summoning as much force as she could, she brought the torch down on the back of his skull. It connected with a sickening crunch. The man jerked and reared back. His hands loosened on Archer's neck. For a moment, he hovered in the air, fingers convulsing. Then he toppled sideways and lay still.

The torch tumbled from Harry's numb grip as she scrambled towards Archer. With strength born of fear, she dragged him from the water and hauled him into a lopsided sitting position, banging her fist hard against his back. He coughed, weakly, and a torrent of fen water gushed from his lungs. Another cough, and another, as Harry continued to pummel his back. Finally, he opened his eyes. Blinking, his gaze came to rest upon Donaldson, who lay groaning. 'Did I do that?' he croaked. 'I've never been in a real fight before. It's quite different to what we do on stage.'

On the other side of the clearing, Eliza glared at them. 'Call off your dog.'

'That depends on you,' Harry said, undoing the belt from her skirt to knot around Donaldson's hands. 'Are you going to tell the police everything? Or shall I leave you out here with Barrymore?'

The woman's eyes narrowed. 'You wouldn't.'

As though on cue, the dog snarled. 'Oh, I would,' Harry said. She smiled thinly. 'Among all the commotion this evening, I believe Donaldson forgot to feed him. He's probably hungry.'

Eliza seemed to be weighing her options. 'Don't leave me out here,' she said, with a nervous glance at Barrymore's flattened ears and bared teeth. 'I'll come quietly.'

'Sensible,' Harry said and turned her attention to Archer. 'Are you able to walk?'

He nodded. 'Strong as an ox,' he said, wincing as he clambered to his feet and glanced at Donaldson. 'Stronger than him, anyway.'

Hiding a smile, Harry decided not to mention her role in the fight. She tugged on the makeshift handcuffs, earning her a glare from the groundsman. 'You've got a nasty head wound and probably a concussion,' she told him severely. 'I doubt you'd last ten minutes out here on your own, so don't even consider trying to run.'

Scowling, he evidently saw the wisdom of her words because he allowed her to help him to his feet. She handed the end of the belt to Archer, who took it with steely determination and turned to Eliza. 'You. In front of me. Don't try anything or I'll set the hound on you.'

With an apprehensive look, Eliza nodded. Satisfied the fight seemed to have gone out of her, Harry squared her shoulders. 'Let's go,' she said to Archer. 'Barrymore, take us home.'

With a final baleful growl at Eliza, the dog turned and trotted into the reeds. Archer followed, keeping Donaldson close. Eliza went next, leaving Harry to bring up the rear. Progress was slow – it seemed to take an age to reach the edge of the fen and Harry's shoulders ached with the tension of watching their captives – but no sooner had the ground firmed up beneath their feet than Eliza let out a scream. 'What's that? Out there, I can see a light!'

Warily, Harry looked around, certain it was a trick meant to distract her. But Eliza was right – there was a light bobbing among the sedge behind them. It appeared to be coming their way. For one startled moment, Harry stared at it in disbelief. There couldn't be more smugglers on the fen, could there? But the terrified expression on Eliza's face told her it was not someone she was expecting and Harry knew without a doubt what the other woman feared. 'Move,' she commanded, nudging the girl in the back. 'Towards the house. Now.'

Eliza did not argue. She stumbled forward, almost losing her footing, and Harry was obliged to steady her. She did not dare look back. Before they were more than halfway, more lights appeared, this time in front of them. Harry cursed, fearing Donaldson had somehow alerted the other smugglers. They could not go back into the fen – she had no desire to meet whoever – or whatever – bore the lamp floating there. But frantic shouts soon made it clear the lanterns in front of them were held by Agnes and Oliver. As the bedraggled party cleared the reeds, Harry saw them both. Oliver's head was wrapped in a clean white bandage but he seemed otherwise unhurt. The housekeeper's face sagged when she saw Donaldson's bonds. Her gaze slid to Eliza and her obvious confusion deepened. 'I don't understand. What is this?'

'I'll explain later,' Harry said tersely. 'Has anyone called the police?'

Oliver nodded. 'They're on their way. The local constabulary should arrive first but I took the liberty of suggesting they call in Scotland Yard, to sweep up the rest of the gang.'

The news brought Harry a much-needed surge of relief, although she might have known he would have matters well in hand. 'Well done,' she said, further relieved to see the house looming into view. 'How's your head? Are you badly hurt?'

He grimaced. 'It's sore but I'll survive. How are you?'

'Wet,' she sighed. 'Again. But otherwise fine. I'll feel better once we get these two under lock and key. I seem to recall there's a cellar we might use.' She let out a long shaky breath as the magnitude of the night's events began to catch up with her. In the space of a few hours, she had unmasked Philip St John's poisoners, saved John Archer's life and exposed an international drug smuggling ring. No wonder she felt exhausted. 'I did say it would be an interesting night, didn't I?'

'You did,' he agreed, with an amused nod. 'And it's not over yet.'

He meant the arrival of the police, she supposed, but Harry found her gaze straying in the direction of the fen. There was no light there now, the darkness was unbroken. She and Eliza had been mistaken, she told herself with firm resolution – the ferryman was nothing more than a myth. With a determined effort of will, Harry turned her back on Morden Fen. Oliver was right; the night was not over and there were other dangers to face. Forcing her stiff muscles to move, she hurried forward to catch up with John Archer. 'Forgive my urgency but I must ask – has the mystery of your uncle's illness been solved to your satisfaction?'

'Eh?' he said, staring at her for a moment. 'Oh. Yes, I suppose it has, although I must admit it's turned out to be rather more extraordinary than I expected. One might even say an adventure worthy of Sherlock Holmes.'

'Quite.' Harry knew her smile lacked its usual vibrancy but she offered it nonetheless. 'Which brings me onto the favour I must ask. As you know, my employer prefers not to draw attention to himself these days.' She met his gaze, hoping he understood her. 'Do you think you might be able to keep his involvement in the case to yourself when you talk to the police?'

Archer frowned slightly. 'I'm not sure I...' He trailed off, then gazed at her with dawning comprehension. 'Ah. Yes, I don't think that will be a problem. To be honest, the gentleman concerned doesn't appear to have had much involvement at all. You and Mr Fortescue have done all the hard work.'

The observation drew another smile from Harry, but this one felt rueful. 'Thank you. Might I suggest you pass me off as a cousin, visiting for the weekend?'

He considered the idea. 'If I'm going to do that, I might need to know your first name.'

Harry thought for a moment. 'Why don't we go with Irene?'

Archer nodded and she knew he'd caught her reference to one of the earliest of Sherlock Holmes' cases, *A Scandal in Bohemia*. 'Excellent. Come along, then, Cousin Irene. Let's see if Mary has had the presence of mind to slice up some seed cake.'

16

By agreement, Harry and Oliver kept to their rooms while the police spoke to John Archer. As promised, he had glossed over their roles in the drama, describing them as family members who had most unfortunately been caught up in a murderous conspiracy. Mindful of their master's instructions, Agnes and Mary had maintained the deception during their interviews. The police had finally left around dawn, with Donaldson and Eliza as their prisoners, and the package of poisoned tobacco as evidence. Hollow-eyed and exhausted, the remaining members of the household had stumbled to bed. None of them had risen much before midday.

'I gave Agnes and Mary a few days off,' Archer said, when Harry came downstairs to find him sitting at the dining table. 'I believe Agnes intends to go to her mother's and Mary has taken to her bed. I'm not sure what there is to eat in the kitchen but I daresay we'll manage.'

Oliver had appeared soon after and they had pulled together a lunch of cheese and cold meats, with some of the excellent bread Mary had baked the previous day. Harry was pleasantly surprised to find Philip St John's condition had continued to improve, despite the events of the night before. After lunch, he had asked Harry to join him on a gentle stroll around the grounds. 'I want to feel the sun on my face. I've been stuck inside for too long.'

They took things slowly, for which Harry was glad as she had several aches of her own. She had insisted Philip St John wrap up warmly against the cold, and had layered him in several scarves. Very little of his face was visible but Harry felt his eyes upon her as they walked. 'It appears you are not quite what you seem, Miss Moss. You are certainly not my nephew's cousin, as he told the police.'

She kept her own gaze straight ahead. 'Oh? In what way am I not what I seem?'

He smiled. 'Let's not play games. I know you ask questions and find answers. I know you make observations and set traps. And I know you saved my life, and perhaps that of my nephew. You are a detective, Miss Moss.'

Harry did not reply. How could she when everything he said was true? But St John had not finished speaking. 'My nephew tells me you have read several of my books.'

The change of conversational flow wrong-footed Harry. 'Um – yes.'

'And he has revealed the circumstances behind my first novel?'

Harry frowned. 'Yes.'

Philip St John stopped walking. 'I will be blunt, Miss Moss. Were you sent here by the family of Rupert Templeton to make a claim against me?'

She felt her jaw drop in sheer astonishment. 'What? No, I came because your nephew sent a telegram to...' Harry gaped at him. 'Why would Rupert's family send anyone to...?' And then in her mind, several things that had been fighting for her attention tumbled into place all at once. She let out a long breath of under-standing. 'Oh. Because he wrote *The Blood-soaked Soil*. Not you.'

He eyed her coldly. 'If Rupert's family did not send you, how could you know that?'

It took her a moment to formulate an answer, because she wasn't sure herself. 'I didn't,' she said. 'Or not until just now. But there were lots of little clues, really. The night we first met, you kept insisting it was your hand. I assumed at the time that you were distressed by the way it shook. But when I read some of your later works, I realised how different they were from *The Blood-soaked Soil*. I knew how you came to write it, so I thought that explained the differences. The mutilated first edition in your library confused me – I couldn't understand who would do such a thing.' She glanced over at him. 'But it was you.'

He let out a slow sigh, laced with a pain that Harry suspected he had been holding on to for more than a decade. 'You must understand, we had so much time to fill. Most of the men slept, or wrote endless letters home. Rupert and I discovered early on we were both storytellers. We used to dream of being published, of people reading our work, and somehow hit on the idea of using our time to write. But as the months dragged on, a sense of fatalism settled over us. Rupert in particular started to feel he would not escape the trenches and his gloom brought me down too. So we made a pact. If one of us died and the other made it out, the survivor pledged to find a way to see their writing published.' He hung his head. 'I am ashamed to admit that is exactly what I did.'

Harry kept her gaze averted as they walked, wanting to make the story easier to tell. After a moment, St John went on. 'When Rupert died – a stupid, senseless death caused by a moment of carelessness – I was half-maddened by grief. I remember stum-bling to his kitbag, digging out the battered old biscuit tin he kept the pages rolled in against the mould and the rats, and tucking it in my own bag. It sat there for months, untouched. And then there was a flood – some of the sandbags were blown away by shells and the rainwater poured into our billet. A lot of men lost everything – cigarettes, photographs from home, rations – all drenched and thick with mud. My own manuscript was ruined but I didn't care. I'd lost the heart for writing when Rupert died. His tin was safe, though.'

She could picture the scene. 'It sounds dreadful,' she murmured, her heart aching.

Philip St John shrugged her sympathy away. 'About six months later, the war was over. I got demobbed fairly quickly and went home to my old life, moving back in with my mother and my sister, who was raising her boy on her own, having lost her husband at Gallipoli.'

'John,' Harry observed.

He nodded. 'I went back to work at the bank but nothing was the same.' He paused, frowning. 'No, that wasn't it. In a lot of ways, everything was the same but I wasn't. I found it almost impossible to blindly respect the people I'd once obeyed without question – the manager at the bank who had been too old to fight, the vicar who had seen nothing of life at all. I tried to settle back in, told myself the dissatisfaction would pass in time, but all the time I yearned for escape. And eventually, I remembered Rupert's story, and the pact we'd made.

'I hadn't realised how much he'd written. I had only got about half way through the story I'd been writing, but Rupert had pretty much finished his. It was written in the funny sort of shorthand we'd developed between us – I'm not sure anyone could have made sense of it but me. Anyway, I began to write it out in long-hand, spending every evening bent over the kitchen table until my hand ached. My mother suggested I get a typewriter but I didn't want that. Writing Rupert's words made me feel close to him again, somehow. I didn't want anything to get in the way. Before long, I'd transcribed the whole thing and I knew right away that it was something special.'

He smiled sadly. 'He was always so much better than me, you see. At first, I planned to send it to his family but there was the pact we had made. What if they didn't appreciate how good it was, and kept it for themselves, as a piece of the man they had lost? Once it was out of my hands, I would have no say in what happened next. Wouldn't I be letting Rupert down, breaking our pact, if I risked allowing that to happen?'

Harry nodded in slow understanding. The crime was undeniable but it helped to get a sense of why St John had done what he had.

'I couldn't tell you when I first considered passing Rupert's writing off as my own. My mother was telling anyone who would listen that I was writing a book, oblivious to the fact that I hadn't written an original word for years. I thought about sending it to some publishers with a covering letter explaining what had happened but realised that was fraught with difficulty too. In the end, I managed to convince myself that pretending I had written it was the only way.' He let out a hollow laugh. 'If only I had known.'

'You didn't anticipate the level of success,' Harry said.

'No,' St John said. 'Nor – somewhat naively – that the publisher would want more books.' He stared at the ground. 'I've spent the last ten years trying to live up to the promise of somebody else's brilliance. It – it has not been a pleasant experience.'

Harry was quiet for a moment. 'Your other books are good,' she said. 'Different, of course, and now I know why. But still engaging stories.'

'You are being kind,' he said. 'But I am not ashamed of them – they were the stories I was meant to tell. I like to think I did a good thing in getting Rupert's out there too, although taking the credit was very wrong.'

Harry could not disagree. 'John tells me you take meticulous care over your royalty statements, that the payments for *The Blood-soaked Soil* are held separately.'

He nodded. 'My solicitor holds instructions on what to do with the monies after I die. I do hope poor John will not be too disappointed not to inherit the income. He will, of course, have Thrumwell Manor. I bought it with some of the royalties from *The Blood-soaked Soil* but have long since repaid that money with my own earnings.'

There was no denying Philip St John's actions had been criminal but Harry found it hard to judge him too harshly. It certainly seemed that no one could have berated themselves more strongly, in spite of the advantages he had gained. And she had no doubt Philip St John had worked hard at making the shorthand writings of his friend into something that would catch a publisher's eye. He had probably put more of himself into the story than he had realised but she suspected that he would reject any suggestion that he had added anything to Rupert's brilliance. 'You did at least fulfil the pact,' she said, after a long silence. 'You found a way to get his story into the hands of readers.'

St John let out a bark of laughter. 'I don't think Rupert would see it that way. The thought of how I cheated him haunts me still, even after all these years.'

Harry shook her head. 'I think it's time to stop that, Mr St John.'

He turned to her then, and she saw resignation mingled with a strange sort of hope on his face. 'Will you shame me, then?' he asked.

Harry regarded him steadily. 'I will not,' she said. 'You cannot change what is done and you have made more than enough effort to redress the balance. I assure you, your secret is safe with me.'

His eyes moistened as he sighed. 'I cannot tell you how much it helps to have told someone at long last.'

'I can imagine,' she said softly. 'Secrets are a heavy burden.'

A strained silence fell over them as they walked. 'I think you are quite a surprising young woman,' Philip St John said, at length. 'I'm not sure I've met anyone quite like you.'

'I know the feeling, Mr St John,' Harry replied, with a self-deprecating smile. 'Most of the time, I surprise myself.'

* * *

'I am sorry, Miss Moss. I refuse to let you go under such circumstances.'

John Archer was standing beside the fireplace in the drawing room, his forehead knotted in the kind of forbidding frown Harry was more used to seeing from her father. 'I am sorry to disappoint you, sir, but both Mr Holmes and I are quite firm on the matter. There will be no settlement of your account, no payment needed. Our services come for free and that is the end of it.'

Archer appealed to Oliver. 'Come now, Fortescue, surely you can make her see reason. I am deeply indebted to her – to you both – for everything you have done here. Please allow me to compensate you accordingly.'

Oliver shook his head. 'It is not my business. I do my best to help where needed, but I am not in the employ of Sherlock Holmes.'

'I have never heard of such a thing,' Archer exclaimed, throwing his hands up. 'It is a ridiculous way to operate a business. However do you make any money, if you never charge your clients?'

Harry smiled. 'As you will know from Mr Holmes' published adventures, the fees he charges are discretionary. In your case, there is no charge.'

'Preposterous!' Archer exploded.

Oliver took a step forward. 'Might I make a suggestion? Miss Moss has certain charitable concerns in which she takes an interest.' He fixed Harry with a meaningful look. 'Perhaps a donation to one of those deserving cases might be appropriate. The Brighton charity, perhaps?'

It took Harry several seconds to catch his meaning but the moment she understood she had to admit it was an excellent idea. The difficulty lay in persuading Cecily to accept help but she did not have to know where the money had come from. 'That could work,' she said, looking at Archer. 'If you agree.'

He nodded. 'I am always happy to support worthwhile causes. Shall we say £200?'

Harry swallowed a gulp of surprise. It was more than she dared hope for, enough to see Cecily settled in a good house away from the slums of Circus Street, with plenty left over for food and living expenses for at least a year. 'That is very generous. Thank you.'

'On the contrary, Miss Moss, it is a small price to pay for all you have done for us here. You both have my undying thanks, as does Mr Holmes. Although I am beginning to suspect his role is rather exaggerated in the accounts I have read.' His eyes twinkled as he regarded Harry. 'Perhaps even the greatest detective is only as good as his assistant, eh, Miss Moss.'

Harry couldn't quite hide her smile. 'I couldn't possibly say, Mr Archer.'

17

The newspapers were full of the narcotics ring that had been uncovered and smashed in rural Cambridgeshire. The story dominated the headlines for several days, revealing how the gang had smuggled drugs in from the coast, using ancient waterways to move their deadly cargo around. The ringleader was named as Ishmael Bloom, although Scotland Yard confirmed he'd had many accomplices, most of whom had been rounded up. No mention was made of Thrumwell Manor, nor of the famous author Philip St John's strange illness, for which Harry was grateful. She knew from Oliver that the tobacco Eliza had given them had indeed been laced with tincture of Ergot. It seemed she and Donaldson would be going to prison for a long time, if found guilty at trial.

It was more than a week later that Harry received another letter from Beth. They met, as before, at the Mother Red Cap, and Harry discovered she was beginning to develop a taste for mild.

'So what have you got for me?' she asked, once she and Beth were seated at a table.

The other woman took a long draught of her drink. 'Firstly,

Polly Spender is a wet drip. I don't know who she's more scared of – her old man, the gang she's fallen in with or me.'

Harry eyed her with some disapproval. 'I hope it's not you. You were supposed to persuade her to talk, not scare her half to death.'

Beth rolled her eyes. 'Who said I done that? I didn't say that, did I? I just pointed out that the girl is terrified of her own shadow.' She sniffed. 'Luckily for you, I made that work in our favour. It turns out she did plant that jewellery under your friend's pillow but get this – she was told to by the housekeeper.'

The housekeeper who had links with Mrs Haverford's Bureau of Excellence. Why did everything keep coming back to that, Harry wondered. 'Does Polly know who told the housekeeper to do it?'

'That's where your luck ran out. She did mention there was a right to-do when Mildred got released from prison – a lot of people got angry, she said.' Beth paused to gaze at Harry. 'She didn't name any names but I got the sense she meant the sort of people you don't want angry with you. It was obvious she knew more but she clammed up like an oyster. That means she was more scared of them and what they might do if they found out she blabbed, than she was of me and what I was threatening to do if she didn't blab.'

'Beth!' Harry exclaimed. 'What were you threatening to do?'

'Keep your hair on,' Beth grumbled, casting a sour look around to see if anyone had noticed. 'I told her I'd put the word out, make it tricky for her to get another job. And she said, it was already tricky. The housekeeper at the Finchem place refused to give her a reference, see. Polly said she might have to go into the family business instead.'

Harry considered the information. It was curious that Polly had been refused a reference from Lady Finchem – Percy

Finchem, in particular, had thought highly of the girl. 'What's the family business?'

'Picking pockets,' Beth said. 'But she'll be no good at that. She's too scared – the mark would notice her before she got fingers anywhere near their pocket. But she might be useful to us in the future. For information.'

'Us?' Harry stared at her, amused at her impudence.

The woman shrugged. 'You said there might be more work for me, if I done all right with Polly. Seems to me I done a good job.'

Harry could not deny it; Beth had done exactly what she had asked of her. She placed four shillings on the table. 'Fair enough. Here's the rest of your payment, plus a little more for expenses.'

Beth stared at the money, then grinned at Harry. 'Thanks very much. I might take myself on a little jolly to the seaside with this.'

Harry nodded. 'Good idea. I'm going there myself at the weekend. Brighton, in my case.'

Beth raised her eyebrows. 'Ain't we lah-di-dah?'

'Just visiting a friend.' She sighed. 'One who's got herself into a bit of a mess, actually.'

'Involving a man, I'll bet,' Beth said knowingly. 'There's always a man at the bottom of it.'

Harry couldn't deny it. 'There is.'

'In the family way, is she?' Beth went on. 'I don't suppose he wants to marry her.'

'No,' Harry agreed absently, her thoughts on how she could persuade Cecily to leave Circus Street. 'She's worried about being an unmarried mother. She says even if she moves somewhere new, people will look down on her.'

The other woman shrugged. 'She's right, they will. But who says everyone has to know?'

Harry stared at her. 'What do you mean?'

'Who's going to tell them?' Beth asked patiently. 'I always thought, if I got myself into that particular sort of state, that I'd just nip down the pawnbrokers and buy a cheap ring. Then, if anyone asked, I could just wave my hand around and tell them how my husband had tragically died before he could see our little babe even born.'

Harry turned the idea over in her mind. It was, she had to admit, a simple but brilliant solution. 'Wouldn't people suspect?'

'They might, but what are they going to do? Demand to see my wedding certificate?' Beth gave her a practical look. 'People don't like to talk about death, especially if you can dredge up a few tears.'

Would it work? Harry wondered. And then decided there was no use in speculating. She would simply have to go to Brighton to find out. She smiled at the woman beside her. 'You're a marvel, Beth Chamberlain. Simply a marvel.'

Beth snorted, although Harry thought she was secretly pleased. 'Yeah, yeah. Tell the whole blooming world, why don't you?'

* * *

Saturday dawned bright and clear. After a leisurely breakfast, Harry took the train down to Brighton. The confectioner did not offer her any advice as she passed by, but she barely spared him a glance. She knew her way to Circus Street, and she knew which house she wanted.

'You.' Joan's expression was flat and unwelcoming as she surveyed Harry.

'Hello,' Harry said pleasantly. 'I've come to see Cecily. Is she here?'

The woman folded her meaty arms. 'No.'

Harry drew in a patient breath. 'I see. Do you know where she is?'

Joan shrugged. 'No.'

'Do you know when she will be back?'

She fixed Harry with a defiant look. 'No.'

Sighing, Harry reached into her bag and withdrew a pound note. 'I appreciate Cecily is your niece, and a good hard worker, but you must be worried about the burden she'll be once the baby arrives. She won't be much use when she's up all night feeding, will she? Keeping you up too – you know how noisy babies are.' She held out the money. 'I'm offering to compensate you. One pound now, if you tell me where she is, and another nine if you let her go.'

The older woman thinned her lips, clearly torn. Harry had calculated the amount with care – ten pounds was a small fortune to a woman in Joan's situation, more than she could expect to recover from Cecily even after several years of laundry work. She reached out to pluck the note from Harry's hand. 'You'll find her at the Palace Pier.'

And stepping smartly backwards, she shut the door in Harry's face.

The seafront was busier than it had been during Harry's last visit. Couples and families were making the most of the sunshine, although there was still a brisk wind blowing in from the sea. The pier jutted out a long way over the water, a confectionery of delicate iron struts and balustrades. There were plenty of people here too, Harry observed as she passed beneath the clock tower that marked the entrance to the pier, and paid the tuppenny toll to enter.

It was hardly surprising the pier was popular. Boards proclaimed the entertainments available for all the family – scooter rides, a rifle range, a children's playground, reading rooms, a theatre... The list went on and on. All of which presented Harry with another problem. How was she to find Cecily Earnshaw among the crowds? She could probably rule out the smoking rooms, and the scooter rides, but the theatre and the Winter Garden were both possibilities. In the end, it turned out to be quite simple. Cecily was in the first place Harry looked – the reading rooms.

She was so engrossed in her book that she did not see Harry approach. It was only when Harry gently cleared her throat that Cecily looked up, and covered her mouth to mask the gasp that escaped her. 'Miss White,' she said, once she had recovered herself a little. 'I didn't expect to see you again.'

She looked pale, Harry thought. Her belly, covered by the coat she wore, seemed to have expanded further, although it had only been a few days since their last encounter. The dark circles beneath her eyes were more pronounced and her lips were dry and chapped. Even so, she managed to radiate a serenity that attracted more than one passing glance. 'How have you been, Cecily? May I join you?'

The younger woman waved a hand, although Harry thought the motion was a shade reluctant. 'Please do.'

Harry sat beside her. 'I will come straight to the point, Cecily,' she said in a low voice. 'Last time we spoke, you expressed reservations about accepting charity, because you were afraid you would still be a pariah.'

Cecily's gaze dropped to her lap, where Harry saw her hands were red and scabbed. 'That is still the way I feel. It is better to be accepted somewhere like Circus Street than an outcast by society.'

'What if I were to tell you I had not only the means to offer you a new life but a way to avoid becoming the subject of gossip?'

She looked up then, her expression suspicious. 'I would wonder what was in it for you.'

Harry sighed. Clearly, Cecily had spent too much time with Joan already. 'There is nothing in it for me. A benefactor has pledged enough money to find a new home for you and your baby, a long way from where you live now.' She paused and took a breath, because this was the trickiest part of the proposition. 'And I have in my pocket a second-hand wedding ring, which will allow you to claim a sadly departed husband as the father of your child.'

Cecily shrank back, horrified. 'A dead husband? You cannot mean that!'

'But I do,' Harry said quickly. 'It is only a small lie, after all, and one that will enable you to make a fresh start away from Circus Street. Think of the life you might have, Cecily,' she urged. 'Think of the life your child might have.'

'My aunt would never allow it,' the younger woman whispered, her expression torn.

'She will,' Harry said firmly. 'But I have no intention of telling her about any charitable donations and nor should you. The money will become available to you only when you leave her house and agree to start again somewhere else.'

She sounded horribly overbearing but she did not plan to let the proceeds of John Archer's generosity fall into the wrong hands. The cheque had been made payable to Oliver Fortescue and, when cashed, would enable Cecily and her baby to make a better future. If Cecily decided she did not want to take up the offer then the cheque would remain undrawn.

'But where would I go?' Cecily asked.

'Wherever you like,' Harry replied. 'There are more new houses being built every day and many are available to rent. You might even be able to use some of the money as a deposit for a mortgage, if you are able to find work at a later date.'

At this, Cecily eyed her with even greater uncertainty. 'A

deposit. But that would be £30 or more. What sort of charity gives that much to one person, much less a – a fallen woman like me?'

'An extremely generous one,' Harry said, with complete honesty. 'But the offer is there, all the same. All I ask is that you go somewhere far away from Circus Street.'

Cecily shook her head, her expression hopeful and wary at the same time. 'I don't understand. Why are you doing this?'

Harry reached for her hand. 'Because you have been treated terribly – by your parents, by your aunt and by the man whose child you carry. But I don't believe you should be made to suffer the consequences alone.' She met the younger woman's gaze and held it firm. 'Have courage, Cecily – you are not without friends. Take the money and build a new life for yourself. You will never have a better chance.'

For a moment, Cecily seemed to waver. Then she looked away. 'I'm afraid you have too high an opinion of me, Miss White. I have no courage, in fact, I am a coward. I – I cannot accept your offer.'

Harry's shoulders sagged. From what she knew of Cecily Earnshaw, the last word she would use to describe her was coward. But she also knew obstinacy when she saw it. If such an opportunity could not induce the young woman to make a fresh start, then nothing would. 'Then I am sorry for you both,' she said quietly, and left the reading room.

Outside, the sky was still blue and the sun was still bright. Harry stood gripping the iron balustrade for several minutes, allowing the wind to buffet her while she gazed out to sea. Somewhere further along the pier, a band had struck up; snatches of music faded in and out on the breeze. The smell of salt danced on the air, mingled with the piquant scent of vinegar from an oyster bar not far from where Harry was standing. She allowed the wind to scour away her disappointment and, when at last she felt less melancholy, she began to make her way back along the pier.

She had almost reached the clock when she heard her name being called. Glancing over her shoulder, she was astonished to see Cecily hurrying over the wooden slats. The young woman had one hand supporting her belly and was puffing with the effort of moving at speed. 'Miss White, wait!'

Harry did as she asked. Cecily huffed to a halt, her cheeks rosy from the exertion and her eyes suspiciously bright. 'Do you truly mean it?' she asked, half gasping the question as she struggled to get her breath back. 'There is no catch?'

'There is no catch,' Harry repeated. 'I promise. If you don't know where to start then there are those who can help with that too.'

Cecily caught her lip between her teeth and gnawed at it. 'My aunt will be angry.'

'Then don't tell her,' Harry suggested as an idea occurred to her. 'In fact, come with me now. We can take the train to London and you can stay with me while we make a plan.'

She almost regretted the offer as soon as it was made – her apartment was luxurious compared to the slums of Circus Street but it had only one bedroom. It was too late to take the words back, however. The other woman shuffled anxiously. 'I can't. I have some things in my aunt's house – a few trinkets and what little I have left of my savings. It is not much but I would hate to leave it all the same.'

Harry understood her attachment to her possessions. Cecily had already given up so much already. Why should she also give up what little she had left? 'We will go to collect them together,' she said decisively. 'And then we shall board the train and the next chapter of your life will begin.'

'You are so brave,' Cecily said, as Harry took her arm and led her from the pier. 'Is there anything you're afraid of?'

Harry considered her recent adventures in the fens, when she had been scared of many things, including a strange bobbing light she was still not convinced she could entirely explain. 'Yes,' she said. 'But your Aunt Joan is not one of them.'

As Cecily had predicted, Joan took a dim view of her niece's departure. 'Who's going to help me with the laundry tomorrow, that's what I'd like to know,' she growled when Cecily explained in a halting voice.

'I'm sure you'll manage,' Harry replied briskly. 'Go and collect what you need, Cecily. I'll wait here.'

As her niece climbed the stairs, Joan rounded on Harry. 'You never said she was going today. I've got three loads of laundry coming in the morning, and another four on Monday.'

Reaching into her bag, Harry took out the wad of notes she had counted out in case she needed to give them to Joan. 'You'll find someone,' she said. 'Here's your compensation, as agreed.'

With sour-faced acceptance, Joan snatched the money, just as Cecily appeared on the stairs with a small suitcase in one hand. 'Show me what you've got in there,' she demanded, nodding at the case. 'I want to make sure you're not taking anything that's not yours.'

Cecily's cheeks flamed. 'I would never do such a thing, Aunt Joan.'

The older woman did not dignify her with an answer. Instead, she rummaged through the contents of the case, undoing Cecily's carefully folded clothing. When she came to a small drawstring bag, she jangled it menacingly. 'Where did you get this?'

'I brought it with me,' Cecily said, raising her chin. 'It's my savings, from when I worked at the bank.'

Joan hefted the bag, considering. Harry took a step forward. 'We had an agreement.'

The air hummed with tension. If it came to a fight, Harry knew she would lose. Joan was strong and Cecily would be no help. But thankfully, Joan seemed to think better of her greed. She dropped the bag into the case and slammed the lid shut. 'Go on, then, if you're going. And don't think I'll forget how ungrateful you've been.'

Harry felt her eyes upon them all the way along Circus Street. 'Here,' she said, once they had turned the corner and reached the safety of Victoria Gardens. 'Let me take your case. It's over now.'

They reached the station with just minutes to spare before the non-stop train left. With each step along the platform, Cecily's mood seemed to lift, until she was almost laughing as they tumbled into an empty compartment and shut the door. She leaned back against the seat, panting a little, her eyes gleaming. 'I feel better already,' she said, as the train lurched and began to pull out of the station. 'But I don't know how I'm ever going to repay you.'

'You don't have to,' Harry said, as the young woman turned to gaze out of the window. 'All I ask is that you do your best for yourself and your child.'

Cecily let out a weary sigh. 'There is so much to think about.'

'But it doesn't all have to be thought about today,' Harry replied. 'Most of it can wait until tomorrow.'

'Tomorrow,' Cecily echoed, and closed her eyes. 'At least I won't have to wash the bed linen. It hurts my back so to bend over the tub.'

Harry shook her head. 'You don't have to do anything you don't want to. You're going to be fine, Cecily.'

'Fine,' the girl murmured softly. Moments later, she was asleep, lulled by the gentle motion of the train. Harry allowed herself a smile of satisfaction, then reached for her notebook and pen. *The Case of the Cursed Writer*, she wrote, *By R. K. Moss.*

EPILOGUE

It was Christmas at Abinger Hall. Harry had finished work on 23rd December and gladly taken the train to Surrey, where she had been met by Seb in his speedy red MG. The drive to Abinger Hall had been a little hair-raising, since Seb seemed to have forgotten what the brake was for, but they arrived without incident. Harry had watched the house from the moment they had passed through the gate and its never-changing solidity warmed her heart. Once inside the magnificent entrance hall, decorated with an enormous, shimmering fir tree cut from the estate, she had been enthusiastically greeted by both family Labradors, Tiggy and Winston, her older brother, Lawrence, and her mother.

'Darling, you look so pale,' Evelyn White had chided, holding her at arm's length to study her properly. 'I'm not sure the London air agrees with you.'

Behind her mother's head, Harry saw Seb pull a sympathetic expression. 'I'm fine, Mama,' she said. 'Just a little tired. You know what a whirlwind the run-up to Christmas is.'

Her mother nodded. 'Of course. But you're here now and needn't do a thing until New Year's Day. Won't that be lovely?'

It would, Harry thought, but she knew her mother better than that. 'No parties?' she said, raising both eyebrows. 'No guests to entertain?'

Evelyn sighed. 'Of course there will be parties, Harry. We are not bears, hibernating for the winter, after all.'

Now Seb was grimacing and even Lawrence looked pained. 'I wouldn't mind hibernating so much,' Harry said. 'I feel as though I could sleep for a month.'

'Don't be so dramatic,' her mother said briskly. 'We have our usual Christmas Eve drinks tomorrow, and then the Gladstones are coming for Boxing Day.'

'So much for not doing a thing,' Seb said dryly. Their mother had made no secret of her hope he might marry one of the Gladstone girls.

Evelyn pretended not to hear him. 'But before I forget, your grandmother asked to see you, Harry. She's in her study, when you're ready.'

Dutifully, Harry went upstairs to freshen up and change, then made her way to her grandmother's study. As usual, it was in a state of disarray. Baroness Abinger sat at the cluttered writing desk, a pair of spectacles perched on her nose as she bent over a letter. She looked up when Harry knocked on the open door. 'Ah, there you are,' her grandmother exclaimed, rising to kiss her on the cheek. 'How glad I am to see you.'

'Hello, Grandmama,' Harry said, breathing in the familiar scent of gardenia and roses. 'How are you?'

'Simply splendid, my dear, although there is always so much work to be done.'

Harry smiled, because she had never known her grandmother to be idle, even for a moment. 'I hope you'll find time for your family at Christmas,' she said. 'I know Mama has several parties planned.'

'I'm sure she has,' her grandmother said, her eyes twinkling. 'But one of the benefits of being old is that one can safely leave partying to the young.'

'I'm almost jealous,' Harry said, and it wasn't altogether a lie.

Her grandmother held out a letter. 'This came on Wednesday. I thought you might like to read it.'

Curiously, Harry took the sheet of writing paper.

3, Salt Cottages
Arundel
Sussex
19th December 1932

Dear Baroness Abinger,

I am writing to express my sincerest thanks for the help given by you and the Abinger Foundation in finding my new home. I am now settling into the cottage recommended by the charity, and feel hopeful for the first time in many months that my future, and that of my child, may be a happy one.

I would appreciate it if you could also pass on my thanks to Miss Harry White, with whom I believe you are acquainted. She has been kindness personified and I am further indebted to her for the money deposited in my bank account this week. I would be most glad to see her again, if she ever finds herself in Arundel.

Yours sincerely,
Cecily White (Mrs)

Harry was not sure what pleased her the most – the knowledge that Cecily was safe and well and settling into her new life, or the signature at the end that showed she had taken Beth's suggestion and decided to invent a husband to fend off unwanted questions. The whole matter had turned out most satisfactorily, Harry thought as she read the letter again, and she owed some of that to her grandmother. 'This is excellent news. Thank you for your help in finding her a home.'

The baroness waved her thanks away. 'It's no more than the Foundation tries to do for every woman in need. The cottage is on a friend's estate. She'll be safe there.'

Harry smiled. 'I appreciate it.'

Her grandmother smiled. 'I know you do, dear. And I won't ask how you came by the money to help this girl relocate.' She peered over the top of her glasses. 'I trust it was all above board.'

'Of course, Grandmama,' Harry said, relieved she would not have to lie.

'Good,' the older woman said, and waved her granddaughter away. 'Now, run along and I'll see you at dinner.'

* * *

Christmas came and went in a blur of too much food and drink, of presents and cocktails and small talk, and the occasional well-meaning bout of matchmaking by Harry's mother, which her children bore with good grace. Harry spent a refreshing morning riding one of her aunt's horses, took Tiggy and Winston for several long walks around the estate, and caught up with the family gossip. Even Rufus, her youngest brother, had been allowed permission to return from exile in Great-Uncle Douglas's Scottish estate. Harry was glad to observe that his banishment appeared to have done him no harm, although he had learned some colourful new swear words.

She was surprised to be approached by the family butler, Chesterton, just after breakfast on New Year's Eve. 'It's the telephone, Miss Harriet. Mr Fortescue is asking for you.'

Seb let out a low whistle as Harry got her feet and left the dining room, making her grateful more family members had not been present to observe his teasing. She hadn't talked to Oliver since leaving London, when they had spoken briefly to wish each other affectionate season's greetings. 'Oliver?' she said. 'It's Harry. How are you? Did you have a good Christmas?'

'Never mind that,' he said, in a tone Harry couldn't quite decipher. 'Have you seen the *Times* this morning?'

She frowned. 'No, we haven't had the papers yet. Why, what's wrong? Is it the Morden case?'

There was a brief silence, during which she heard a rustling noise that she assumed came from Oliver rifling through the paper. 'No, not that. Ah, here it is – Page 34. There's a letter addressed to Sherlock Holmes.'

Whatever Harry had been expecting Oliver to say, it was not that. 'Oh! What does it say?'

Oliver cleared his throat. '*My dear Sherlock Holmes, you are invited to prove your status as the world's greatest detective by solving an impossible crime. You have seven days. Yours sincerely, Professor James Moriarty.*'

Harry laughed. 'It must be a joke of some kind. It doesn't say what the crime is, or when it will be committed.'

'That's what I thought at first,' Oliver said. 'But there's another, darker possibility. It could be a gauntlet, designed to draw Holmes out.'

She felt her forehead crinkle, because the suggestion sounded very much like the start of a classic Sherlock Holmes adventure. 'But who would go to the trouble? And why? There's no such person as Professor Moriarty.'

'There's no such person as Sherlock Holmes and yet he seems to have developed a knack for solving real-life crimes recently,' Oliver pointed out. 'Do you think it's a game of some sort?'

'It certainly sounds like one,' Harry said, shrugging. 'But it has to be a coincidence. No one knows Holmes had anything to do with the Mildred Longstaff or Morden Fen cases.'

'True,' Oliver conceded and huffed out a breath. 'I suppose the safest thing to do is ignore it.'

'I don't see what else we can do,' Harry replied. 'Unless a fiendishly difficult crime presents itself in the next seven days.'

Oliver snorted. 'In which case every amateur detective in England will take up the challenge. Scotland Yard will be delighted.'

When the papers arrived, just before lunchtime, Harry took the copy of the *Times* up to the library to study the letter for herself. Whoever had written it appeared to have a reasonable passing knowledge of Sir Arthur Conan Doyle's stories; Sherlock Holmes had frequently described his encounters with Professor Moriarty as a terrible game, often with deadly consequences. But Harry found it hard to believe that the letter in the newspaper was anything more than a joke between friends. It couldn't have anything to do with her, and her own activities on Holmes' behalf.

Could it?

AUTHOR'S NOTE

In 1932, the rapidly expanding Abbey Road Building Society moved into their new headquarters in the heart of London. The offices spanned numbers 219–229 Baker Street, which any fan of crime fiction knows includes a very famous address, and sure enough, the bank immediately began to receive letters addressed to Mr Sherlock Holmes. There were so many that they were forced to employ someone to reply – a secretary to Holmes who played along with the belief that the great detective was a real person – and the role continued for many decades, perhaps even until the bank left Baker Street in 2002. It's not too much of a stretch to imagine that a bright and enterprising secretary might be tempted to investigate one of the letters on Sherlock's behalf, even though the mere suggestion was enough to cost them their job... And so *The Baker Street Mysteries* was born.

Harry White is, of course, as fictional as Holmes but I had great fun envisioning her following in his footsteps, albeit it many years on from the cases he solved. *The Cursed Writer* is my little homage to the most famous adventure of them all – *The Hound of the Baskervilles* – and I hope I did it justice. The game is once again afoot.

Holly Hepburn
July 2024

ACKNOWLEDGEMENTS

It takes a village to write a book (or something like that) and there are many people who helped me produce *The Cursed Writer*. I've tried to mention most of them here – apologies to those I have missed.

My first thanks go to Jo Williamson of Antony Harwood Ltd, my agent and friend and champion. I am indebted to everyone at Boldwood Books, but most specifically to my editor Rachel Faulkner-Willcocks, whose insightful suggestions and comments made this a much better book.

A heartfelt thank you to Helena Newton for her excellent copy-editing skills, and Rachel Sargeant for her brilliant proof reading. Your eagle-eyed attentions are worth their weight in gold. Another grateful tip of the deerstalker to Hayley Russell, for making the words into a book, and to the Boldwood design team for coming up with such an evocative cover. Thank you to Nia Beynon and Jenna Houston for their marketing and PR inspiration, and the rest of Team Boldwood for their hard work.

Thank you to the very lovely Katie Marsh, for cheerleading through the gloomier bits of the writing process, and to Kathryn and William of Tea Leaves and Reads bookshop for their excellent support. I think my friend Charlotte Dennis contributes something to every book I write and this one is no exception – thank you again. And as ever, my thanks and undying love go to T and E, as well as to Luna the Labrador for general writing cuddles and adorable interruptions. I can throw the ball now, yes.

Last of all, I want to thank my readers, who encourage me to improve with each story I write. I hope you've enjoyed Harry's second adventure.

ABOUT THE AUTHOR

Holly Hepburn writes escapist, swoonsome fiction that sweeps her readers into idyllic locations, from her native Cornwall to the windswept beauty of Orkney. With *The Missing Maid*, her first book published by Boldwood Books, she turns her hand to cosy crime inspired by Sherlock Holmes himself. Holly lives in leafy Hertfordshire with her adorable partner in crime, Luna the Labrador.

Sign up to Holly Hepburn's mailing list for news, competitions and updates on future books

Follow Holly on social media:

x.com/HollyH_Author
instagram.com/HollyH_Author

ALSO BY HOLLY HEPBURN

The Baker Street Mysteries

The Missing Maid

The Cursed Writer

Poison
& Pens

POISON & PENS IS THE HOME OF
COZY MYSTERIES SO POUR YOURSELF
A CUP OF TEA & GET SLEUTHING!

DISCOVER PAGE–TURNING NOVELS FROM
YOUR FAVOURITE AUTHORS &
MEET NEW FRIENDS

JOIN OUR
FACEBOOK GROUP

BIT.LYPOISONANDPENSFB

SIGN UP TO OUR
NEWSLETTER

BIT.LY/POISONANDPENSNEWS

Boldwood

Boldwood Books is an award-winning fiction publishing company seeking out the best stories from around the world.

Find out more at www.boldwoodbooks.com

Join our reader community for brilliant books, competitions and offers!

Follow us
@BoldwoodBooks
@TheBoldBookClub

Sign up to our weekly
deals newsletter

https://bit.ly/BoldwoodBNewsletter

Milton Keynes UK
Ingram Content Group UK Ltd.
UKHW042008311024
450194UK00001B/1